Dark Forces

Harry stumbled through the fog in the direction Alexander had indicated, and within a few minutes he'd noticed the air become thicker and heavier, while at the same time more translucent. Another minute, and he was on a winding path lit by the moonlight, leading up to what was the ugliest building Harry had seen in his entire life. About a hundred feet in the distance, it was just like Tonia had described: an enormous public toilet block. Yet even as Harry stared it seemed to change shape, morphing into what Harry considered to be the worst example of public housing ever built—a filthy, decaying tenement block for the poor and dispossessed. He took a few, hesitant steps along the path, limping forward reluctantly. His sprained ankle ached at the motion, and his legs felt heavier than usual. Walking seemed a much bigger effort than normal, as if the building itself was repelling him, trying to force him back the way he'd come. He could feel the thick forest encroaching on either side the path. The gnarled, leafless trees were the same dark color as everything else in this landscape, barely touched by the moonlight. The moon focused its pale light on the path, leaving the trees to fall back into the shadows.

Dark Forces

Kathy Anderson

A Wings ePress, Inc.
General Fiction Horror Novel

Published by Wings ePress, Inc

Edited by: Leslie Hodges
Copy Edited by: Shonna Brannon
Senior Editor: Dianne Hamilton
Executive Editor: Lorraine Stephens
Cover Artist: Pat Casey

All rights reserved

Names, characters and incidents depicted in this book are products of the author's imagination or are used fictitiously. Any resemblance to actual events, locales, organizations, or persons, living or dead, is entirely coincidental and beyond the intent of the author or the publisher.

No part of this book may be reproduced or transmitted in any form or by any means, electronic or mechanical, including photocopying, recording, or by any information storage and retrieval system, without permission in writing from the publisher.

Wings ePress Books
http://www.wingsepress.com

Copyright © 2008 by Katherine Anderson
ISBN 978-1-59705-892-6

Published In the United States Of America

Wings ePress Inc.
3000 N. Rock Road
Newton, KS 67114

Part I

Tracking The Beast

One

Dragging himself out of bed in the middle of the night was a lot harder than it used to be, and Harry was wishing he'd drunk a little less bourbon last night. Still, he'd managed to get himself here, and from the looks of the crime scene—which was still being taped off— the police hadn't got there long before him. He walked towards Mario and Jo, who were watching the police photographer lean awkwardly over an industrial bin to take photos. He felt their eyes move from the photographer to him, and his gut contracted at the thought of talking to Jo.

"Hey guys." He went for the cheerful approach. "Did you just get here?" Mario bobbed his head hesitantly in recognition, looking glum. His suit looked slept in and he was chewing his gum despondently. His partner was also looking worse for wear. Which wasn't surprising, given the time. Her dark curls hung limply down her shoulders, like she'd just stepped out of the shower. She frowned at Harry.

"What are you doing here?"

"I got a call from Pam Grinstone." Her frown deepened.

"How'd she know we were here?"

"She didn't. I called the station."

"You shouldn't be here, Harry".

"C'mon, Jo, give me something. It's four in the morning." Mario was watching closely, staying quiet.

"Go home, Harry. We'll have a comment later in the day."

"It's the Wolfman, isn't it? Come on, Jo. Pam said it was another young boy, ten or eleven. Is she right?"

"That bitch is crazy, Harry." Mario's voice held a warning, and Harry knew he couldn't push it much further. They'd been friends for a couple of years, but lately they hadn't been too close. Mario wasn't much of a conversationalist, but Harry missed hanging out with him at the Metro, where they used to drink together sometimes. The Metro was a cop bar, so Harry didn't drink there anymore. A young officer approached, looking like he didn't want to be there.

"Detectives, we're going to take the body out now".

"Have you called the coroner?" Jo's voice was flat and drained of emotion.

"Yes. She's already down there, waiting for the body." Jo looked over at the homeless man loitering about twenty feet away. At least, he looked homeless to Harry, with his grungy beard and dirty, mismatched clothes. The clothes were several sizes too big for his lean frame.

"Is he the one who called it in?" The officer followed her gaze.

"Yeah, there's a public phone box just down the road. A miracle it still works."

"Okay. We don't want to leave the body hanging around any longer than it has to." She turned to Mario. "You ready to go through the bin?" He grimaced and Jo remembered Harry.

"You better leave now, Harry." He knew the tone—there was no use arguing.

"Can I call you later this morning?" She nodded reluctantly and walked towards the photographer, dismissing him.

~ * ~

Jo looked at the big Italian who'd been her partner and friend for the past four years and sensed in him a reluctance that matched her own. Mario had two kids under twelve and the case had been hard on him. On both of them. They both slowed as they neared the end of the dark, silent corridor, and Jo took a deep breath before pushing on the heavy doors. Marcy Dawson was standing over the body and didn't look up when they entered.

"Have you got anything for us yet?" They'd both stopped a few feet from the table, neither of them keen to see the body again. Jo hadn't been able to erase the earlier image she'd gotten from the top of the industrial bin. She could hear Mario's jaws going as he chewed hard on his gum. He always chewed gum when he wasn't eating, which wasn't all that often. Jo had never known anyone who loved food as much as Mario.

"Well, I can confirm what I guess you already know: same puncture marks on the skin." When Marcy had identified the puncture marks on Victim Number One, they'd hoped it would lead them to the killer. If they were actually teeth marks, the man Harry had infamously dubbed 'the Wolfman' had gotten some fancy orthodontic work done. There was nothing natural about the fangs he used to tear victims apart. But despite hundreds of detective hours spent ringing New York dental surgeons, they hadn't found anyone who'd fitted steel-capped teeth. And because the killer scrubbed the wounds with industrial-strength bleach, he left no DNA behind with the bite marks.

"The bite marks match those on James Matheson. His wrists and ankles have been bound. You can see the older marks here." Jo and Mario were forced to move closer to see what she was pointing to. "I found some rope fiber in the cuts on the ankle, where the rope rubbed the skin off. Evidence of extended captivity. Some muscle deterioration." Jo felt the bile rise in her throat as she forced herself to look at the young boy's mangled body. Half his cheek was missing, and huge slabs of flesh had been ripped from his sides and inner left thigh. The raw, red flesh looked like it had been mauled by a pack of hungry dogs.

"Jesus Christ." Mario's voice was a shocked whisper as he edged closer to her side. He'd been on the force for twenty years, and the only time Jo had ever seen him break down was four weeks ago, when they'd found Victim Number One: Mandy Gleeson. Ten-year old daughter of Mitch and Patricia Gleeson, whom Jo had watch disintegrate. Mitch, the loving husband and father of two, had initially struggled to keep his family together, comforting his wife when she'd collapsed at the station. But he'd lost control when he saw his daughter's body. Mario was standing next to him at the time, while Patricia waited outside, and Jo had watched her partner fight back the tears.

"Jesus Christ," Mario repeated, louder this time. His horrified eyes were fixed on the mangled flesh that had once been the boy's genitals.

"Part of the right shoulder and left buttock have also been torn off," Marcy informed them with clinical detachment. Jo flashed back to the image of the victim face down in the garbage, the frail body ravaged by the killer.

~ * ~

It was after nine when they left the Coroner's Office and headed back to the precinct. The atmosphere there had been subdued since Mandy Gleeson's body had turned up, and as she walked in that morning Jo sensed the mood slipping from subdued to gloomy. They headed straight for the coffee machine, where they were met by Captain Alton. Like them, he looked like he'd suffered an interrupted sleep. A tall, authoritative man with intelligent brown eyes and a military hair cut, Captain Alton was normally well groomed. But this morning gray stubble covered his cheeks, and Jo recognized the suit from yesterday.

"We've already sent Donaldson and Petersen to break the news to Sylvia Matheson. I decided we'd go with Marcy's identification. She couldn't do anything with the body, to make it fit for a mother's eyes. When they bring her in, I want you two to do the interview. Donaldson can sit in with you." Marie Donaldson was their trauma counselor. She'd been working with the parents, and staff, since Marge James, mother of Victim Number Two, had committed suicide two days after seeing her son's body. Since then, they'd tried to ID the bodies without the parents' help. Grimacing at her first bitter sip of coffee, Jo remembered what Harry had said.

"Harry O'Brien arrived at the scene soon after us. Claimed Pam Grinstone called him about the murder." Mario snorted, and Alton replied carefully.

"I know the woman's highly strung, but she seems to know something. We need to find out what it is, and how she knows it. She called the station around midnight last night, claiming he had another boy.

"Who took the call?"

"Petersen. He was pretty shook up when we heard about the body. You might want to talk to him about it. The call's on tape, but he might be able to tell you something. We're going to have to bring her in again." He didn't sound like he relished the prospect. They'd had her in for questioning before, and the woman was bordering on hysteria.

Two

Harry decided Pam was unlikely to be resting, and phoned from the car. She accepted his request to call over with almost grateful readiness.

"Mr. O'Brien, come in."

"Please, call me Harry." He followed her into a long, dark sitting room, where all horizontal surfaces and available wall space were crowded with porcelain plates and other knick-knacks. The dark, ornate furniture and excessive ornamentation made the room seem even smaller and darker than it might otherwise appear, and the room's owner reminded Harry of one of her own fragile collectables. She was long, thin and angular, and had a brittle appearance about her. As if she might suddenly snap apart. Even her hair seemed thin and brittle, and she walked with the abrupt movements of someone who didn't really occupy her own body. More like an awkward teenager than a women in her early forties. Completely lacking in sensuality, she reminded Harry of one of those dry, nineteenth century spinsters: the maidenly aunt you read about in a Jane Austen novel. Not that he'd read a Jane Austen novel since college. The quiet desperation of loneliness hung about her like a cloud, and made being in her company a rather uncomfortable experience.

As he edged onto a tapestry couch Harry dislodged a sleepy-looking Persian, which shot him a disdainful glare before leaping to the next chair. He could feel the contempt in the cat's eyes as it watched him fold his too-big body into the couch, pulling in his legs to avoid knocking over the small coffee table.

"Did the police find the body?" she asked abruptly. "I'm sorry, I should have offered tea. Would you like some?" She stood suddenly.

"Thanks."

"Peppermint, Jasmine or Chamomile?" Harry was really hanging out for caffeine, but she was already up and looking at him anxiously, so he settled for peppermint. He glared at the cat while listening to her move around the kitchen, foolishly defying its contemptuous assessment of him. He was forced to look away when Pam returned with a wooden tray, and could sense its smugness from across the room. The tray was laden with a delicate china teapot and matching cups and saucers, and she laid it carefully on the small table, before pouring the tea with jerky movements.

"Yes, they found a body," he continued, answering her earlier question. "A young boy, just as you described." She fell back into her chair with a startled expression. But Harry had learned that startled was pretty much her normal expression, and didn't necessarily denote surprise in this instance. "Pam, can you describe what you saw tonight?" Holding the saucer up towards her face, her hands shaking slightly, she drew the dainty cup to her thin lips before beginning.

"I was dreaming. I could see the boy. The man was pulling him from some kind of giant tub." The cup clinked as she returned it to the saucer. Her speech echoed her movements: abrupt and disjointed. "He put his hands in handcuffs. They came down from the ceiling. Attached to a long chain. The boy seemed groggy or something... he might have been drugged. He didn't really struggle. Then the man started to..." She paused, and her voice broke. "...Eat him." She choked on the words, and with shaking hands she returned her saucer to the coffee table. Harry smiled encouragingly, but she didn't smile back. A cloud descended on her as she went somewhere Harry couldn't follow.

"I didn't want to see it. I didn't want to watch. I woke up, but I could still see. He just kept eating. Like an animal. The boy was screaming. Not groggy anymore. I could see the fear in his eyes as he hung there, screaming." Pam's eyes were clouded, and she seemed lost in some kind of trance. "I covered my ears, but I could still hear the screaming. I shut my eyes but I could still see. It was awful. I prayed to God. I walked into the sitting room, but nothing was familiar. It seemed like I was still there, in the room with them. I thought I might be dreaming, and started to feel myself wake up. The room came back into focus. I found the phone and dialed 911. I tried to tell them, so they could stop what was happening. But even as I spoke I kept fading in and out, going back to that awful basement."

"What made you think it was a basement?" She stared blankly at him for a few moments, as if she didn't recognize him.

"It was so dark, but he'd put a light against the wall. It lit the tub, and then the handcuffs. The boy was lit up against the wall. I could see stairs, leading upwards."

"Was there anything else in the room?"

"I couldn't see anything." She lowered her voice. "There was whimpering in the corner."

"Whimpering? Was it the boy?"

"No, the boy was hanging from the ceiling. It was coming from somewhere else. Someone else. Another boy. I don't know. I could only see the boy the man wanted. He wasn't interested in the other one." Harry felt a chill pass through his body. He still didn't know what to make of Pam, or her visions, but listening to her filled him with a sense of dread. He didn't like what she was saying.

"Can you describe the tub? Was it a bathtub?"

"No, more like... a giant fish tank. Much bigger than a tub, and transparent. I think it was made of glass... I could see right through it. I saw the boy in the water. He was leaning against the back wall, keeping his head above the water. The smell of the water was oddly familiar. It seemed out of place."

"What did it smell like?" Her answer came suddenly and surprised them both.

"Lavender."

"Lavender?"

"Yes, like he'd put lavender oil in the water. I use it myself. Although I won't anymore. I'm quite sure it was lavender." The bizarre image of the killer scenting the water with lavender oil made Harry wonder if Mario was right about Pam. He gulped at his tea, and found it cold. He poured another cup and took a long sip, finding the warm liquid comforting. Harry didn't know if he wanted to keep listening. Although her last revelation seemed bizarre, there was something about her that made him anxious. Maybe her own anxiety was infectious. Listening to the tick-tock of her old Grandfather clock, he asked what he'd wanted to ask since arriving. And for some reason had put off.

"Could you see what the man looked like?"

"No. It was like I was looking through his eyes. I couldn't see him, only what he saw." Her voice was quiet, her speech disjointed. "I could feel what he wanted. When it was all over, he wanted to get rid of the body. He rubbed bleach into the wounds while the boy hung there. Then he undid the boy's hands. I could see his gloves, that's all. He wrapped the body in a sheet, then loaded it into in the back of his car. And the garbage bag. Then he drove. There wasn't much traffic on the road, and he hummed along to the music as he drove. Then he stopped at a dumpster and took the body out. No one was around. He threw it in the bin."

"Can you remember what kind of car he drove?" Although he wasn't sure whether he believed her or not, he was starting to feel the excitement of the chase.

"I don't know much about cars."

"Try to visualize him putting the body in the boot. Was it a hatchback or sedan? Could you see a logo on the back of the car? How about the color?"

"It wasn't a car; it was an SUV. Dark blue. He opened the back to put the body in." She paused for a moment, thinking. "There was some kind of symbol on the back. What's it called... the oblong shape with the U through it."

"Toyota?" Harry's excitement was growing.

"Toyota, yes."

"Pam, you said he put something else in the SUV. A garbage bag. What was in the bag?" Pam shuddered, and her voice quivered.

"Garbage, from the boy."

"Was it his clothes?" Harry asked, not understanding.

"Yes, his clothes. But also the mess. He had to clean up after the boy." The chill took hold as Harry realized what she meant. Her eyes had widened with the horror of remembering, and her voice had risen, verging on hysteria. Harry wanted to help her, calm her down, but he didn't know what to say.

"It's okay," he consoled, but he knew it wasn't really. "Think about the drive instead. You said he was humming to music? Do you know if it was a CD or radio? Maybe a local station? Can you remember any of the songs?"

"No, I don't know. The music was classical. I don't really know it. I mean, it sounded kind of familiar, but I don't know what it's called. I'm not really familiar with classical music. I prefer something with words. You know, something you can sing along to." She paused, trying to remember. "He knew it though—he was humming along. And he had the volume up quite loud. I told the policeman what he was doing with the body, but he wasn't really listening to me. He kept asking irrelevant questions." Harry was confused.

"Did you stay on the line while you were seeing it?"

"No, I rang back after he dumped the body. I can't even remember ending the first call, but I know I rang back. I was fading in and out that first time. I couldn't concentrate. It was like I was there, in the basement. The room kept fading out. I don't think he believed me. Especially the second time. And by then it was too late anyway: he'd already dumped the body. That's when I came back, to my own house."

Her voice dropped to a whisper. "Oh God, I don't think I can stay here." Her wide eyes moved around the room as if confirming it was still the same.

"Is there somewhere else you could stay for a while? Maybe with a friend? Or family? She shook her head. "Isn't there someone else you can talk to about what's happened?"

"Not really."

"Haven't you discussed this with anyone? Apart from the police, I mean?" She shook her head. "Not even the first time?" he persisted. "Didn't you talk to anyone else then?"

"No. Well, apart from you. And Doctor Winton." Harry wondered if she was seeing a psychiatrist, but didn't want to make her defensive by asking.

"Is he your doctor?"

"No, just someone I know from work." She seemed evasive, but that didn't mean she was seeing a shrink. She was a medical receptionist, so she must know a few doctors. Indeed, from what he knew of her, from her respectable profession to her rather spinsterly decorating tastes, she might be tightly wound but she didn't really fit Mario's depiction of 'psychic Pam'. The house was full of porcelain plates and china cats, not crystal balls and batik rugs.

"How would you describe what you saw? Do you think it was some kind of psychic experience?" She looked puzzled at first, and took a few moments to respond.

"No, not really. I mean, psychics claim to see the future, don't they? What happened to me seemed to be happening in the present. Like I was seeing through his eyes. As if we were connected." She shuddered. "Through some kind of telepathic relationship. I'm not really sure. I don't know much about psychics, but I've got to admit I'm cynical. But ESP has been tested and verified, unlike fortune-telling. Perhaps that's all psychics really do: read their audience. Exercise some type of telepathic ability. If they're not complete charlatans, of course." Harry wasn't sure how to respond.

"It sounds like you're quite informed on the subject." A tentative smiled passed across her normally serious face.

"Yes, well, I've done a little internet research at work, since that first experience. During my breaks, of course."

"Why do you think you've developed this ability now? Has anything happened to prompt it?"

"Well," she blushed, "I'm not sure whether I should tell you this..."

"Anything you tell me will be off the record," he assured her. She began wringing her hands nervously, suddenly demure, like a shy schoolgirl.

Yes, well, the thing is, I'm a little embarrassed talking about this."

"Please don't be." Harry smiled encouragingly.

"A couple of months ago I met a man." She faltered, before rushing on. "There's nothing happening between us, it's just that he and I, well, we've been developing a friendship. I think there's a special bond there between us." She stopped speaking, shy again, and Harry prodded her gently.

"What's his name?"

"Gary Pitman. He's the new cleaner at the clinic. He usually arrives at the end of my shifts. We've started chatting. He's recently divorced. And lonely." She gave Harry a shy smile. "We understand each other," she explained. But Harry still didn't get it.

"So this Gary and you have started dating?" She looked startled at the suggestion.

"Oh no, nothing like that. His divorce was only finalized a few months ago; I doubt he's ready to start dating again. We just talk. He tells me about his marriage. And I understand what he's going through. The loneliness. There's nothing romantic between us. Not yet, anyway." Harry detected a hint of coyness in her last statement, and tried not to smile. "Things are still developing."

"Have you told him about your visions?"

"No." She hesitated. "I don't want to scare him off." Harry was still struggling to see the point.

"But you think there's some connection—between your visions and this... developing relationship... with Gary?"

"Well," she began, wringing her hands again, "it's just that I've read that ESP can develop in pre-verbal relationships. When you form a special bond with someone. Like the relationship that develops between mother and infant—they can understand each other without speech. And I think that's what's happening between Gary and I." She blushed when she said his name. "As our relationship develops."

Harry wasn't sure what to say. He still didn't know what to make of Pam Grinstone, but this latest confidence wasn't enhancing his faith in her. While she might not fit the 'psychic Pam' depiction, he could understand why Mario dismissed her as crazy. But there was still something about her story that profoundly disturbed him, and which he couldn't easily dismiss. It wasn't that she herself was so credible, although Harry didn't think she was lying. If there was some truth to what she was saying, and so far there did seem to be some, than Harry had to find out how she knew what she knew. If she was honest about not discussing her visions with anyone else, and Harry thought she was, then no one else could be feeding her this stuff. He knew there was something about her story that required further investigation. The things she'd told him left him feeling uneasy, even anxious. He needed to talk to Jo.

Three

Jo was about to call Harry when her phone rang.

"Jo, it's Marcy Dawson. Listen, there was something a bit unusual about the latest body. It was very clean, despite being dumped in the bin."

"I'm not following. Doesn't he use bleach on the bodies?"

"Yes, although that's concentrated on the wounds. Apart from the victim's own bodily wastes—urine, feces, blood, tissue—the back of the victim remained clean. When he dumped the others, they rolled out of the sheet. He must throw them over. Which he also did this time, but the body remained partially covered. And because it was face down, and found soon after being dumped, the back wasn't covered with garbage like the others were. So it was still clean. As if it had been soaked for some time, prior to the homicide. But not by bleach."

"What then?"

"Well, strangely enough, lavender oil. We found oil residue on the body. I'm guessing he'd been soaked in it." Jo tried to digest this latest finding.

"Lavender oil? You're saying our killer soaks the bodies in oil before eating them?"

"Before biting them," Marcy corrected. "Some of the flesh from the wounds is missing, including the genitals and buttocks, so he might eat it. Or simply collect it. But he doesn't eat everything he bites off. The remains in the bag were cleaner, but they'd been completely soaked in bleach, so we didn't detect any oil on them. It was on the intact body. We must have overlooked it with the other victims, if he used it, because they were more contaminated. And the oil is very diluted, which is why I'm guessing that small amounts of it were placed in water, and used to soak the victim before the homicide." Jo shuddered at the image of the killer cleaning his meat before chewing it.

~ * ~

Peter Holdman dug his elbow into the woman lying next to him.

"Get up, Leanne". She groaned and rolled over. Fat, lazy cunt, he thought, elbowing her again, harder this time. "It's seven a.m. Get up." He saw her eyelids flicker as he rolled out of bed, scratching his balls through his cotton boxers. Leanne wouldn't bother getting up at all if he didn't insist on her getting his breakfast before he went to work. She'd be content to lie around until the midday talk shows came on, and she could lumber from bed to couch.

"Lazy cow," he muttered as he moved towards the shower. "I'm going for a shower now," he snarled loudly, "so I'll be ready for breakfast in about ten minutes." That ought to get the slut moving, he thought with satisfaction.

~ * ~

Leanne was frying his sausages and eggs when he walked in and sat himself at what he'd deemed to be the head of their small kitchen table. She placed a cup of black coffee in front of him, and he tugged at his tie. It was already irritating the rash on his neck, and that wasn't his only problem. Gray polyester stretched tightly across his crotch, making his balls itch. The cotton of his short shirtsleeves cut tightly across his arms, almost cutting off the circulation above his elbows, and he could already feel the perspiration forming under his armpits. All these things served to infuriate Peter Holdman. Leanne was going to have to start cooking healthy meals, rather than all this fried crap. But before he could broach the subject, the cow started talking.

"Do you think you could give Jody a lift into school?" Her voice had that whinny tone that made him want to reach across and slap her.

"Why?" She tried this on every so often, but he knew if he did it once she'd be asking all the time, and he'd be stuck with the job.

"She needs to get there early, before the bus gets in. They're doing some group project."

"You'll have to take her then." His voice was firm—he wasn't having any argument on the subject. "Sorry, but I've got an appointment this morning. Besides, there's no point in you having a car if you're not going to use it. She's not even up yet, so I don't see how she's going to get there early." Jody and Jason were lazy slugs like their mother, barely capable of dragging their fat asses out of bed each morning to get to school for a few hours. He'd hate to see them try to do a full day's work. Still, he preferred it when they slept in— the kitchen was too small for all of them to be in here eating breakfast at the same time.

Peter hated the small bungalow they'd bought fifteen years ago, when they'd first gotten married. And he hated the fact that it had been bought with money borrowed from Leanne's father—a stupid old prick who'd slaved in a factory all his life, taking orders and giving his paycheck to the wife each week to pay the bills and 'save a little of what's left over'. Despite being a drone all his life, the old prick liked to look down his nose at Peter, and never seemed to tire of reminding him of the loan he'd given all those years ago. As if he hadn't more than repaid it by taking his fat, useless daughter off his hands. If he'd known what an asshole he was going to be about it, Peter would never have taken his money. But he and Leanne had been young and stupid at the time. Excited about their first home. Peter had always assumed they'd upgrade before the kids arrived, but somehow the time had never been right. The bills kept rolling in. Leanne wasn't good with the finances. Now the place seemed to be closing in on him, too small to escape his family, their pressing demands suffocating him. He finished his breakfast in silence and left for work.

~ * ~

The ringing woke him up.

"Hello."

"Harry? It's Jo. Can we meet sometime today?" Still half-groggy from sleep, he struggled to wake up properly.

"Sure. Thanks for ringing back."

"Sorry?" She sounded puzzled. Maybe she hadn't checked her messages.

"Never mind. I called earlier. How about lunch? We could meet at that cafe on Elizabeth Street—down from the precinct." She hesitated briefly before answering.

"Okay. About twelve? I'll call you back if I'm running late."

"Hey, Jo, I don't know if it means anything, but Pam seemed to think the Wolfman had another kid. Besides the one that turned up this morning. Have you identified the body yet?"

"We can't release the name yet—there'll be a press statement tomorrow morning." She hesitated. "It was James Matheson. We're talking to Pam again today. Someone's already gone to pick her up." Although the Daily Courier had been among the many papers following the James Matheson story, it still came as a shock. Harry had personally interviewed Sylvia Matheson after her public appeal for information, so his heart went out to her at hearing her son was the Wolfman's third victim. Third that they knew about, anyway. The police had been inundated with calls about missing kids.

"Do you think he might have another kid?"

"I don't know. We'll talk at lunch. I gotta go."

"Okay, see you at lunch then." As he hung up Harry rubbed his eyes, still trying to get the sleep out. His tired eyes moved around the room, taking in the sparse furnishings like a stranger inspecting someone else's apartment. The suede sofa he'd fallen asleep on was one of the few decent pieces of furniture he owned. Which didn't make it comfortable to sleep on, he reflected, rubbing the back of his very stiff neck. He must have dozed off after calling the paper. He'd rung to let Lou know about the story, but as the deadline for tomorrow's edition was seven p.m., he'd decided to hold off on writing it up. Hopefully he'd have more to report by then. Glancing at his watch and seeing it was almost eleven, he decided there wasn't much point going into the office now. He'd leave it until after lunch. He was just heading for the shower when the phone rang again.

"Hello."

"I'm going to be thirty minutes early—can you be there?" He looked at his watch.

"Sure."

"See you there." She hung up.

~ * ~

The cafe was already filling up by the time Harry arrived, but he managed to get an outside table. Jo hadn't arrived yet so he ordered a cappuccino and lit a cigarette. She walked in five minutes later and arched an eyebrow at the cigarette.

"Started again a few months ago," he explained sheepishly, stubbing it out.

"Pam Grinstone killed herself this morning," she announced. Harry felt like he'd just been punched in the gut. "We got a report from a neighbor just after I talked to you this morning—the first time. That's why I wanted to meet earlier. You might have been the last person to see her alive."

"I don't believe it. How?"

"She shot herself." Harry struggled to digest this unexpected information.

"Shot herself? I can't even imagine her touching a gun."

"It was registered. She bought it about a month ago. What time were you there?"

"I went straight from the scene. Left about six a.m. I guess I was there about an hour. Jo, this doesn't seem right. She was scared, but not suicidal." A waitress came over and Jo stared at her for a few seconds, as if trying to work out what she wanted.

"Can I take your order?"

"I'll have a cappuccino, thanks."

"I'll have another one too, please." Harry lit another smoke, even though he knew Jo didn't like the smell. She didn't say anything.

"Do you want to see the lunch menu?"

"Yes. Thanks." Harry wasn't feeling hungry but they'd come for lunch, so it seemed an appropriate response.

"What did she say? What was she scared about?" The waitress left, and Harry recounted his conversation with Pam. Jo listened without interrupting. The cappuccinos arrived and she waved the waitress away, telling her they weren't ready to order. By the time Harry finished her face was pale.

"She was right about the lavender oil. And the garbage bag with the victim. There was a bag with the other victims, too." That was a detail he hadn't known before, but it was the image of him soaking his victim that really creeped Harry out. Lavender oil was something he associated with old ladies, not homicidal cannibals.

"How did she seem to you? I mean, did you find her credible?" He'd been wondering the same thing himself pretty much since Pam first contacted the Daily Courier. After Mandy Gleeson's body showed up. Jo had just given her a bit more credibility by confirming the oil and bag.

"I don't know. I mean, she does seem kind of loopy, as if she could be feeding off the public hysteria, but there's something about the way she tells the story. All the details. And she's been right about some stuff that we know of. Including the fact that a boy was killed last night."

"Do you think she might know the killer? Perhaps she knows who he is and doesn't want to say. Maybe she doesn't even want to admit it to herself." He'd been giving that one some thought, too.

"I guess that's possible, but I don't know if I believe it. She seems a bit of a loner. No boyfriend—nothing serious anyway. I suggested she might want to stay with someone, and she said there was no one. I think she was telling the truth. She seemed so scared about being alone in that apartment. I still can't believe she shot herself. Are you checking her background?" Jo nodded.

"So, she couldn't tell you the license plate of the SUV? Or if it was a late or early model?"

"Sorry."

"What about the direction he took? Or the distance he traveled?"

"Sorry, Jo, I've told you everything I know." He wondered if they were both avoiding the other subject. "If she was right about James, maybe she was right about another boy."

"I hope not. We still have a lot of missing kids." Although Jo was being vague, Harry knew she must be thinking about one kid in particular: Billy Williamson.

"You look tired." She acknowledged the observation with a weary smile.

"I'm fine." Jo was obsessive about work, and she and Mario had been working this case since the first body showed up. She wasn't likely to be fine until the killer was caught, which didn't look like happening any time soon, despite the resources the city was throwing at it. But Harry knew how she felt—he'd gotten more than a little obsessed with the Wolfman himself.

"Do you want to order?" Although the question seemed inappropriate, and he'd lost his appetite, he couldn't think of anything else to say. She nodded and he signaled for the waitress.

Four

"Hey, Harry," Paul greeted him cheerfully. "Heard about your scoop this morning. Pity you couldn't get it into today's edition. Have you heard any more?" Paul Preston occupied the desk next to Harry's, and they'd been friends pretty much since he joined the Daily Courier four years ago, soon after Harry. They'd both been following the story closely, covering different angles since it first broke. Although Paul had now moved on to the latest scandal in the Senate. Not that the paper had finished with the Wolfman—Paul just had a limited attention span. The public was still hungry for any news of the killer. Indeed, Paul and Harry weren't the only ones who'd been covering the story for the Daily Courier. While the citizens of New York generally shared Paul's limited attention span, this was one story they hadn't tired of. The idea that some madman was running around eating their children had outraged the citizens of New York, and they no longer just wanted him found—they wanted his blood. They wanted him to suffer.

"The body's been identified: James Matheson." Paul let out a low whistle.

"Poor kid. When's the press conference?"

"Not till tomorrow morning."

"Shit, that's great. We'll still be able to break the story before anyone else." Paul was a nice guy, but he was a reporter first and foremost. Harry nodded.

"Yeah, I came in to write it up. We can't release the name yet." Well, Harry reflected, they were both reporters, first and foremost.

~ * ~

Harry omitted the details about the oil—the police didn't want that made public—but included the information about the Toyota. He wasn't yet ready to follow up with the grieving mother, and figured any other interviews could also wait until after the press conference. He didn't want his information flow to freeze up. The story on 'Informant in the Wolfman Case Commits Suicide' offered further scope for speculation.

"Hi, Harry." He turned at the sound of Anne-Marie's voice.

"Hey, how's it all going?"

"Good. I hope I'm not disturbing you." Anne-Marie was one of the newest additions to the staff, and in the tradition of the paper, had been informally assigned to a senior reporter for supervision. In this case, Harry was the senior reporter.

"It's fine. I'm just finishing up something."

"Yes, I heard you got a scoop this morning. Congratulations!" Anne-Marie was young and almost agonizingly enthusiastic, and liked to use words like 'scoop'. With her thick, black ponytail; bright, white, even teeth; short skirts and preppy manner, she could easily pass for the paper's cheerleader. Harry knew from experience that the 'eager beaver' routine wasn't always genuine. Some used it to flatter those who could help them. Used it to mask their cynical ambition. But while he didn't doubt Anne-Marie's ambition, he hadn't detected any cynicism yet. That was something she'd grow into. And a bit of cynicism never hurt anyone. Harry always found himself a little uncomfortable in the presence of undiluted enthusiasm—it was so easy to disappoint. A little cynicism made a person so much less effort. Still, she was a sweet kid, and from what he'd seen so far she was far from dumb.

"I wondered if we could talk, when you've got time." She dazzled him with one of her bright smiles.

"Sure, let's go to the balcony. I'm dying for a smoke." Although unofficially a non-smoking zone, the seventh floor balcony of the New State Building, home to the Daily Courier, was the unofficial gathering place for the paper's poor, disenfranchised smokers. Lighting up, he turned to Anne-Marie.

"So, how's the Market Promise story coming along?" He'd started looking into the story about a month ago, when the company's half-yearly report revealed a ten million dollar contribution to the private research of Doctor Robinson. The renowned neurologist had established a private research clinic after abruptly leaving his position as Head of Neurology at the Hyman-Newman Institute for Neurology and Neurosurgery. Although the contribution wasn't the company's first, it was their largest, and they were being vague about what they were funding.

"Well, that's what I wanted to speak to you about. To get your opinion on something." She smiled brightly and he nodded at her to continue. "No one at Market Promise is interested in talking to me, and Doctor Robinson won't return my calls."

"Well, that's not really surprising. Private business is never too keen to reveal its secrets. What about Robinson's former research? Was he working on something that might interest a marketing company?"

"Well, he hasn't published anything for the past two years, but prior to that he was working on hypnotic states and the patterns of activity in the brain's central cortex. Looking at how behavior is affected by different levels of activity in the right and left hemispheres." Harry had a general idea of Robinson's work on hypnotic states, which is why he'd thought there might be a story in it. The public was always interested in accounts of mad scientists attempting to control human behavior.

"So, if he's still looking at hypnotic states, he could be researching ways to simulate buying behavior. That'd be my guess, given that it's a marketing company which is funding his research. Did you find out whether they're the only ones funding him?"

"I haven't uncovered any other investment. Although he does have a private income—a family trust."

"Okay. So if Market Promise is his only private contributor, I guess they're not going to want their competitors to hear about the research. Technically they own it, rather than Robinson, so even if he wanted to he couldn't publish his results. Not without their permission. They'd have to provide some general information to the shareholders, but we don't really know what stage he's at. Only that he must have found something to warrant a ten million dollar contribution. You said he hasn't published for a couple of years—is that since he established the private research clinic?"

"Mountview, yes. His last article was published while he was still at Hyman-Newman."

"Did you actually speak to anyone at Mountview?"

"Just the receptionist. A woman named Dorothy Porter. She said Doctor Robinson was 'unwilling to discuss his research at this stage'. But the clinic has advertised for more subjects. That's what I wanted to talk to you about. I thought it might be a good way of getting in and finding out what they're doing in there. What do you think?" Under the pressure of her expectant gaze, Harry lit another cigarette.

"Well, they'd probably make you sign a confidentiality agreement. So you wouldn't be able to write about what you learned."

"I thought about that. And I wouldn't tell them I was a reporter, of course. But if I had a better idea of what they were doing, I might be able to get the information another way." Harry thought about it. He wasn't even sure the story would go anywhere, although it might have potential. He'd given it to her when the Wolfman story came up as a way to occupy her time. But she seemed keen to follow up on it, and who was he to thwart young ambition and initiative.

"Where did they advertise?"

"In the New York Times. They offered 'generous remuneration' for research subjects.

"Well, it can't hurt. At the very least, you'll earn a bit of extra cash." Junior reporters were paid a pittance.

"Thanks, Harry, I'll get right on it." She shot him an admiring gaze before bouncing back inside, leaving Harry to lean heavily against the balcony, dragging the smoke deep into his lungs. While her admiring glances might be flattering, her youthful enthusiasm only made him feel old. Although he was only ten years her senior, give or take a year, his own youthful enthusiasm seemed like a distant memory. As he glanced down at his feet he worried that even his clothes seemed faded—his jeans and boots were worn with age. For the past year or so Harry had found it increasingly difficult to get enthusiastic about anything. Until the Wolfman, which was probably obsession rather than enthusiasm. His mind was fixated with the modern monster—with what he must be thinking. The thought of him keeping his young victims bound in the basement for weeks on end, and then bathing them in lavender oil, seemed almost as unthinkable as what he did next.

Five

The young blonde on reception was the antithesis of Pam Grinstone, with her thick mane of bleached hair and her carefully made-up face.

"Can I help you, sir?

"Hi, my name's Harry O'Brien. I'm from the Daily Courier. I wondered if I might talk to you for a few minutes." A puzzled expression flickered across her face.

"Well, I'm kind of working at the moment. What's this about?" Harry had noticed the scattering of people in the waiting room on his way in, and guessed she wasn't too busy to talk.

"Well, perhaps when you've finished work then. It's about Pam Grinstone." The puzzled expression was replaced with a look of concern.

"Oh, wasn't it horrible? The police have been in already, talking to Doctor Wong. They were going to talk to Doctor Morrison too, but he was busy with patients, and then a lady detective went in, but she didn't really stay very long."

"Did you know Pam very well, Miss..."

Oh, call me Julie. Everyone does. Well, I've been here about eight months now, so I've worked with her since then. She was here for forever, so she did my induction, but we haven't been working together lately. I'm usually on when she's off. We're not that busy here. It's only Doctor Wong and Doctor Morrison—and Doctor Johnson, but she's gone part-time since she had the baby. She only works twice a week these days."

"Does a Doctor Winton work here?" Her face went blank.

"No, not since I've been here. Maybe he was here a long time ago."

"I could have made a mistake with the name. So you and Pam never really socialized?"

"No, not really. She wasn't the type to pop down for a drink after work or anything like that, if you know what I mean. That's really the only downside of this job. Don't get me wrong, Mr. O'Brien, but—"

"Please, call me Harry," he interrupted.

"All right then, Harry," she smiled. "Like I was saying, the conditions here are good and everyone's very nice, but there's not much of a social element, if you know what I mean. Not like my last job, at Murphy and Simpson. That's an accounting firm. Quite a large one, too. Lots of staff. Lots of younger people. I went out quite a bit with the other girls in the office. But I was only a Temp, so when a permanent part-time position came up here I thought I'd better jump at it. Although I wasn't trained as a Medical Receptionist. Still, it's really not much different to being a receptionist anywhere else. Once you get used to it. Of course, I would have preferred if it was full-time." A thought struck her.

"Well, perhaps now it will be. Pam was permanent full-time." She blushed. "Not that I'm happy she's gone—not like that. What happened to her was horrible. Really horrible. I can't imagine what she must have been thinking to want to go and do something like that. I doubt I'll be able to sleep tonight for thinking of what she must have been going through." Harry couldn't really imagine her losing too much sleep over it. A middle-aged Asian man in a white coat steered a woman and her young son into the area behind Julie's desk, unlatching the half door to the waiting room. He picked up a folder and glanced at the waiting patients, looking right past Harry, before shuffling back to his office.

"I'll send Mr. James through now," Julie called after him. "Mr. James," she called shrilly, "Doctor Wong will see you now." She hopped off her chair to unlatch the door for an elderly man. "Down the corridor, first door on your right," she advised briskly, before sitting back down.

"Did you know what was bothering her?"

"Pam? No." She paused briefly, as if thinking it over. "She was a very private person. Didn't ever really talk about personal matters."

"So you don't know if she had a boyfriend? Or anyone else she might have been close to. Someone she might have talked to." Julie seemed amused by the question.

"A boyfriend? No, I shouldn't imagine so." She became more serious. "I never knew her to meet anyone for lunch or after work—male or female."

"Do you know someone called Gary Pitman?" Julie groaned and rolled her eyes.

"Our cleaner?"

"Yes. Pam mentioned him. Do you think she might have been having a relationship with him?"

"You'd have to be a real loser to have a relationship with that creep. No offence to Pam—I don't think she would have been. She would have just seen him after work, like I do. That's when he comes in. Thinks he a real ladies' man—you know the type. Gold chain around the neck, hairy chest." She shuddered for emphasis. "Hairy ears, too. And he seemed the type to have a hairy back. Real gross. Always wanted to talk. Had an opinion about everything. The guy is a complete wanker." Harry found himself feeling even sorrier for Pam.

"How about the doctors here? Would Pam have talked to one of them about things? Maybe there was one in particular she felt close to?"

"Oh, I really don't think so. You'd have to ask them, but it's like I said, Pam was a very private woman." Another middle-aged man in an identical white coat walked into reception, shepherding a young woman to the door. This one had less hair and looked at Harry, prompting Julie to introduce him.

"Doctor Morrison, this is Mr. O'Brien from the Daily Courier. He was just asking whether poor Pam might have spoken to either you or Doctor Wong about why she might have, well, you know..." She trailed off.

"Harry O'Brien. Pleased to meet you, Doctor Morrison." He held out his hand, which Morrison took without much enthusiasm. "I know you must be busy but I wonder if I could just have a few minutes of your time."

"Ah, well, my colleague and I have already spoken to the police today, and I'm not sure it's such a good idea for us to be speaking to the press."

"I understand your concern, but I just wanted to check a couple of things Pam said to me this morning—before the incident. I promise I won't keep you from your patients for too long. A couple of minutes, that's all." Julie was now staring at him wide-eyed.

"Ah, right then. It will have to be quick. Follow me." He strode ahead and Julie whispered into Harry's ear as she opened the door, "Second door on the right."

"Have a seat," Doctor Morrison offered perfunctorily. He was already seated in front on his computer, and Harry took the chair closest to his desk. "You mentioned speaking to Pam this morning." Despite his reserved demeanor, he didn't try to disguise his curiosity.

"Yes, I'm not sure whether you're aware or not, but Pam had been talking to me, as well as the police, about the Wolfman murders." A look of distaste flickered across his face, as if he'd just smelled something bad.

"Quite. The police first contacted us a few weeks ago to confirm her working hours, and ask a few questions." Harry remembered something Jo said about Pam having an alibi the night of Mandy Gleeson's murder. Not that she'd ever really been a suspect. But they'd clearly checked out her story, just in case.

"Does the clinic open at night?"

"Only Thursdays."

"And does Pam usually work Thursday nights?" He nodded.

"Always. She is—was—very reliable. We were very upset to hear about what happened. She's been a valuable employee for almost eight years. Been here almost as long as I have. We're going to miss her."

"Yes, I imagine it must be very upsetting for you." Morrison didn't look like he was in mourning. Poor Pam didn't seem to endear herself to anyone. "Did Pam ever speak to you or Doctor Wong about the case?"

"No. Not at all. Paul—Doctor Wong—informed her that the police had contacted us, but even then she didn't say much about it. And it hasn't really come up since. Not that I can speak for Paul, mind you, although I do think he'd say if she'd said anything."

"Do you and Doctor Wong have a close relationship then?"

"Oh yes, very friendly. We started the practice together, and still play the occasional round of golf on the weekend."

"Do you know of anyone else in Pam's life she might have spoken to?"

"Well no, not really. I know it sounds terrible, but despite working with her for eight years I don't really know much about her life outside the office. I told the detective who was here the same thing."

"Okay, well, thanks for your help. I really appreciate you taking the time to talk to me today." Morrison remained seated as Harry stood up to leave.

"That's fine. Can you ask Julie to send in my next patient?"

"Of course. Oh, one more thing. Do you know a Doctor Winton?"

"No. Why? Should I?"

"Just something Pam said. Do you think she would have been seeing another doctor?"

"I shouldn't think so. I'm her general practitioner, and I haven't referred her to anyone else." He'd lost interest in Harry now, and was peering into his computer screen. Harry slipped Julie his card on the way out.

"Thanks for all your help today, Julie. Please give me a call if you think of anything else?"

"So you don't want to meet after work then?"

"I think I've got all I need—you've been very helpful." As he left the clinic Harry felt her disappointed gaze following him. She looked like she had some questions of her own.

Six

The Taskforce had been meeting twice a day for the past two weeks, and the atmosphere in the room that Monday afternoon was far from buoyant. Doctor Henry King, the Homicide Squad's profiler, was addressing the room.

"The biting and possible eating of the flesh is a form of sexual fetishism. The killer doesn't need to have sex with the children—the biting itself provides the gratification. It's also significant that the only missing parts have been the buttocks and genitals. If he does actually devour the flesh, it seems he only devours these sexualized areas, and is content to dispose of the rest of the flesh he tears off."

"This tends to reinforce the notion that for him the biting is the primary form of gratification. Sexualized cannibalism prioritizes the eating of the flesh; our killer is more concerned with the biting itself. And as we have just recently learned, he is quite particular in the preparation. Not only does he keep the victims for some time, which is perhaps part of the preparation, but he also soaks them carefully. This is not someone with great hunks of meat in his freezer, or filthy surroundings. He is quite fastidious in his habits. This is also demonstrated by the care he takes to remove any traces of DNA. We would therefore expect our killer to be an intelligent and probably well-groomed man."

"If our killer gets off on biting, can we assume he has a history of it?" The question came from Detective James, an African-American man in his mid-thirties.

"Yes. I don't know that this in itself will help us to track him down, but it will help once we have a suspect. Our killer will most probably have a history of biting. I believe Detective Thompson has been looking into this." A dark-haired woman at the front of the room rose and addressed her colleagues.

"Unfortunately, this biting thing isn't all that uncommon. I've done a computer search of child abuse and other assault cases in the New York area, and the incidences of children being bitten runs into the thousands. Even discounting those offenders who are dead, imprisoned or over sixty, the list is too extensive to be very useful."

"Furthermore," Doctor King added, "biting is notoriously under-reported, particularly when performed by siblings. Child counselors commonly encounter the problem of children who bite."

~ * ~

Jo felt despondent. It seemed like every clue they followed wound up at the same dead end. There was nothing linking the kids, and the abductions were spread out across the city, in Queens and Brooklyn. They'd retraced the steps of Mandy, Tony and James on their last days, talking to hundreds of neighbors and friends, and had come up with nothing. The list of missing children under investigation was long and growing daily. The switchboard had been jammed for weeks. If someone's kid was thirty minutes late getting home from baseball practice the parents called the police. The national search for similar crimes in the past ten years hadn't revealed anything. There was Pam's information about the Toyota SUV, but the source wasn't all that credible, and the information was too general, so they weren't devoting any detective hours to it. It felt like they were no closer to catching the killer than they'd been a month ago. It was like they were all just waiting for him to slip up. Kill another kid, and make a mistake this time.

~ * ~

Billy Williamson was having a very bad dream. The black hole was sucking him in and he was suffocating, drowning in the darkness. He woke gasping for breath, and the nightmare became real. Billy felt the rope around his wrists and ankles and remembered. He was alone in the dark, and he wanted his mother. He wanted to be out riding his bike with his best friend, George Johnson. He didn't want to be here. He didn't know how long he'd already been here, for the darkness disorientated him, but it felt like forever. His other life was becoming more and more like the dream, and this was his reality.

It seemed so long ago now that he'd stopped crying. That he'd stopped praying to God. He'd told God that if He got him out he'd never do anything bad again for the rest of his life. He'd help his mother with all the chores around the house, and he'd be a better big brother to Gracie. He wouldn't get mad at her when she came into his room and touched all his stuff, or when she followed him and George around asking what they were doing. He'd let her play with them, even if George didn't want her to. And he'd help his dad wash the car on the weekends, and do the yard. He'd mow the lawn too, if his dad let him, but he didn't think he would because Billy had wanted to have a go with the mower once before, a long time ago, and his dad had said he was too little. That something might spring up and hit him in the eye. That he could do it when he got older. Maybe he'd be old enough when he got out of here. If he got out.

He'd also told God that he'd make friends with Gary Patterson, who always sat by himself at recess and watched the others play. No one ever wanted to play with him because he was fat and stuttered. But Billy would try to make friends with him because he now understood what it felt like to be all alone and it was horrible. Billy had thought and thought about all the things he would do to be better, and all the promises he could make to God. But it hadn't done any good and now he'd stopped talking to God.

Billy wriggled himself into a sitting position and squinted, trying to see in the darkness. It was no good. He had to pee, but he didn't like using the bucket because it smelled so bad, and he knew his poo was in there. He hadn't heard the Man come and take the bucket away yet. He reached out into the darkness for the bucket of water the Man left for him, splashing water on the floor as he tried to use his bound hands as a cup. Not much made it to his mouth, but it was enough to take the dryness away. At first he'd been terrified by the sound of the Man coming, but now he listened out for him to come with his food. He'd never spoken to the Man, even though he'd wanted to ask him when he could go home. He was scared that the Man would tell him he was never going home. The Man didn't speak to him either—not when he brought the food, and sometimes a new bucket of water, and a clean bucket for Billy's toilet. The only thing he'd ever said to Billy was "eat your food, little boy", and though his voice wasn't loud or angry it still scared him. It had made his stomach ache.

He remembered opening his eyes that first time and seeing the Man standing there beside his bed. He'd come into Billy's room like some kind of ghost, and Billy thought he must have some kind of magic, even though he'd heard the window creak. Black magic. Because Billy had known he was coming even before he saw him there. He'd felt the darkness first, and it had woken him up. It had made the room feel cold, and every violent scene in every movie Billy had ever watched had flashed through his mind. He'd closed his eyes, and even though he'd wanted to run next door into his mum and dad's room, despite being too old for that now, his legs wouldn't move. The Man was dressed all in black and he'd only gotten a glimpse of him before the hand reached out over his nose and mouth and everything else had gone black, too.

~ * ~

When Richard Tamworth read the Daily Courier with his morning espresso that Tuesday morning he experienced a heavy sinking feeling.

"Oh shit," he'd muttered to himself. His wife Debbie was still asleep when he dialed 911.

~ * ~

Shelly Williamson was also reading the Daily Courier before her husband joined her at the breakfast table. When Dan walked into their colonial-style kitchen-diner he found his wife staring blindly across the table, the paper still unfolded, its front page screaming up at them: Wolfman Claims Third Victim. He picked up the paper and read the first few paragraphs, feeling sick to his stomach. He felt the frustrated rage build within him, before dissipating into helplessness at the sight of his dazed wife.

"Shelly honey," he began. But he didn't know what to say next, and she didn't seem to be listening anyway. Dan Williamson stood over six feet tall and weighed two hundred and eighty pounds, and every day he took charge of the many employees and contractors who worked for his construction company. Yet he felt as helpless as a small boy before his grieving wife. He clenched and unclenched his big hands uselessly as he tried to think of something to say.

"Honey," he tried again, but she continued starting blankly ahead. "The police will find him."

"Mummy, is it time to get up now?" Their four-year old daughter stood in the doorway, looking small and fragile in her nightdress. Shelly usually got her up with Billy so they could all have breakfast together, before Dan went to work and Billy went to school. Gracie stood there looking uncertain about the change in her routine. Dan glanced across at his wife, who hadn't even turned to look at Gracie, before moving quickly across the kitchen and scooping his daughter up in his big arms.

"Morning, angel. Mummy's not feeling too good this morning so Daddy's going to cook your breakfast. Anything you want." He deposited her at the table next to his wife, hoping Shelly would be forced to acknowledge her. But she looked past her daughter as if she didn't really see her, and continued staring blankly ahead. Gracie looked from her mother to her father with the same uncertain expression.

"How about pancakes? They're your favorite, aren't they?"

"Yes, Daddy."

Seven

Jo was briefing the Taskforce about the call. It wasn't much but at least it meant they could justify spending some time looking for dark-blue Toyota Landcruisers. Richard Tamworth had seen the Landcruiser drive off not far from the Matheson's place at approximately 3.40 a.m., on the morning James was kidnapped. He hadn't come forward before now because he'd been leaving his girlfriend's place at the time, rushing to get home before his wife finished her night shift at a local Aged Care facility.

"Not that I saw anything anyway," he'd blustered. "That vehicle could have belonged to anyone. But when I read that report in today's paper, about the SUV, I thought I should ring in. My wife won't have to know about this call, will she?" Assuring Mr. Tamworth that there was no need to inform his wife, and satisfying herself that he'd told her all he knew, Jo had taken his contact details and written up the report.

It still wasn't much to go on. One of the most troubling aspects of the case was not knowing how he targeted the kids. They believed all three kids—possibly four—had been kidnapped in the middle of the night, but otherwise the pattern seemed random. The families lived nowhere near each other, and as far as the squad had been able to determine, there were no common friends or acquaintances. No one remembered any unusual visits in the weeks leading up to the kidnappings. No tradesperson or courier had visited the three houses.

The only common thread was an unsecured entrance to the houses, and the fact that the kids all had their own bedrooms. All three rooms—four if they were counting Billy Williamson's—were located on a ground floor, and had been accessed by an unlocked window. In all but the Matheson case the window had been the child's own bedroom window. In the Matheson case the unlocked window was in the kitchen, and they believed the killer had entered there and left through James' bedroom window. But it was just a theory—he'd left no fingerprints or any other sign he'd been there. He'd even pulled the windows closed after him, leaving everything just as he'd found it. There were no signs of struggle in the bedrooms, suggesting that he knocked his victims unconscious as they slept. Maybe he drugged them—none of the parents had heard anything. Richard Tamworth's information supported what they already believed: that he struck in the middle of the night, when everyone was asleep and there was less chance of being seen by neighbors. In every case a distraught parent had discovered an empty bedroom the next morning. If nothing else, thought Jo, the media frenzy was at least making it harder for him, as the citizens of New York began bolting their children in.

"So we'll need to check out everyone with a late-model, dark-blue Toyota Landcruiser, believed to be licensed in the state of New York," Jo concluded, and a few of her colleagues groaned.

As Detective Morrison rose to report on the investigation into the current list of missing children, a young Officer knocked on the door and waved to Jo and Mario, beckoning them outside. There they were confronted by an enraged Dan Williamson.

"What are you doing to find my son?" he raged. "It's been over a week now and that madman's already killed another kid." A thick purple vein throbbed on his forehead.

When Jo and Mario first interviewed Dan and his wife, and heard how Shelly had gone in to wake Billy for school, only to find his bedroom empty, a feeling of cold dread had passed through Jo. That feeling intensified yesterday when Harry recounted Pam's comments about another child. The fact that Billy was still alive at least gave them some hope of finding him before he was murdered. The other victims didn't turn up for three to four weeks after they'd been taken, and all had been found relatively soon after their deaths. But the thought of the young boy trapped there for another two to three weeks haunted Jo. She couldn't rid herself of the image of him, scared and alone, and it was a heavy burden on her shoulders. She knew it was her responsibility to find him. She'd been working sixteen hour days for the past few weeks, and the fatigue was numbing her mind and body. But not enough to erase the images of the children, and what he'd done to them, and might still be doing to Billy.

"Mr. Williamson, let's talk in the interview room." The compassion in Jo's voice seemed to melt his fury, and the big man allowed himself to be led away.

While Jo and Mario dealt with the distraught father, Rebecca Lui was waiting for her ten o'clock appointment. He was already fifteen minutes late, and she found herself half hoping he wouldn't show. Paul Gribble had been referred to her by Doctor Marshall, who'd only seen him twice before deciding that the sessions weren't going well. He thought Paul might be more inclined to open up to a woman; he certainly wasn't opening up to Doctor Marshall.

"Pretentious prick," was Paul's assessment when Rebecca referred to his previous therapist. Although she'd only been seeing him a few weeks, she was already feeling the strain. Rebecca had been practicing psychiatry for over seven years and had extensive experience with repressed anger and dissociation. But her newest patient roused in her an unease she hadn't felt for a long time, and she wasn't entirely sure how to respond. She took her ethical responsibilities very seriously, and patient confidentiality was sacrosanct. This was the first time in her professional career she'd given any thought to breaching it. She'd thought about discussing the case with Doctor Marshall, who'd been practicing for almost fifteen years, and with whom she'd discussed cases in the past. But lately she'd been wondering whether to discuss it with someone else. Her thoughts were interrupted by the arrival of her patient, looking hot and bothered as he lumbered in and sank into the armchair facing her.

"Good morning, Paul," she greeted him, getting a grunt in response.

"I had another dream last night," he began abruptly. Rebecca crossed her legs and smiled in what she considered an encouraging manner. "The little boy's still in the basement and he's afraid. He's all alone now, since the Man came for the other boy." A line of perspiration had formed across his forehead, and he bit down on his lower lip, lost in the image.

"What happened to the other boy?" Rebecca prompted.

"He hung him up and ate him," he blurted out. His pupils were dilated and he continued biting down on his lip until it started swelling. Paul's therapy sessions were always about the man and the children. Sometimes he seemed to associate with the children, sometimes with the man. Rebecca's attempts to encourage him to open up about his past were always angrily dismissed. Paul insisted he "wanted to talk about my dreams, not my frigging childhood." He seemed genuinely afraid of the Man, fidgeting when he talked about him, becoming like a small child himself.

"I think he's the Wolfman," Paul announced, and Rebecca was startled. He was watching her with a sly expression, waiting to see how she responded to this newest piece of information. Although Paul's dreams reminded her of the case, he'd never before referred to it explicitly. It was something that had hung unspoken between them, the source of her unease. But Rebecca knew that it wasn't uncommon for such a public story to strike a chord with a patient, to fuel a patient's existing fantasies, and she tried not to read too much into it.

"What makes you think that?" He raised his eyes to meet hers, and the sly expression was gone, replaced with one that looked like fear, and which fed Rebecca's uneasiness.

"He's got steel teeth. Like a bear-trap. There's something wrong with the kid. Like his mind has snapped or something. But when he sees the teeth he's back, and there's fear in his eyes. He's hanging there and he must know what's about to happen, but he goes missing again. Like he's not really there. Until the teeth starting ripping into him and then he screams." Paul was perspiring heavily now, the sweat dripping from his forehead. "What the fuck is wrong with me, Doc? I keep having these images of him, and the other one—the boy who's still there. But I don't want them. I just want them to stop. Even when I'm awake I'm seeing them." Paul was visibly distressed, his state increasingly agitated.

"It's important that you talk about this. If we can work together to understand what these dreams mean to you, you'll gain greater control over them. They won't stop until we understand them. Are you listening to me, Paul?"

"Yes." His voice was almost meek, in contrast to the aggressive, hostile tone he sometimes adopted in these sessions. As if he was the little boy now, rather than an angry man. Waiting to be led. But Rebecca wasn't sure where to lead him. Paul had resisted all previous attempts to get him to talk about his experiences and feelings. She'd suggested hypnosis as a way of unblocking and understanding the root of the dreams, but he'd refused.

"Paul, can you tell me why the man is eating the boy? Has the boy done something to make him angry?"

"No. He does it because he likes it. He enjoys ripping the flesh from the body. He enjoys the boy's screams." Rebecca shuddered involuntarily and glanced down at her watch.

"Our time is up for today. But I think you need to come back later in the week. Especially since you missed last Thursday's appointment. How about this Thursday?" The old Paul was returning to his body. She could see the anger in his eyes, and the frown on his face.

"I only just got here—I was running late."

"I realize that, Paul, but my eleven o'clock appointment will be here by now. If you arrive on time for your Thursday appointment we'll have the full hour together. How about ten a.m. again?"

"I assume I'm still paying for a full hour today, but fine. I'll see you then."

~ * ~

When Doctor Terry Robinson arrived at work, his friend and colleague looked like he'd been there all night. His jacket was draped over the back of his chair, and Terry recognized the shirt from yesterday.

"John, I hope you haven't been here all night entering that data." The short man swung his chair around at the sound of his friend's voice, rubbing his bleary eyes underneath the thick rims of his glasses.

"Terry, you startled me."

"I apologize." Terry gave his friend the broad smile so familiar to the countless medical professionals who'd heard him speak. The tall, charismatic neurologist had become slightly gaunt over the past year, and the thick dark hair had turned silver, but he was still the handsome, articulate man who'd been so popular on the conference circuit. Whose magnetism and confident authority had charmed such difficult audiences. "I can't imagine either of us will be very popular with Amanda if you don't start going home every once in a while."

"Oh God, I forgot to call her back last night." John ran his hands through his thinning brown hair, and looked sheepishly at his friend. John had really lucked out when he'd met Amanda Jones at college. Never much of a ladies man, he'd been a little surprised, and afraid, when the good-looking English major had accepted his invitation to coffee. His fear had turned to amazed delight as the courtship blossomed, and Terry Robinson had been his best man when he'd finally married his college sweetheart. They'd lost touch over the years, as Terry traveled the world lecturing on his research while John practiced neurology. But they'd resumed their friendship when Terry became the Head of Neurology at the hospital where John worked. It hadn't taken much effort for Terry to persuade his friend to join him in private research. But then, Terry was a very persuasive man.

"I think it's time we report our preliminary findings," John suggested. "I've been going over all the data, and it's very promising." A frown flickered across Terry's face before he replied.

"We're not ready. I still want to duplicate some of the tests with the next round of subjects."

"But don't you think we should report what we've already found? Market Promise will be expecting something."

"I'm not interested in their expectations."

"But they're our main sponsor. It's their research—well, much of it is, anyway." He knew Terry was more interested in his private research—the research that Market Promise was subsidizing, but which Terry considered their own.

"We'll report soon. Don't be so anxious." His voice held a note of finality, and John knew not to argue with him. He rarely won any arguments against his friend.

Eight

The muffled screams pierced his brain, and he woke cold and trembling. The blanket had been flung from his small, naked body, and he'd wet himself in his sleep, something he hadn't done for years. The thin mattress beneath him was cold and damp against his lower back, where the urine had seeped through.

"It's okay, Billy, calm down, it's okay." He'd taken up talking to himself ever since he'd stopped talking to God, but he couldn't convince himself that everything was really okay. He must have dozed off again. It was only when he slept that the screams came now. When he was awake he'd talk to himself and had managed to convince himself that they weren't real. They were just part of his nightmare. Everything was mixed up in here anyway—it wasn't always clear what was real and what wasn't. But deep down Billy knew there'd been another boy, and that the screams belonged to him. He'd tried to talk to the boy, but he just whimpered all the time, like a frightened animal. There was a song he used to sing to himself sometimes but Billy didn't know it, and he couldn't catch any of the words. The Man had taken him into another room, and even though the sounds had seemed far away, Billy had known they were close.

He'd heard the boy scream and scream, and he'd been trying to forget the sounds of his screams ever since then.

"It's okay, Billy, it's okay. Maybe the boy got away." He used his bound wrists to pull the blanket up over his legs, letting it soak up some of the urine. It already stank of urine anyway, because Billy hadn't known that the bucket was there at first, and it had taken him a while to work out what it was for. Despite its stink the blanket was precious to him, something he hid beneath.

He pulled himself to his knees and crawled cautiously in the darkness, letting his hands go first to avoid knocking over any bowl that might be there. Sometimes the Man would come when he was asleep and he wouldn't hear him. But he couldn't feel anything in the darkness, and he couldn't smell anything either. Normally Billy would be able to smell the food when he woke up. At first he wouldn't eat what the Man brought. He hadn't been able to bring himself to eat what he couldn't see. But his hunger had overtaken his revulsion, and now he waited for the food. He hoped it would come soon. He took another sip from the bucket to try to fill his stomach.

~ * ~

"Hey, Harry, looks like our newest reporter is checking you out." Most of the Daily Courier staff were at the Exchange, the bar down from the State View Building. Paul and Harry had arrived early and scored their normal table. Harry's first couple of beers had gone down quickly and he had a slight buzz. So far he'd been resisting the urge to switch to bourbon.

"She's twenty-three, Paul."

"Exactly."

"You're such a prick, Preston," came a voice from behind them, and they both turned to see Kelly Sloane standing there. Kelly had been with the Daily Courier for about three years, and about eighteen months ago she and Harry had worked together on a story about corrupt politicians. They'd ended up at the Exchange and later back in her bed. Afterwards she'd told Harry to go home to his girlfriend— she didn't want to be nursing any broken hearts. She was the bluntest woman he'd ever met. The next day it was business as usual, and they'd finished the story without anyone at the paper suspecting there'd been anything between them.

The fact that Paul had been burned in the past didn't stop him trying, and he allowed his eyes to move over her tight jeans and up to her tightly fitted sweater. She dismissed him with a roll of her cool green eyes and turned her gaze on Harry.

"Harry's Catholic guilt would prevent him from sleeping with a child, wouldn't it, Harry?"

"Hardly a child—look at those breasts." Paul's gaze had returned to Anne-Marie.

"I find it hard to believe you can convince any woman to sleep with you." Her voice was scornful but Paul actually did okay, even if he'd never been able to persuade Kelly into bed. With his large brown eyes and halo of light-brown curls, he had a cherubic innocence about him—some slight resemblance to a Dickensian orphan—that was wildly misleading.

"Hey, what can I say—they're persuaded by my boyish good looks and charm." Kelly took long sip from her beer, losing interest in him.

"And I see you're going for the scruffy, macho look these days, Harry. How's that working out?" Harry assumed she was referring to the stubble. Paul sniggered, and offered his opinion.

"Harry here enjoys his state of celibacy—he's just too lazy to shave."

"Thanks, both of you. Can we talk about something else now?" Kelly seemed happy enough to oblige.

"How's the Wolfman thing coming along? Nice name by the way. Seems to have really stuck. I'm surprised some orthodontist hasn't come forward yet to claim his handiwork. Did today's press conference reveal anything interesting?"

"It was pretty unenlightening really. But that's not really the topic I had in mind." It seemed like Harry couldn't escape the Wolfman lately, but he still felt like trying.

~ * ~

Peter Holdman loosened his tie as he came through his front door, frowning at the sight of his family lounging in front of the television. His son and daughter were sprawled across the faded couch, while his wife had made herself comfortable in his recliner.

"What's for dinner?" Leanne started at the sound of his voice, eyes falling from the TV screen as she jumped to her feet.

"You're home late. We've already eaten. I put yours in the oven." She spoke quickly, spewing out the words like a kid caught doing something wrong. "It's meat pie so it should heat up all right—I'll just turn the oven back on." Peter removed the offending tie and left it draped over the coat stand.

"I'll have it in the kitchen." He unbuttoned the top buttons of his too-tight shirt as he sat down. Leanne had scurried in behind him. "Get me a beer would you, I've had a cunt of a day." Peter had wasted almost two hours with some fat housewife only to see her waiver at the last minute, when she asked him to come back when her husband was home. The snotty prick hadn't even bothered listening to what he had to say.

"We don't need any life insurance, Mr. Holdman," he'd insisted, holding open the door before Peter had even finished speaking.

"Yeah," he'd fumed on the way to the car, "well I hope you drop dead of a heart attack, you tight prick, and your wife and brats end up on the streets." To make matters worse, the fucking car wouldn't turn over and he'd had to sit there for five minutes before it finally started, all the while feeling sure that the smug bastard was watching from his window. He'd had the Commodore for almost nine years now and hated it with a vengeance. He'd take his wife's car if it was any better, but it wasn't. He took a deep sip from the bottle and watched his wife's fat ass as it bent over the stove. The bitch had really let herself go over the past fifteen years—not that she'd been any great prize to start with. At least she hadn't been fat. If she hadn't been pregnant with Jody he probably wouldn't have bothered marrying her. Over the years he'd thought a lot about cheating on her. He probably would too, if the right opportunity presented itself. He'd get himself a nice piece of young ass—one that knew how to look after a man.

Nine

Harry woke with a blinding headache and a parched throat. He'd been having a bad dream and it took him a while to orientate himself into a sitting position. The sudden movement sent a rush of pain to his head, and he groaned. The room was dark. He looked at his wristwatch: 4:20. Steadying himself with his hands behind him on the bed, he pushed himself upwards and groaned again as the blood rushed to his head. He stumbled into the kitchen to make coffee, trying to shake the feeling of foreboding that enveloped him. While the bright light hurt his eyes when he flicked the switch, it felt comforting. He couldn't remember the dream but it had left a bad feeling in the pit of his stomach. Maybe it was the alcohol, but Harry's stomach seemed to be telling him that something bad was going to happen.

"Superstitious crap," he admonished himself. He tried to remember how he'd gotten home last night and the memory started coming back, replacing the dark dream-time images that were flickering across his mind too quickly for close examination. At some point in the evening Anne-Marie had come across to their table, and told him about her call to the research clinic. She was going in for her initial interview tomorrow—which was actually today. Paul had smirked and Kelly had rolled her eyes, but the young reporter seemed oblivious in her enthusiasm for the story. He'd had a few more beers with Kelly and Paul before catching a cab. Thankfully, he'd waited until he got home before switching to bourbon.

~ * ~

Anne-Marie felt a thrill of excitement as the gray-haired woman ushered her through to a private office. She'd dressed casually in jeans and a light sweater, and had decided that, if asked, her profession would be bar attendant at the Central, where she'd worked throughout college. There was no one else in the office. She'd kind of expected to be in a room full of other research subjects.

"Please take a seat. Someone will be with you shortly." The woman smiled like it was an effort, then left Anne-Marie alone. She settled herself on one of two chairs facing the large oak desk, then leaned across to study the photograph in front of her, turning it towards her to get a better look. An attractive, dark-haired woman and a young, dark-haired boy smiled into the camera.

"Good morning, Miss Benson." Startled, she pushed the photograph back to its original position, then half stood and held out her hand. He took it with a bemused smile on his face. "I'm Doctor John Winton. Please, sit down."

"Hi, Doctor Winton, it's Anne-Marie." He settled himself into the worn leather chair across from her and peered over his glasses, a faint smile still on his face.

"Well, Anne-Marie, I'm going to be asking you quite a lot of questions today so please try to make yourself comfortable. The purpose of this interview is to determine your suitability for the research we're conducting. Before I start, do you mind if I tape-record this session?" He was already pulling the recorder from his desk drawer.

"Go ahead."

"Good. So, first and foremost, are you prepared to give up two or three afternoons a week over the next six weeks? The testing will start next week."

"Yes, I can arrange my shifts at the bar around the times you'll need me here. Can I ask what the research will involve?"

"Certainly, although I can only give you an overview. The research is being conducted on behalf of a private company, so it must be kept confidential for commercial reasons. Which brings me to my second question, before we go any further. Are you prepared to sign a confidentiality agreement?" She nodded. "Good, then I can tell you that we're studying the affect of various visual images and audio recordings on brain activity. At no stage during the research will you be expected to take any drugs, nor will you be subjected to any testing that could have negative effects on your physical, psychological or emotional well-being. All research procedures adhere rigorously to ethical guidelines. Broadly speaking, we'll be looking at how the brain responds to certain stimuli."

"How do you measure that kind of thing?" He leaned back in his chair.

"With very safe, non-invasive technologies. We use electroencephalographs—or EEGs—to measure electrical activity in the brain. We'll also look at patterns of brain activity, as well as more non-technological data, including information gathered through interviews like this. The person actually conducting the tests is a renowned neurologist: Doctor Terry Robinson. I can assure you that Doctor Robinson places the safety and comfort of his subjects first and foremost."

"So you're not actually involved in the testing?"

"Apart from these initial interviews, I tend to stick to the analysis and collation of data." He ran his fingers through his thinning hair and smiled at her, and Anne-Marie found herself warming to him. He reminded her of a friendly uncle. "From next week you'll be dealing directly with Doctor Robinson. But of course, I'm always here if you have any questions you'd like to ask me. Not that you can't ask Doctor Robinson; I'm sure he'll be happy to answer any questions you might have, about specific procedures and the like."

"That all sounds okay."

"Good. So, why don't we find out a little more about you then." She found herself relaxing in his presence, and for the next twenty minutes she answered questions about every aspect of her life—her sexual habits, shopping habits, financial habits, eating habits, sleeping habits, goals and ambitions. When he was finished he clicked off the tape-recorder and leaned across the table.

"Well, Anne-Marie, thank you for your time today. If you're happy to participate we'd like you to come in next Monday at one p.m. If you agree I'll get Dorothy to give you the confidentiality agreements and other documents to sign, and make arrangements for your remuneration. You'll also be remunerated for your time today, of course."

"That sounds great." He pressed the button on his speaker phone and leaned over.

"Dorothy, can you please show Miss Benson out now, and make all the necessary arrangements for her." He rose and offered her his hand.

~ * ~

He felt his mind shift into another place, and took a cautious step forward, trying to adjust to the darkness. He clenched his eyes shut for a few seconds and when he re-opened them the darkness receded, but only in places, leaving a trail of gray up to the steps of a large concrete building. He squinted again, trying to make out the shape of the ugly concrete. But the darkness blurred the edges, so that it seemed to waver in the gray light. Something about the place frightened him, but he continued slowly moving forward. As if his legs were walking by themselves. He was drawn forward and repulsed backwards at the same time. He'd only gone a few steps before he heard the muffled screams coming from the building, and he felt his heart beat faster.

The beating of his heart grew louder and heavier, until it was like a heavy weight pressing against his chest. He continued moving forward even though his legs felt heavy, like he was walking through water. The water was rising, and with each step forward the screams grew louder, so that he wanted to turn and run the other way. But he kept moving forward, listening to the other sounds seeping up beneath the screams. The sounds of whimpering, of children and babies crying. He put his hands over his ears and tried to catch his breath. The weight in his chest was getting heavier. Suffocating him. Something kept moving his legs forward, even though he was now trying to turn and run. He looked down at the offending limbs and realized for the first time that he was naked. And that there was something wrong with his feet. They were covered in blood, and as he looked closer the flesh seemed to move. The ground was made up of small, sharp rocks, but something else, too. Something was moving down there. The ground itself seemed to be pulsating with life. With great effort he shook his foot, realizing with horror that it was covered in bugs. Although his legs still wanted to move he had become frozen to the spot, as if his body had turned to stone. The heaviness in his chest was becoming unbearable.

Just when Billy thought he couldn't bear it anymore, just when he thought his head and chest were going to explode, he felt something brush against him, then envelop him in a warm embrace. The darkness faded as the light washed over him, blocking out the screams. He thought he heard voices, whispering in his ears.

"Be strong, Billy, you're not alone." Two or three voices, whispering at once. A man and a woman, or maybe two women. The heaviness started to leave his body, and was replaced with a lightness and calm Billy had never experienced before. "We're here, Billy. We're with you." The building disappeared and was replaced with a shimmering light. He saw the sky above and it was brighter than he'd ever seen it before. His mind reeled, spinning furiously, and Billy was back on his thin mattress, his wrists and ankles bound.

Ten

Seeing Anne-Marie walk through the front doors, Harry walked across to meet her, his head protesting at the movement.

"How'd it go at the clinic?"

"Pretty good," she smiled. "I go back next Monday to start the actual tests."

"Good work. Let me know how it goes."

"Sure thing," she beamed.

~ * ~

Robinson knocked gently before entering, and found his friend dozing at the desk, his head down. He cleared his throat and spoke loud enough to rouse him.

"John, I've told Dorothy to reschedule your three o'clock appointment for tomorrow. I'm giving you a lift home so you can get some sleep."

"Huh?" John struggled to sit up. "What's up? I'm just taking a rest between interviews."

"You, my friend, need to get home to your wife and bed. The rest of the interviews have been scheduled for tomorrow and Friday, so there's nothing left for you to do today."

"I told Dorothy to keep it to fifteen this time," he explained unnecessarily. "And just take names and numbers after that. That should give us ten to start next week." These testing rounds were a lot less arduous than the initial ones, when they'd seen sixty subjects at a time.

"Quite. So I take it that's settled then. I'll give you a lift. You're not up to these all-nighters anymore." John wasn't really bothered by the observation, figuring it was pretty accurate. While he sometimes resented that Terry could work sixteen to twenty hours straight for days on end without showing any signs of fatigue, John knew those days were behind him now. As a practicing neurological surgeon he'd done his own fair share of sixteen to twenty hour shifts, particularly in the early days, but he wasn't sorry that those days were over. Especially with Amanda and Thomas waiting for him at home.

"Maybe you're right, but you don't need to give me a lift. I'll give Amanda a call."

"Don't be foolish. She'll be leaving to pick Thomas up from school, won't she? And you know I never mind an opportunity to drive my baby." The reference to Terry's sleek, black Jag convinced him. John had never learned to drive. The bustle and noise of New York traffic intimidated him, and he'd never really believed he could navigate it successfully. A sense of direction wasn't his strong suit, and he'd always preferred to leave it to the cab drivers. Amanda had nagged him about it at first, but she'd soon stopped mentioning it, and never seemed to mind driving him around when the need arose. He was quite content to take a cab, he always told her, but sometimes she liked to drive him.

"Well, if you're sure you don't mind, I'd appreciate it."

"Let's go."

~ * ~

"Hi, Jo, it's Harry." There was a brief pause on the other end of the line.

"What's up?"

"I was going to ask you the same thing. Anything happening with our killer?"

54

"I can't really talk right now. We're just pulling up. We're interviewing SUV owners." Harry let out a low whistle.

"Must be a few of those, huh?"

"Well, we narrowed it down a bit more. To dark-blue Toyota Landcruisers. Someone else confirmed the make and color."

"Can you give me a name?"

"Sorry, but you can print the make. Dark-blue, late model."

"So, how many people own a vehicle like that?"

"Thousands," she groaned. "We've got eight officers out on it. Listen, Harry, I've really got to go."

"Okay. Can we get together later to talk about the case? Maybe have a drink? Tonight? Or tomorrow?" There was a longer pause.

"It's pretty hectic here. I'm not sure when I'll get away." He heard her say something to Mario, but didn't catch the words. "I've really got to go—I'll talk to you later."

"Take care, Jo." But she'd already hung up.

Eleven

Rebecca didn't have a nine a.m. appointment scheduled that Thursday morning, so she was taking advantage of the rare opportunity to catch up on her patient file notes. She'd come in early to finalize it, but at 9:45 she found herself still sitting there, staring at the same file notes she'd been holding for the past thirty minutes. She hadn't been able to get Paul Gribble out of her mind since Tuesday. Well, it had been bothering her before that, but their last appointment had intensified her unease. She found her mind wandering when she was supposed to be listening to other patients. She still didn't know that much about him. Other than that he'd recently married a younger woman who "liked to be fucked hard from behind". And had no children, "thank God".

Like the rest of New York Rebecca had been following the Wolfman case, but she didn't have any proof that Gribble knew anything about it. Other than the unease he aroused in her. Tuesday had been the first time he'd mentioned the killer. But it had been on Rebecca's mind since their first session, when he'd started talking about his dreams as soon as he sat down. It was why he was there, he'd told her—to work out why he was having them.

But Gribble was no different to the rest of New York's citizens—he had to be aware of the murders. It was in no way remarkable that they'd crept into his sub-conscious, fuelling his dreams. She knew he wasn't alone in that regard. And it wasn't like he'd ever said anything that he couldn't have read in the paper. He'd always described his dreams after the children had been found. But despite rationalizing her patient's dreams, Rebecca couldn't shake the uneasiness she felt whenever she was in his presence.

~ * ~

Dan Williamson had agreed to talk to Harry. When Harry rang him last week Dan had screamed abuse, calling him an "insensitive bastard", and telling him to "go to hell." Harry had run the story with the standard police-issued photo used by every other newspaper and television station. He'd managed to get a quote from a neighbor about what a "sweet, happy boy" Billy was, but so far the parents hadn't been speaking to the media. So Harry was surprised when the distraught father called him this morning, saying he wanted to give an interview.

~ * ~

Billy had been trying to hold on to the voices for as long as possible. At first he'd felt like they were still there, in the room with him, keeping close, protecting him. But the longer he'd sat there, waiting for the Man, the softer the voices had become, until he couldn't hear them any more. The darkness had drowned them out.

He knew who the Man was. He'd always known, at some level, even though he'd pushed the knowledge away. He'd seen the news coverage of the Wolfman on TV, before his mum had come in and turned the channel. But his mum couldn't control what the other kids at school watched, or what they talked about in the playground. The Wolfman had been a favorite subject.

"He eats kids," George had told him, but Billy hadn't really believed that. The Man was suddenly there without Billy even realizing he was coming, even though he'd been listening for the footsteps. Sometimes it didn't matter how hard he listened—the Man would just creep up on him. He usually smelled the food first.

"Eat up, Billy," the Man whispered as he put the food down. Billy hungrily stuffed the meat into his mouth, shoveling it in with his bound wrists, trying not to drop any. He gulped it down without bothering to chew too much, almost choking on it. "Do you like it, Billy?" His voice was the same high whisper. "He's called James." He felt the Man walk away rather than hearing him. And he felt something burrowing into his brain. Something like a giant worm.

Twelve

On the drive over Harry replayed his interview with Sylvia Matheson, unable to shake the knowledge that not long after the interview her kid had turned up dead. He hoped history wasn't about to repeat itself. The Williamsons lived in a large single-story new build in Queens.

"Come on through." Dan met him at the door before he'd even had time to knock. He looked like he hadn't slept in weeks, and stared at Harry's hand for a few seconds before taking it, as if unsure what to do with it. Harry followed him through to a large sitting room, whose walls were adorned with family photos. Dan and a smiling woman on their wedding day; Dan and the same woman with a smiling, blond-haired boy of eight or nine; the same boy, a little older, in his baseball uniform; a young girl on a swing; the four of them together. Harry recognized Billy from the police photograph.

"That's Billy, our boy." Dan saw him looking at the photos. "Have a seat. Can I get you something? Tea or coffee?"

"No, I'm fine. Thanks." Harry settled into the three-seat sofa and Dan took the armchair beside it. Taking out the small notebook he usually carried in his jacket pocket, Harry turned to Dan.

"Mr. Williamson..."

"Dan."

"Dan, do you mind telling me why you changed your mind about talking to me?"

"I want him caught. I thought it might help. I remembered your name—I suppose I was a bit rude."

"It's fine."

"The police say they're following every lead but they don't have much to go on. They're still hoping someone will come forward with information." He was struggling to keep it together.

"I know this must be hard for you. And I know you've already been through this with the police, but can you think of anyone who was hanging around before the kidnapping? Maybe someone who came to the house—like a plumber or something?" He shook his head.

"No, I've been thinking about it, trying to think of anything. I use my own trades people—I'm in construction—but there's been nothing done to the house recently. We only built it in the last few years. And there's been no one else I can think of."

"Billy was kidnapped in the middle of the night, wasn't he?"

"Yes. We didn't hear anything. I keep going over it, trying to understand how someone could get into the house like that without us hearing anything. Billy always liked to sleep with a window open. There's a screen there, but I guess they're pretty easy to remove. The windows had security locks—he just didn't like it fully closed. We should have made him close it. I'd been thinking of putting in extra security, bars on the windows, but I hadn't got around to it. We've got an alarm on the front and back doors, extra locks, but the window was open. Pretty stupid, hey?" He cradled his head in his big hands and when he looked up again he was fighting back tears.

"You never think something like this is going to happen to your family. At first I couldn't believe it. I thought he must have gone off to a friend's place or something. Even though he'd never do something like that. Not without saying. And not on a school day. When Shelly called me, I knew from her voice that something was wrong, really wrong, but I just couldn't believe it. She was holding Gracie, our daughter. She must have thought..." He started to break down again, and Harry watched his painful struggle to regain control. "Anyway, she'd gone to the next room to check on Gracie, and Gracie was looking scared. Being woken up like that. And the way her mother was holding on to her. The look on her face. I knew, but I couldn't believe it."

"Where's your wife and daughter now?"

"Gracie's in her room, playing. I didn't want her to hear our conversation. She knows Billy is missing, but we try not to discuss things in front of her. My wife is resting." He looked uncertain. "Shelly hasn't been taking things very well. At first I thought she was going to be okay. Well, she was very upset, of course—frantic with worry. Ringing everyone we knew, all of Billy's friends, hoping someone had seen him. But for the last few days she seems to have given up hope. She hardly talks. Gracie's been getting upset—it's like Shelly doesn't even see her sometimes. I don't know what to do. The police don't seem to know anything." Harry didn't know what to say. It was too hard to imagine what he must be going through. And he didn't want to give him any false hope, although he felt like Dan needed something.

"It's still possible that there's someone out there who knows something. Someone who saw something. It's important we keep putting it out there. Can you describe what Billy was wearing that night? And if you could give me a recent picture, that might jog someone's memory."

"Blue pajamas. He was just wearing plain cotton pajamas. Short sleeved, with boxer shorts." He stood abruptly, looking relieved to be doing something. "I'll get you some photos."

Thirteen

Jo and Mario had been out all day interviewing the owners of blue Toyota Landcruisers. Like yesterday, it had been a long and so far fruitless task. As she sat down at her desk to write up the notes, Jo felt the weariness overcome her. A young officer appeared at her desk.

"Detective, there's a woman outside who wants to talk to someone about the murders." Jo glanced from the officer to Mario, who was already out of his chair.

"Thanks, Burton, we'll get it." The well-groomed Chinese-American woman looked uncomfortable standing in the grimy station. She was looking down at her expensive leather shoes, avoiding eye contact with those around her, and only looked up as Jo and Mario approached.

"Hello. I'm Detective Hanson and this is my partner, Detective Laspina. We were told you might have some information about the recent killings."

"Yes." She seemed unsure. "My name's Rebecca. Doctor Rebecca Lui."

"Why don't you come with us, Doctor Lui."

~ * ~

Jo eyed the woman who sat before them in the interview room, clearly uncomfortable with her surroundings, and was curious to hear her story.

"So, Doctor Lui, what brings you here? And if you don't mind me asking, what type of doctor are you." Rebecca met Jo's gaze.

"I'm a psychiatrist. I've come about a patient. It's not something I'd normally do, and I'm not completely comfortable with the fact that I'm here." Jo could hear the uncertainty in her voice, as she rushed to explain herself. "I've never broken patient confidentiality before, and I'm not completely sure it's the right thing to be doing now."

"I can assure you that anything you tell us in this room will be treated with the utmost discretion. And if it turns out that the information you provide has no direct bearing on the case, your patient won't have to know you've been here." Rebecca seemed to relax at that, and glanced up gratefully.

"Good. I've been struggling with this all day, not knowing whether or not to come. But, in the end... well, here I am." Jo nodded.

"This patient of yours—do you think he or she might know something about the crimes?"

"He. And I'm not sure. He's been having some very disturbing dreams about a man eating children. And earlier this week he told me he thought the man was the... Wolfman." She seemed to have trouble with the nickname. "Which wouldn't normally prompt a visit to the police," she rushed on. "It's quite common for patients to project aspects of themselves into fantasy figures—even drawing on real people to further the fantasy. Like the boy in the basement, or the man who threatens the boy. It could just be a way of dealing with repressed memories or emotions. Perhaps he was abused as a child, and he identifies with the boy. Maybe he's angry—and my patient does have a lot of anger—and he identifies with the killer. It's not uncommon for the media to feed into a patient's pre-existing alter egos, and normally I wouldn't see them as necessarily linked with the patient's real life. Patients don't act out all their fantasies, thank God."

"So, you wouldn't normally worry. Wouldn't normally report such fantasies. What makes this case different?"

"I'm not sure of that myself. He says the dreams spill into his waking life, but it's more about the way he describes the acts. The detail he goes into. When he describes the murderer's actions, it doesn't sound like a dream. It sounds like he's right there, describing something he's actually lived through. And at today's appointment he was distraught about a boy called Billy, who was trapped in the basement." Mario, who'd been silent up until now, interrupted her.

"He knew the boy's name?"

"Yes. Of course, he could have got that from the media. I understand the police are currently looking for a missing boy called Billy."

"Billy Williamson, yes. What did he say about him?" Mario was scrutinizing her closely, and she met his gaze evenly.

"Well, just that the boy was very frightened. To be perfectly frank, he was rambling quite a bit. He was very agitated this morning. He believed the killer was going to feed the other boy to Billy." Jo spoke carefully.

"Do you have any reason to suspect that your patient might actually be the murderer?"

"I don't have any evidence. I can't even confirm whether or not my patient is dangerous. I simply haven't spent enough time with him. He does sometimes identify with the murderer, which suggests that he could be dangerous. Normally, of course, I'd want to spend a lot more time with someone before making that kind of determination."

"Time is something we don't have in this case," Mario commented, and she nodded. "So, Doc, what's your patient's name?" She hesitated before answering.

"Paul Gribble."

"What else can you tell us about him? Appearance, occupation, family life—that kind of thing." Mario was directing the interview now.

"He's in his late thirties. Average looking, I guess. White. Average height. Brown hair and eyes. He sells insurance—apparently the top salesman, although perhaps he's just boasting. He doesn't really strike me as a successful man. He recently married a younger woman, and has no kids." Mario was scribbling notes.

"Do you know what type of vehicle he drives?"

"Sorry."

"And you're not overlooking anything obvious—like steel-capped teeth or something?" She gave Mario a strange look.

"Detective Laspina is just joking," Jo interrupted, glaring at Mario for the revelation they were keeping from the general public. "Please disregard that comment." Mario shrugged, clearly unconcerned. "Do you have an address for Mr. Gribble?"

"He did say the man had steel-capped teeth," Rebecca said softly. "He described them as being like a bear-trap." Although they hadn't released information about the puncture marks, Jo told herself it didn't necessarily mean anything. The public were no doubt forming their own opinions. But the detail gave her a small thrill of hope. Rebecca hesitated before continuing. "His address is 375 South End Avenue. Apartment 4A. Are you going to talk to him?"

"Yes," Jo responded, "but this information doesn't make him a suspect. We're not about to make an arrest based on what you've told us. We've been talking to hundreds of people in relation to this case, so it won't be difficult to find some pretext for questioning him. There shouldn't be any need to mention your name." She looked relieved.

"Thank you."

"By the way, Doctor Lui, where is your practice situated?"

"16 West 81st Street."

"Is that on the Upper West Side?"

"Yes, down from the American Museum of Natural History."

"Long way from South End Avenue," Mario reflected. "Does he work over that way?"

"I don't know. Patients don't always like to seek psychiatric counseling near to where they live or work. But I don't really think location has much to do with this case—he was referred to me because I specialize in anxiety disorder."

"Yeah, okay," Mario conceded. "When are you seeing him again?"

"We have an appointment scheduled for next Monday afternoon."

"It would be good if you kept that, and let us know if anything new turns up." She looked at Mario uncertainly.

"We understand your predicament," Jo intervened. "And if this turns out to be nothing, there will be no need to breach your patient's confidentiality again. But if, in fact, he has committed homicide, or intends to do so, you are ethically bound to report it to the police. You've done the right thing by coming here today, even if it turns out to be nothing." Rebecca still didn't look convinced.

Fourteen

"Hi, Harry. Are you going to the Exchange this afternoon?" Anne-Marie seemed to have developed a knack for surprising him from behind.

"Ah, hi," he replied, turning to face her. I'll probably give it a miss today—I'm still working on something."

"Is it anything I could help you with?" she asked hopefully.

"Not at the moment, no. Thanks anyway." He'd thought of Anne-Marie on the drive back to the office, and felt guilty about not involving her more in the case. He could have taken her along to the Williamson's today. He wasn't really doing too much mentoring. She couldn't have much background left to do on the Mountview story, and would just be waiting around until next week's appointment.

"I've just been to see the father of the latest missing boy, Billy Williamson. And I'm thinking of doing some follow-ups with the other families. A 'retracing the steps' type of thing. It could be a bit sensitive—I don't know if they'll all want to talk to us. But it would be good to get your input on that. Maybe we could get together in the morning and talk about it some more?" She nodded enthusiastically.

"That sounds great. I'd love to work with you on it."

"Good, keep you busy until you get further with the Mountview story."

"Yes. I've finished the background—I've written some of it up if you'd like to see it."

"We can go over it in the morning, when we discuss the other story."

"Sounds good."

"So, you're off to the Exchange then?"

"I'll probably pop in. I haven't had much time to get to know Glenda, but I think it's good to make an appearance. Good for me, I mean—I'm not saying you should go. It helps me get to know people a bit better. Gives me a chance to talk to them when they're not busy. Tuesday was my first time there, and I got to know a few people better." It took Harry a few minutes to realize what she was talking about.

"I'd completely forgotten it was Glenda's last day. I guess quite a few people will be down at the bar."

"Yes, Paul said she'd worked here for two years." Harry experienced another twinge of guilt at his lack of supervision. He should have been the one to tell her about the event, not Paul.

"Maybe I'll get down later for a quick drink. After I finish up here."

"I might see you down there then. I should let you get on with it."

"Yeah. Listen, I meant to ask you before—did you get to meet the great Doctor Robinson this morning?" She giggled.

"No. His partner did the interviews. Doctor John Winton. He seemed like a nice guy. Guess I'll meet Doctor Robinson next week— he's doing all the actual testing."

~ * ~

Mario groaned as they pulled up in front of a large industrial shed.

"Ah shit... I knew there was something wrong with that address."

"Guess we'll have to see how many Paul Gribbles are listed in the phone book."

"Could be an unlisted number." He didn't sound keen.

"We'll start with the listed ones."

"I'm stopping for a burger first," he insisted glumly. "Don't reckon we'll be getting home for dinner tonight." As it turned out there were only five Paul Gribbles listed, along with seventeen P. Gribbles. Thank God it hadn't been Paul Smith, Jo reflected. They started with the Ps, and after only thirty minutes had eliminated eight Peters, four Paulas and a Percy Gribble. That left two Pauls and two Ps who didn't answer. They'd eliminated one P for Paul because he sounded about seventy on the phone, and eliminated the other one because he didn't know what Jo was talking about when she asked if he was the Paul Gribble who'd spoken to her about insurance. That left five Pauls and two maybes.

"Time to go for a drive," Mario announced. He was sounding keener now that he'd demolished two burgers and a large fries.

The first Paul turned out to be retiree, as was Paul number three. Paul number two was an angry man who'd been in the middle of dinner, and who was continually distracted by what sounded like a dozen noisy children in the background. When they knocked at the apartment of Paul number five, they were greeted by a woman in her mid-twenties, with bleached blonde hair and a skimpy dress. Mario took the lead.

"Afternoon, Mrs. Gribble. We're Detectives Laspina and Hanson." He flashed his badge. "We wanted a quick word with your husband, if he's in."

"Paul? What about?" She eyed them suspiciously.

"Just a routine matter, Mrs. Gribble. Is he in?"

"No, he's still at work."

"What time are you expecting him home?"

"I don't know," she responded sullenly. "Don't expect he'll be too much longer, but I can't say for sure."

"Perhaps we could just come in and wait then?" Mario took a step forward, forcing her to take a step back into the house.

"It's not really a good time for me right now—I'm in the middle of cooking dinner."

"You can go about your business while we wait. Like I said, we're just here to ask some routine questions, so as soon as your husband arrives and we can ask them, we'll leave. The sooner we can clear this up, the sooner we'll be out of your way. If we leave we'll just have to come back later, and that won't be convenient for any of us."

"We really would appreciate it," Jo added. "As Detective Laspina says, it will save us coming back." Mrs. Gribble thought it over and heaved an exaggerated sigh of resignation.

"Guess you'd better come through then. Perhaps I should give Paul a call."

"No need to interrupt him at work," Mario commented. "He might be busy. What kind of work does he do?"

"Sells Insurance."

"What company is he with?"

"Hartleys Insurance. In Lower Manhattan." She ushered them into a small sitting room which looked recently decorated. It was dominated by a state-of-the art entertainment system with big screen and surround sound. The furniture was modern and loud. Mario moved towards a red leather recliner and folded his bulk into it, while Jo took the other one. Mrs. Gribble hovered nearby, looking uncertainly at the sofa, as if she was trying to decide whether to sit down.

"So," Jo addressed the hovering hostess, "does your husband often work late?"

"Just depends really. Sometimes he has to see clients after business hours."

"How long have you and Mr. Gribble been married?" Jo maintained a light, friendly tone, trying to draw her into conversation. But Mrs. Gribble wasn't having any of it.

"About a year." Mrs. Gribble remained standing, a slight frown creasing her face.

"Do you have any children?"

"No. Why do you need to know all this?"

"Detective Hanson's just making conversation, aren't you, Jo?" Mario joined the conversation and Mrs. Gribble looked at both of them as if there was something she should know.

"I think I'd better give Paul a call. Let him know you're here." But Mrs. Gribble's plans were interrupted by the man in question coming through his front door. He made it into the sitting room before his wife had time to go out and warn him, and he seemed startled to see them.

"What's going on?" Paul Gribble was in his late thirties, of average height, with brown eyes and a thick head of brown hair. He looked like he might work out a few times a week. Mario glanced briefly at Jo before unfolding to his full height.

"Evening, Mr. Gribble. I'm Detective Laspina. And my partner over there is Detective Hanson. We were just waiting for you to get home. As we informed your wife here, we had a few questions we wanted to ask you. In private, if that's all right—your wife mentioned she had to go and finish dinner." Mrs. Gribble looked uncertainly at her husband, waiting for his nod before retreating to the kitchen.

"What's this all about?" His tone was slightly imperious.

"Why don't you have a seat," Mario offered graciously, playing host in Gribble's sitting room. Gribble hesitated before taking his place on the sofa, looking displeased at the way things were going. Mario sat back down, and waited until Gribble was settled before speaking. "A man fitting your description was seen on East 81st Street when two burglaries took place. One occurred on Tuesday morning, and the second took place earlier today."

"That's ridiculous," Gribble spluttered. "I haven't been in that area all week. Who is this witness? And what do you mean someone who looked like me? Surely lots of people look like me. How did you get my name? Has someone actually said I was there?" Mario dismissed the string of indignant questions.

"What kind of vehicle do you drive?"

"What?" He was temporarily disarmed by the question. "A white Lexus. Why do you want to know that?"

"Is that a private vehicle or a company car?" Gribble snorted.

"Hartley's doesn't give its employees company cars. Even its top salesman. It's my car."

"Where were you today and Tuesday morning between ten and eleven a.m.?"

"I was working. On Tuesday I was actually in a staff meeting, and this morning I had a meeting with one of my clients—a Mrs. Goodman. At her home in Lower Manhattan."

"We'll need Mrs. Goodman's full address, along with that of your office. We'll have to verify this information."

"Fine, go ahead. I'll write the addresses down for you. But do you mind telling me what you're going to tell these people? I don't want anyone getting the wrong idea about this. I'm expecting Mrs. Goodman to buy insurance in the next few days—I don't want that to go sour."

"You're not a suspect, Mr. Gribble—we'll make that very clear. But as you've been identified as a possible witness to a crime, we do need to eliminate that possibility. Just write down the names of the people who were at Tuesday's meeting."

"But it was a staff meeting. That's about twenty people."

"Who's your manager?"

"Anthony Garrison."

"And was Mr. Garrison at this meeting?" Gribble nodded. "Okay, we'll start with him."

~ * ~

Back in the car Mario turned to Jo.

"What did you make of that?"

"Pretty strange. He seems to fit, especially with that 'top salesman' crap. I mean, if he's not our guy, there's a lot of coincidences. The insurance salesman with the young wife, recent marriage, no kids. But his story seems pretty tight. And if he was in meetings this morning and Tuesday, how could he have been at Doctor Lui's?"

"You want to check out Paul Gribble number five then?" Jo thought about it briefly.

"We can call in—we're nearly there anyway. But I think we need to talk to Gribble's colleagues. There's just too many details that fit. Maybe Doctor Lui's patient knew our friend here."

"You think he borrowed his name? And a few details from his life?"

"Maybe. We have to go to Hartley's Insurance anyway, to check out his alibi. We might as well check out his colleagues at the same time. Perhaps Doctor Lui can give us a better description."

Paul Gribble number five was a young bachelor who answered the door with a plastered leg and a pair of crutches. "Broke it about two months ago now," he informed them glumly. Guessing that Doctor Lui would have mentioned a broken leg, they thanked him for his time. Although it was almost eight p.m. when they left his place, Jo rang Doctor Lui from the car and arranged to pick her up on the way back to the station. They'd need a more precise physical identification of her client.

Fifteen

While Mario and Jo were making their way back to the station, Harry was still at work, waiting for a call. Like them, he was struggling with coincidences, and hadn't made it down to Glenda's farewell drinks. Anne-Marie's reference to Doctor Winton had stirred his memory instantly, and while he knew there must be plenty of Doctor Wintons in New York, the coincidence had struck him. He'd phoned a college buddy who occasionally did some of the trickier background checks for him. Nothing Harry could print, but useful nevertheless. For a healthy fee JP could hack into anything. His phone rang.

"It's done." JP was a little paranoid, and despite using a scrambler on his phone, tended to speak in two or three word sentences.

"Can you fax it over? You've still got the number, right?

"No problem."

"I owe you, pal."

"I know. I'll be home tomorrow."

~ * ~

Pam's bank statements appeared at the fax machine a few minutes later. Harry noted the three payments from Mountview. Going through the phone book, Harry lucked out on his fifth John Winton. He hadn't got far into his speech with the first four.

"Hello, is this Doctor John Winton?"

"Yes, who's this?"

"This is Harry O'Brien from the Daily Courier. I'm sorry to be calling you at home this late in the evening, but I needed to ask you a few questions about Pam Grinstone."

"Pam?" Harry could hear the surprise in his voice.

"Yes. I understand she participated in some studies you conducted at Mountview Private Research Clinic."

"Where did you say you were from?"

"The Daily Courier."

"Mr. O'Brien, I was very saddened to read what happened to Miss Grinstone, but I'm afraid I don't talk to the press. Good evening." Harry interrupted quickly, before he could hang up.

"I understand what you're saying, Doctor Winton, but I'm not interested in writing anything about Mountview. I interviewed Pam shortly before her tragic death, and I just wanted to follow up on some things she said."

"As I said, I really don't think it's appropriate for me to talk to the press. Whether it's about Mountview or anything else. And, I assure you, there's very little I could tell you. I'm afraid I really don't know Miss Grinstone all that well, so I can't imagine why you think I might have something to say on the matter. In light of what's happened, I think the best thing we could do for the poor woman is let her rest in peace, rather than dragging her name through the tabloids. Good evening, Mr. O'Brien." This time Harry couldn't prevent him from hanging up.

"Oh well, I guess that's that then," Harry muttered to himself. He wasn't sure there was much Winton could have told him anyway. Looking at his watch, he wondered if anyone would still be down at the bar.

~ * ~

The farewell for Glenda had wound down by the time Harry arrived; only the diehards were left. Paul waved him over to the table he was sharing with Gina Sproats, the editor's secretary.

"Hiya, Harry, where've you been all night?" Gina's speech was slurred, and she swayed ever so slightly as she talked. Paul winked over her blonde, curly head, and his own curly head and effeminate features created a strange kind of mirror image behind her. Harry blinked as the two heads seemed to blur into one for a minute. They'd clearly been having a bit of a session.

"Just finishing up a story. I'm going to the bar—can I get you two a drink?"

"I've really got to get going. Nothing personal, Harry," she giggled. "I've been telling Paul for the last hour I've got to get home to feed my cat."

"Thanks, pal." Paul waved his beer bottle at Harry. Gina was still standing in the same place when Harry returned with two beers.

"You sure you don't want another drink, Gina?"

"No, really, I'm fine. I've definitely had enough—Paul just called me a cab."

"Yeah, mind my spot buddy. I'm going to walk Gina out." Harry took a long sip from the bottle as he watched them weave their way across the floor. When Paul returned five minutes later he had a smug look on his face.

"What's happening, Preston?"

"Not much—you know how it goes." He became sheepish. "Hey, by the way, I might have told Gina that you and I were hanging out tomorrow night. In case she asks. She probably won't."

"Hanging out where? Why'd you tell her that?"

"Ah, well, it's just that I got a date with Angela. You know, that girl I was telling you about. The redhead from the cafe. Well, I worked up the courage to ask her out, and tomorrow's the big night."

"Why not just tell Gina that?"

"Well, we've been getting on so well tonight. You know how it is. I didn't want to close any doors. She mentioned some party she was going to tomorrow. Asked if I was interested. I think she likes me." He grinned. "I'm taking her to lunch on Sunday."

"You can be a real prick sometimes, Paul." Harry was annoyed at him for dragging him into it.

"What's wrong with that? Gina's been around the office a few times—it's not like she's going to stop dating just because she's having lunch with me. Everyone needs options, right? Or maybe I'm talking to the wrong guy here."

"Why can't you just tell her the truth? I like Gina. I don't want to lie to her. It'll be awkward."

"Don't be such a pussy." Paul grinned. "Besides, what are the chances it'll ever come up? Look at it this way—you're just saving her feelings. Just because we might see other people doesn't mean she'd want her nose rubbed in it at work. And think of it from my perspective. I'm not a rich man. I'm a reporter. What have I got to offer a woman except for my charm and good looks." He ran a hand through his thick, wavy hair. "But my looks aren't going to last forever, Harry. I don't want to waste my pretty years. I have to keep my options open while I've still got options." Harry laughed, unable to stay annoyed, and Paul became more earnest. "Besides, I think I might really like Gina. Don't you think she's got great tits?"

"You really are one of the most shallow people I know." But Harry actually found Paul's shallowness rather refreshing. It was the foundation of their low-maintenance friendship. And at least he was honest about it.

"What's wrong with shallow?" Paul was grinning, but then he turned serious on Harry again. "You know, pal, it wouldn't hurt you to drop the Mr. Serious act for a while and get yourself a bit of pussy. You've been looking a little stressed lately."

"Thanks for the advice."

"Hey, really, I worry about you. How long's it been, anyway?"

"I really don't want to talk about this."

"That long, hey? You're not still hung up on the lady detective, are you?"

"Leave it alone, Paul." Harry was starting to get annoyed again.

"Oh, come on. How long has it been since you two broke up? Over a year, isn't it?

"I'm serious. I don't want to talk about this."

"Okay, but I'm only saying something because I worry about you. You need a root, my friend." Before Harry had a chance to respond Paul groaned. Following his gaze across the room, Harry saw Jeremy and Jasmine heading their way. Jasmine had started at the paper around the same time as Harry, and for a while the two of them were always together at the Exchange. When Paul started it was the three of them. Sometimes Brian, Jasmine's partner, would join them there, and occasionally the four of them would hang out together on the weekend. Jasmine had met her soul-mate at the Exchange, which was as good a place as any, Harry supposed, given the amount of time they all used to put in there. She'd been with Brian at the time, and he'd been with Dana. Sometime during the evening they'd swapped alliances, and never looked back. Together they'd mutated into some dark force that everyone blamed Brian and Dana for.

Harry didn't know whether it was love at first sight, but that's what they were saying now. No one else noticed at the time, and Jasmine had reproached them for it ever since then. Retrospective love at first sight, perhaps. Certainly a flicker of something. Mutual contempt for everyone else, perhaps. The relationship between Jasmine and Brian had been breaking down for as long as Harry knew them, and she only used to bring him out to try to get rid of him for a while. He was her albatross, hanging around to make sure she had no fun, counting her drinks and sniping in a sulky voice whenever she suggested anything.

"We should go on a picnic tomorrow—take some lunch and go down to Central Park."

"Funny, we've been together for two years now and I don't recall you ever wanting to go on a picnic before". And picnic spat out with contempt, like she'd wanted to go and beat fags for the evening.

"It'll be nice."

"What, suddenly you're the outdoorsy type, are you?" And of course she wasn't, not at all, and her picnic would never eventuate, but it was part of the rules back then that they'd all agree to any halfway plausible suggestion and then just not go.

"Fuck off, Brian". And of course that's what he'd been waiting for, the chance to play the injured martyr. She'd traded in her sad martyr for the emphatic Jeremy. As a social worker, empathy seemed to come with the territory. But the identical partners were a drag, and Harry didn't feel like engaging with Jeremy in some long, complicated conversation about how their capitalist society was marginalizing its weak and vulnerable. He drained his beer and said his goodbyes, leaving Paul at their mercy. Paul gave him a reproachful glare as he made his escape.

Sixteen

At 8:25 that Friday morning Jo and Mario were drinking coffee out the front of Hartley's Insurance. Mario was also eating donuts. They were missing the morning Taskforce meeting, and had gained a temporary reprieve from interviewing Toyota owners. Mario stuffed the last donut into his mouth and turned to Jo.

"Ready to go in?" Taking the elevator to the third floor, they stepped into a well-appointed reception area, and Mario approached the young woman at the desk.

"We're looking for Mr. Anthony Garrison."

"Do you have an appointment?"

"No need. I'm Detective Laspina, and this—" he nodded in Jo's direction, "is my partner, Detective Hanson." Mario flashed his badge.

"Well, I'll have to call through and let him know you're here." She sounded somewhat reluctant, and Mario leaned over the desk as she made the call, a friendly smile on his face. "Mr. Garrison—there's two detectives out here to see you... No, they didn't say... Okay then." She looked up at Mario. "He said to come through—down the corridor and last door on your right." Mr. Garrison was a smooth, snappily dressed man in his late fifties, who looked like he wore a toupee. He stood as they entered and gestured to the leather chairs facing his desk like a television host pointing to the prizes.

"Good morning, detectives—please, have a seat. What can I do for you?" He sat back down and smiled smoothly as they took their seats. Mario took the lead.

"We just wanted to confirm that a Paul Gribble attended a staff meeting here on Tuesday morning, between the hours of ten and eleven.

"Paul? Why, has he done something wrong?" The concern in his voice didn't reach his smooth face.

"Not at all, this is just a routine inquiry. We need to confirm his whereabouts."

"Yes, he was here. The meeting started at 9:30—went for about two hours."

"So you're sure he stayed for the whole meeting?"

"Detective, Paul Gribble is our top salesman." He imparted this information like it was something they should already know. "I would have noticed if he was missing."

"Was anyone else missing?"

"Well, I think most of the staff were there. Perhaps one or two were absent. It's a sales meeting, so all our salespeople are expected to attend. Of course, for one reason or another, people miss the occasional meeting. But unless they're actually sick or out closing a sale, it's pretty frowned upon. We consider them an important component of our motivational strategy." Mario reached into his jacket and drew out the computer image they'd generated from Doctor Lui's description.

"Do you know this man?" Garrison leaned over to inspect the picture, and they could tell from his frown that he recognized the face.

"Yes. Peter Holdman. One of our less outstanding salespeople. What's he done?" The smooth concern was replaced with a disdainful curiosity

"Was he at the meeting on Tuesday morning?" Garrison thought for a minute.

"Actually, he wasn't. I had to have a word to him when he got in, because he's one of the team that really needs to attend these things.

He said he'd had a medical appointment." He offered the final bit of information in a contemptuous tone, as if a doctor's appointment might be a sign of weakness. Mario returned the picture to his pocket.

"Do you know if Mr. Holdman is at work this morning?"

"I'm not sure. Our sales staff generally come in before and between appointments. If you like I can check with Crystal—the girl on reception. She has access to all their computer diaries—in order to transfer calls and the like. They have to record all their appointments in the dairies, and let her know when they're in." He provided this information proudly, as an example of the technological efficiency of Hartley's Insurance. Mario nodded, and he pressed the button on his speaker phone with authority.

"Crystal, is Mr. Holdman in his office?"

"No, sir, he hasn't come in yet. Do you want me to check his diary?" Garrison looked across at Mario, who nodded.

"Yes, please."

"He had an appointment with a Mrs. Jones—Long Island." She gave them the address, and Mario leaned over Garrison's desk to talk into the phone.

"Crystal, in case we miss him there, can you access Mr. Holdman's personal details and give us his address and phone number?" There was a long pause on the other end, and Garrison leaned into the phone.

"It's all right, give them what they want." Mario leaned back in, his head only inches from Garrison's.

"And, Crystal, this conversation is strictly confidential. Any discussion of this matter would be considered interference with the course of justice." Crystal sounded suitably impressed.

"Yes, Detective. I'm just getting the details for you now. He's in Long Island too, which must be why he didn't come in first." She gave them the details, and they stood to leave. Garrison remained seated, looking slightly uncomfortable now.

"I'm not sure what's going on here, Detectives, but I hope it's not going to bring any discredit to the name of Hartley Insurance." Jo smiled reassuringly.

"I assure you that we have no intention of questioning Mr. Holdman in front of a client. Neither Mr. Gribble nor Mr. Holdman is actually a suspect in any crime at this stage. As Detective Laspina said, we're just following through on some inquiries, which we hope your employees can assist with. But as my partner informed your receptionist, this conversation is strictly confidential, and we'd appreciate it if you didn't mention it to anyone. Including the employees in question."

~ * ~

They pulled up behind a white Holden Commodore, taking note of the red Honda Accord parked in the driveway. Jo reached for the radio, and Mario shot her a quizzical look.

"I'm calling in the license plate. Confirm that this is our Mr. Holdman. And check whether he has any other cars registered in his name." Mario grinned.

"Like a blue Toyota?" It only took a few minutes to confirm Holdman's car.

"He does have another vehicle registered in his name," the officer informed them, and they held their breath. "Ford Falcon sedan."

"Ah, well, couldn't have been that easy," Mario observed philosophically. They had to wait another twenty minutes for their man to leave the house. He matched the picture, which had failed to capture his beaten demeanor. Mario was out of the car and heading towards him before he had a chance to put the key in the lock. "Peter Holdman?" The man turned, a puzzled expression on his face. "I'm Detective Laspina. We'd like to ask you a few questions." The puzzlement turned to anxiety.

"What about? I haven't done anything." Mario took a step closer, his huge frame dwarfing the insurance salesman.

"No one's saying you have. Now if you'll just come with me, we won't take up too much of your time." Holdman shrank back.

"But my car's here."

"We'll give you a lift back to your car when we're through. But it would be best if we asked our questions at the station, rather than here."

83

"Can you make me do that? I mean, don't you need a warrant or something? What's this all about?" Mario put on his patient voice.

"We don't need a warrant just to talk to you, Mr. Holdman. But you're quite right, you don't have to come down to the station. We could ask your client to let us inside, or maybe you'd prefer to go back to your place. It's up to you. Once you decide we'll be happy to explain what all this is about."

"No, no, that's okay. I guess I can answer a few questions at the station. But I'm supposed to be at work. I should call in."

"We'd be happy to call your employer for you." Holdman glanced about himself furtively, as if he was looking for an escape.

"No, that's okay. If it's not going to take too long I guess it will be okay. It's not, is it? Going to take too long?"

"The sooner we get back to the station the sooner we'll be able to drop you back to your car, and let you get on with your day." The reluctant salesman let himself be directed to the back of the car.

Seventeen

Harry knew it was cowardly of him, but he'd given Anne-Marie the job of interviewing Sylvia Matheson. They'd given her a few days grace now, but he knew her feelings would still be as raw today as they were when the police called with the news. Still, they were reporters—it's what they did. And Harry knew that sometimes people wanted to talk. Sylvia did. At least she had. Before Monday. Her distress that last time had been physically evident in the red rawness of her hands and arms, which she'd scratched frantically throughout their interview. She didn't seem to realize she was doing it. The only time she'd stopped scratching was when she had a cigarette in her hand. Harry had to resist the urge to stop her scratching, and instead had chain-smoked in sympathy.

But he wasn't being a complete coward, he told himself. Although Robert James was refusing to talk to anyone since his wife's suicide, the Gleesons had agreed to do their first interview with the press. And that unpleasant task was Harry's responsibility. He'd outlined the story to Anne-Marie, and they'd spent some time going through the questions.

"But don't push it, if she doesn't want to talk," he'd advised. Although he felt like he should be talking to Sylvia, he knew it was good experience for Anne-Marie, and she didn't seem overly daunted by the responsibility. There was a tough streak in her, although it wasn't callous. All reporters who covered homicides had to learn how to deal with grieving family and friends, so he guessed he shouldn't feel too bad about pushing her forward on this one. Besides, he'd already talked to Sylvia, and had gone over most of the information Anne-Marie would be checking today. But no one had interviewed the Gleesons yet.

~ * ~

"Can you tell us where you were between the hours of one and four on the morning of this Monday and last Monday, Mr. Holdman? Mind if I call you Peter? Or do you prefer Pete?" Mario was leaning over his very uncomfortable looking suspect.

"I don't mind what you call me. I was home in bed like I always am at that time of night. Are you going to tell me what this is about?" Mario pushed his face closer to Holdman's.

"We've got reason to believe your vehicle was in the area when a crime was committed." The color drained from Holdman's face.

"My car! That's ridiculous! I wasn't out anywhere at that time of night. Ask my wife. Besides, I thought you were looking for a blue SUV. I drive a white sedan."

"Just what crime are you referring to, Pete?" Mario paused for a few seconds, as if he was thinking about it. "You're not referring to the Wolfman crimes, are you? I certainly didn't mention them." Holdman was perspiring now.

"I, well, I just assumed. I mean, I read the papers. That's all they seem to be talking about lately—this Wolfman case. I knew the police were looking for the driver of a blue SUV—I read it."

"Do you know how many crimes are committed in this city every day, Pete? It strikes me as a little odd that that's the first thing you think about." He turned to Jo, who was leaning against the back wall with her arms crossed. "Doesn't it strike you as a little odd, Detective?" Jo thought about it for a while.

"Well, it is a little strange. Maybe he knows something about the case." Mario turned back to Holdman.

"Is that right? Do you have something to say about the case? You don't ever drive a blue SUV, do you, Pete?"

"No, you've seen what I drive. And my wife drives an old Falcon. I don't even know anyone with a blue SUV. I don't know anything about the case—except what I read in the papers."

"Well, Pete, as it turns out, I was going to ask a few questions relating to that case. But the fact that you brought it up first, well, that raises some issues for me. I'm having some trouble getting over the coincidence."

"Like I said, that's all you read in the papers lately. I'm not the only one in New York thinking about that case. I got kids you know."

"Is that right? Must make you a bit nervous then, does it? Knowing there's a madman out there eating kids. How old are your kids, Pete?"

"Sixteen and fourteen."

"Oh, I reckon you've got nothing to worry about then. This guy seems to prefer the younger kids. I wonder what makes a guy like that tick. What do you think, Pete?"

"How the hell should I know?"

"Well, you've been following the case and all. Must have some theories. What about all this media attention he's getting—do you reckon he likes being famous?"

"I've got no idea. Look, are you going to tell me what this is all about?" He was panicking now, the fear making him ramble. "I don't know why this guy does what he does. And what did you mean, about my car being seen? Who saw it? And what's that got to do with this case anyway, if you're looking for an SUV?" Mario took a step back, taking his hands off the table and pulling up a seat across from Holdman.

"Hey, settle down there, Pete. That's a lot of questions. But about your car, you should know we don't release all our clues to the press.

You know what I mean? Have to keep some things back. No one knows about the white Holden."

"Like I told you, it can't have been my car. I was home in bed. Call my wife, she'll tell you."

"Well, we'll certainly do that, Pete." He nodded at Jo, who left the room quietly. When she returned Mario was still staring across at the unhappy salesman. Jo nodded to Mario across the room.

"Well, Pete, you've been very helpful. Thanks for your time." Mario stretched himself upwards and folded his arms across his chest. Holdman looked confused.

"You mean I can go? You're finished with the questions?"

"Yep. If we need anything else we'll be in touch. In the meantime, you're free to go." Holdman stood and regarded them both uncertainly.

"You were going to give me a lift. Back to my car."

"Of course." Mario tapped his forehead, and Jo suppressed a smile. "I completely forgot. Let's go then."

Eighteen

Harry's morning had been harrowing. It wasn't even lunch-time yet and he felt like a stiff drink. The Gleesons had been understandably traumatized by the experience, and hadn't been able to add much to what he'd already learned from the police. He'd gotten another photo, but he already knew what Mandy was wearing on the night she was kidnapped. Andy Gleeson had looked at him with pleading eyes, appealing to him to find their daughter's killer. They needed him caught.

The story he'd written about Billy Williamson had already run on page two of today's paper, so it was a matter of cutting and pasting it to what he'd gotten from the Gleesons, and what they already knew about James Matheson. He was still working on it when Anne-Marie walked up behind him. This time he heard her coming.

"How'd it go with Sylvia?" Sylvia had readily agreed to a follow-up interview when Anne-Marie outlined their proposal.

"Pretty good I think." She hesitated, her smile faltering. "It was horrible. That poor woman." Her enthusiasm seemed to have taken a bit of a beating. Harry reached across to pull Paul's empty chair towards him, motioning for her to sit down.

"Are you okay? It's never easy interviewing the victims, and this case is worse than most."

"Yeah. It's okay. I'm okay, really. I mean, it's good experience, right?" She looked at him for confirmation.

"Yep. Look, the best thing to do is just go away and write it up. Okay? Get it out. Maybe what we're doing will jog someone's memory—someone might come forward with new information." The smile she gave him was shakier than usual. "Tell you what. We'll finish writing this up and I'll take you for a late lunch. What do you think?" The smile brightened a little.

"Thanks, Harry."

~ * ~

As soon as Holdman was out of the car Jo turned to her partner.

"Do you think we should have let him go?

"We don't have anything to hold him on."

"He didn't say anything else after I left the room?"

"Nope. He was getting pretty nervous though. I've got a feeling he knows something he's not telling us."

"Do you think he could have done it?"

"I dunno. Do you think his wife was lying?"

"Could be I guess. You didn't ask him about the other nights?"

"Not much point. If he's innocent he probably wouldn't remember where he was seven weeks ago, when the first one went missing. Probably wouldn't even remember a month ago. Unless he's always at home nights, like he says. Besides, it doesn't really matter, does it? If he was home the past couple of Monday mornings, he's not our guy. We don't have enough to go checking into his alibis for the past two months."

"His wife said he's always at home in the evenings—doesn't go out much. They don't seem to have much of a social life. She claims he never even goes out for a beer—prefers to drink at home."

"Well, that's that then, don't you think? The guy's got an alibi. If she's telling the truth. What do you want to do?" Jo thought for a few moments.

"Let's pull his bank records. If he does stay in all the time, he shouldn't have any nightly expenses. And we can check whether he's rented any SUVs lately."

~ * ~

"Peter, is that you?" Leanne Holdman met him in the narrow hallway, dressed in bike shorts and an oversized tee shirt. "What are you doing home at this hour?" He squeezed past her.

"For Christ sakes put some pants on, will you? I've come home for lunch—I don't want to lose my appetite." She followed him through to the kitchen, wincing at his tone. Her voice was a whine when she spoke again.

"Peter, a policewoman rang me earlier today. She wanted to know where you were the last two Monday mornings. Early mornings."

"I know. Make me a sandwich, will you?" He'd been driving back to the office when he'd turned the car around and headed home. He couldn't stop thinking about what that detective had said, about someone seeing his car. Why would someone say that? He knew he'd been at home. He'd had trouble sleeping lately, but he wasn't out driving in the middle of the night. He tried to remember if he'd woken up last Sunday night with one of those dreams, but his mind kept coming back to this Sunday night. He'd been really shaken. But he can't have gone out without remembering. It must be a mistake, that's all. A car that looked like his. Despite his rationalizations, Peter felt something slipping away inside him.

"Peter, are you all right?" Leanne was regarding him with curiosity if not concern.

"I'm fine. Just get the sandwich, will you—I should be getting back to work." She moved slowly about the kitchen.

"Do you want it toasted?"

"Yeah. What did you tell her?"

"What?"

"The policewoman. What did you say?"

"That you were home in bed. What else would I say? That's the truth, isn't it?" He grunted in response.

~ * ~

Anne-Marie was back with the story in less than an hour, and Harry gave her the press officer's name and number.

"Check whether there's been any new developments. We want to make sure we've got everything before running the story." He'd already phoned someone this morning, but it wouldn't hurt for her to start developing her network. His contact within the homicide squad had given him something, but it wasn't anything he could use. He'd tried following up on it, but so far it was looking like a dead end. As Harry read through her report he had to concede she'd done a pretty good job. He made a few adjustments before checking back with her.

"Nothing new," she told him. "He said they're still hoping someone will come forward with information." Harry quoted the press officer and filed the story. Walking back past Anne-Marie's desk, he glanced at his watch: 1:30.

"Hey, I've just got a couple of calls to make, and then we can get out of here. Give me thirty minutes, okay?"

"No problem." He was back at his desk when he saw Gina approach Anne-Marie's desk. Gina said something to her, and she shot Harry a worried look, before getting up and following Gina into Burrows' office. Ten minutes later she was moving towards him with a bright smile.

"Harry, Mr. Burrows said you were sharing the by-line with me. I wasn't expecting it. Thank you."

"Is that what he called you in for?"

"He wanted to congratulate me on the story. He said he was going to run it on the front page, and that it would run to page two. Isn't that great? I know it's really your story, but I'm really excited about it."

"Hey, it's our story. You did a good job—Burrows was right to congratulate you. Let's go eat."

Nineteen

"Anything turn up?" Mario peered over her shoulder at the statements.

"Afraid not. Pete's certainly not raking in the cash. No rentals, no late-night spending. There's a few entries here from some private clinic—don't know what that's about."

"Maybe his psychiatric bills."

"No, he must have paid cash for that. Well, I guess he'd have to if he was using Gribble's name. But this is income, not expenditure. Some place called Mountview. He must have been supplementing his income. Three payments of nine hundred dollars over three months."

"What's your theory on him using Gribble's name?"

"Maybe he was embarrassed about seeing a psychiatrist."

"Yeah, or maybe he worried about her talking." Jo had wondered about that too, but it was common practice for her and Mario to adopt opposing sides as a way of thinking things through.

"He shouldn't have. It's not like we get a lot of psychiatrists in here helping with our cases."

"Yeah, but if someone's planning to commit homicide they might get a little cautious. Maybe he saw a TV show about a shrink coming forward, or testifying against her patient. Something like that. The

Doc reckons he was pretty nervous about his story. Certainly struck me as the nervy type."

"So why pick Gribble?"

"Maybe the guy shits him. He could be jealous of Gribble's sales performance, or his young wife. Gribble seemed pretty fond of himself. Reckon he could piss you off if you spent much time with him, particularly if he was doing a lot better than you. Our guy's not doing so well, so maybe he's jealous. Whatever the reason, it wasn't a real bright choice. Not if he's actually done something wrong and wants to talk it over with his shrink. I mean, the guy works with him; he led us right back to Holdman. But then, no one's saying crims are always bright."

"So do you think we should keep an eye on him?" Mario changed track.

"What have we got, really? A nervous shrink and a few dreams. We were lucky to get the warrant for his bank statements. Alton would never go for us tailing him. We can't justify it. Maybe we should just monitor the situation through the shrink." Jo couldn't think of an opposing argument.

"I guess you're right."

~ * ~

"Hi, Jo, it's Harry."

"Oh. How are you?" She sounded tired.

"I heard you interviewed someone this morning." Her voice changed from tired to annoyed.

"Who are you talking to? Is it Edmonton? Everything's supposed to be going through the press officer."

"You know I'm not going to print anything without clearance." He heard her sigh on the other end.

"Yeah, okay. Things are just a bit sensitive at the moment."

"Not having much luck, hey?"

"We don't have a clue."

"So, who'd you interview?"

"You know I can't tell you that. Besides, it turned out to be nothing. False lead."

"Too bad. Hey, it probably won't cheer you up, but I know who Pam's Doctor Winton is."

"Yeah?" Despite the question mark in her voice, she didn't sound that interested.

"Yeah. Apparently she was taking part in some research he's involved with. At a private clinic." There was a long pause on the other end.

"What's it called?"

"Mountview. Do you know it?" Another pause. "Jo, does this mean something to you?"

"It's nothing."

"Come on, Jo, don't hold out on me here." On the other end of the line Jo wrestled with what to say.

"Okay, well, it's probably nothing but the guy we interviewed this morning was also involved with Mountview. They paid him, so I guess he was involved in their research, too."

"Why were you interviewing him?"

"He'd talked to someone about some pretty weird dreams he was having. Dreams about the killer." Harry felt his heart-rate speed up.

"Like Pam!"

"It's probably a coincidence."

"Maybe, but it's a pretty big one, don't you think? Two people participate in the same research, and both of them start dreaming about the killer. There could be some connection to this place."

"What do they research?"

"Brain patterns and electrical activity. I'm not really sure but they could be looking at ways to influence brain functioning and behavior. Hypnosis—stuff like that. They're being funded by a marketing company, so they must be looking at ways to influence consumers. Buying behaviors, that sort of thing. The founding researcher, Terry Robinson, has done work on hypnotic states. One of our new reporters has looked into the place, and is actually planning to participate in the studies, to try to get some more information. I'd be happy to send over what's she gotten so far, if you like."

"Thanks, Harry. Listen, I'll ring you back, okay?" There was a note of urgency in her voice.

"What's up?" But she'd already hung up.

~ * ~

The worm had grown bigger, and was burrowing deeper and deeper into his brain. He tried to remember the voices from before, but they'd been getting quieter and quieter, and since the Man brought dinner he hadn't been able to hear them at all. The darkness was folding in on him, and the worm was starting to hurt his head. Billy curled himself up into a fetal position and whimpered.

Twenty

The name had jolted her memory as soon as Harry uttered it. Looking through the lists, Jo saw that Peterson and Jones had interviewed Doctor Terry Robinson yesterday. She got a copy of the interview from Jones, and read that Robinson had the same alibi for almost every night in question: he'd been at home. His housekeeper, an elderly spinster by the name of Margaret Hamilton, had been able to verify his story. On the two nights he hadn't been home, he claimed to be working at the clinic. He'd been alone on both occasions, but his colleague, Doctor John Winton, had verified that Robinson often worked well into the mornings. In addition to his Toyota Landcruiser, Robinson had a Jaguar registered in his name. He claimed not to use the SUV very often—the Jag was his preferred vehicle for city driving. Closing the file, Jo returned it to Jones' desk.

"What did you think of Robinson?" He looked up from his report writing.

"Bit arrogant. But he didn't strike me as a cannibal, if that's what you're asking." He smirked. "Why the interest?"

"It's probably nothing. The name of his colleague came up in relation to something else. Doctor John Winton. You talked to him, right?"

"Yeah. Not arrogant like Robinson. But he didn't have much to say. Did you read the report?"

"Yeah, thanks for that."

"Anytime." Back at her desk, she reached for the phone.

"Hello, Harry O'Brien."

"How did your reporter get in on this research thing?"

"There was an ad in last week's New York Times."

"Okay. I'll call you back in a minute."

"Jo," he began, but she'd hung up on him again.

~ * ~

"Mountview Research Clinic. How may I help you?"

"Hello. My name is Josephine Brown. I saw your ad in last week's paper—about some research you're conducting—and wanted to register as a participant." The woman's voice was impatient.

"If you read the advertisement, you should have noted that you had to call between four and five on Tuesday afternoon. I'm sorry, but we have enough participants."

"Oh, okay then. Thanks for your time."

"Have a nice day."

She rang Harry back immediately.

"Hello, Harry O'Brien."

"When's your reporter going in for this research?"

"They're starting Monday afternoon. Why?"

"I want to go instead of her."

"So you do think there's some connection between Mountview and the killer?"

"I don't know, but Robinson drives a dark-blue Toyota Landcruiser. Although he also has an alibi."

"You've interviewed him?"

"Not me personally. But yes, he's been interviewed."

"But they'll know you're not Anne-Marie."

"Well yeah, there's that. But I just want to get in, have a look around—they probably won't kick me out straight away, right? Maybe there'll be heaps of people and they won't notice me immediately. Did Anne-Marie mention what kind of format it was going to be? Whether or not it would be a group thing?"

"No, but actually she did say she hadn't met Robinson yet. Apparently Winton did the initial interviews, but Robinson takes over from there."

"There you go then. Maybe it will take him a while to realize I'm not her."

"Anne-Marie's only twenty-three." There was a pause on the other end of the line. "No offence."

"I guess that could be a problem. But I can't get in any other way; they've stopped taking new participants. And I don't have enough to go in an official capacity."

"Well, you should probably talk to Anne-Marie first if you're going to do this. See what she says. She can give you a better idea of what to expect."

"Yeah, that's probably a good idea."

"Do you want to come in on Monday? Or should we meet you? It could be earlier if you want. Well, it would have to be today, before the weekend—I don't know what Anne-Marie's got planned. Maybe we could meet for drinks or something." Harry knew he sounded overly eager to accommodate her, but he couldn't help himself.

"No, Monday's fine. Maybe we could meet for coffee."

"Okay. How about the same place as Monday? We could call into the precinct first if you want, or shall we just meet there?"

"Let's meet at the cafe. Say about ten. If anything changes I'll give you a call."

"Sounds good."

"Bye, Harry."

"Bye."

But when she got off the phone and explained her plan to Mario she got an unenthusiastic response.

"I don't think that's such a great idea. You can't just go in there as a regular citizen."

"Why not? That reporter was going to."

"Yeah, but you're a detective. The Chief's not going to go for it. There'd have to be surveillance."

"That's why I wasn't going to tell him. I thought we could keep this to ourselves." Mario exploded.

"Jo, you have to get clearance. What if you found something, and didn't have any back-up? If you did find something you wouldn't be able to use it. Or what if there's nothing, but they find out you're a cop? They could charge us with harassment." She tried to placate him.

"It's not going to come to that. No one's going to know I'm a detective. If they realize I'm not Anne-Marie, I'll just tell them I'm a friend of hers. That she wanted me to fill in for her so she'd still get paid. And if I do learn something, we'll just work out another way to get the information."

"I don't know. If the Chief finds out what you're doing he's going to freak out. You know that." He still sounded worried but she knew he was starting to back down.

"That's why he's not going to find out—unless something turns up. We can deal with that if and when it happens. Okay?" Mario looked unhappy.

"I don't like this."

"Look, let's just leave it for now, okay? Maybe something will turn up over the next few days, and I won't have to go through with it. Perhaps we'll get something else on Robinson."

"Yeah, we should let the Chief know about the connection with Mountview. Maybe he'll want to put someone on it."

"Pity about his alibi."

Twenty-one

For once it was late when Jo woke up. After ten, according to the alarm clock. She stretched and wondered what she'd do with the day. The whole weekend stretched out like empty space she was going to have to fill. On her days off she generally walked down to the deli on the corner for fresh rolls and a Danish, and came back to bed with breakfast and the paper. But she didn't feel like reading the paper this morning.

She knew she should probably visit her mother, but she didn't feel like doing that either. She didn't feel like leaving the apartment. And her mother lived on the other side of the city, so she'd spend most of the morning on the subway. Jo drove, but she didn't own a car. There was nowhere to park one in this apartment block. On the last Thursday of every month Jo and her younger sister, Sam, typically made the journey to Queens to dine with their mother. But Jo had missed this month's dinner, and still felt guilty about canceling. She hadn't talked to Sam in a while either. She'd returned her call last weekend, and while she'd been pleased to hear her sister sounding happy, she'd been too preoccupied with this case to give Sam her full attention. Sam had recently started seeing one of the other teachers from her Elementary school, and Jo hoped he'd be a better catch than

Bill Eggleston. The best thing Jo could say about her sister's last boyfriend was that he wasn't a complete bastard. Just a boring wanker. Sam had brought Bill to dinner a few times, and Jo had trouble understanding how her sister could be attracted to anyone so dull. She sounded happier with the new guy, George, so Jo hoped he was decent. She'd always felt protective of her younger sister. But she just didn't feel up to conversation right now.

Jo had actually offered to do surveillance over the weekend, after Alton agreed to put someone on Robinson. But he'd told her to take her days off. It wasn't too often they got a weekend off, and she knew Mario valued his weekends with the family. So it was probably a bad idea to have volunteered. Even though she'd planned to partner up with someone else, Mario would have felt obliged to go in if she was working.

"It's not like we've got so many leads to follow up on that we can't cover some surveillance duty," the Chief had told her. "Given the extra resources committed to this case, I think we can spare you and Laspina for a couple of days. It's been a long week—get some rest. Next week might be even longer."

She knew he was right but it still felt wrong, taking the weekend off while Billy was still out there, trapped and alone. It had been almost two weeks now—she couldn't imagine how he must be feeling. He'd been at the back of her mind all week, and she was afraid that two days without work was going to be too much time to think about him. She'd never doubted he was still alive. Since hearing Pam's comments on Monday, she'd known he was waiting for someone to rescue him.

~ * ~

Like Jo, Peter Holdman was lying in bed that Saturday morning, unable to face the day. He hadn't gone back into work yesterday, calling in sick instead. He couldn't stop thinking about what the detective had said, about someone seeing his car, and the more he thought about it the more anxious he'd felt. After dinner he'd done a stupid thing. He'd gone for a drive, looking up the names in the phone book. One hadn't been listed but the other three were. He wanted to see the houses. Wanted to know if they looked familiar. But now as he lay in bed he regretted doing it. He was afraid. What if someone had seen him, and remembered his car? It was stupid. He hadn't even been bright enough to take Leanne's car. He never should have done it. Although he couldn't remember going there before, he'd experienced a sinking feeling of déjà vu as soon as he'd seen the house. Never even bothered with the others. He'd come home and drunk half a bottle of cheap Scotch whisky, but even that hadn't helped him sleep. He must have dozed off after a while, but mostly he'd just lay there. Unwilling to get out of bed.

Twenty-two

It was the start of a new week, but the atmosphere in the room seemed even gloomier than the week before. Countless detective hours had been spent talking to neighbors of the victims, and to owners of Toyota Landcruisers, but they didn't seem any closer to catching the killer. The detectives who'd followed Robinson over the weekend were addressing the Taskforce meeting, but they had nothing to report. He'd worked all weekend. The surveillance would continue today, until the background investigation was completed, but would be discontinued by the end of the day if nothing turned up. So far all they'd learned was that Robinson was raised by his Boarding School, after his family was killed in an auto accident on Route 495. No suspicious circumstances surrounded the accident. Julie Morrison was speaking.

"We did have a report that a white Holden Commodore drove slowly past the Williamson house on Friday night. It was reported to myself and Detective Harleson when we were doing the follow-up interviews yesterday. It occurred to us that this could be the man Detectives Laspina and Hanson spoke to on Friday, although no one got a license plate number. The neighbor was a bit vague about the timing, but thought it was sometime between eight and nine. She'd already eaten dinner. She probably wouldn't have noticed it at all except that she'd gone out to get the cat, and with our interviews and everyone's extra attention to strange cars, she thought she should mention it." Jo rose.

"It could be Peter Holdman, although we don't have much on him. Just his psychiatrist's concerns about his interest in the case. We can bring him again and check it out." Captain Alton, who'd been listening from the back of the room, moved to the front and addressed his detectives.

"Okay, everyone, I think that's it for today. You all know what you're doing, so let's just get on with it. If Billy Williamson's still alive his time's running out, so let's try to find him."

~ * ~

"Hiya, Crystal," Mario greeted the receptionist cheerily. "We're looking for Peter Holdman."

"Sorry, detective, his wife rang in sick for him about an hour ago."

"Is that right?"

"Yes." She leaned forward to whisper conspiratorially. "He took Friday off sick as well."

"Thanks for your help." She watched them leave with curiosity burning in her eyes.

~ * ~

Leanne Holdman answered the door in her dressing gown, pulling it tighter around her neck at the sight of the two detectives.

"Morning, Mrs. Holdman," Mario addressed her formally. "We wanted a word with your husband."

"He's still in bed. He's home sick from work." Mario smiled apologetically.

"Well, would you mind getting him up? I'm afraid we really do need to speak to him."

"What's all this about? Has Peter done something wrong?"

"Now, why would you ask that, Mrs. Holdman?" She looked confused for a minute.

"Well, I just mean, why do you want to talk to him?"

"I'm afraid that's confidential police business, Ma'am. Perhaps we could wait inside while you wake him." Mario had already pushed through to the narrow hallway, not giving her much choice. She shrank back.

"All right. But you better give him a minute to get dressed. Come through to the sitting room." Ten minutes later the dazed, nervous-looking salesman came out in long shorts and a short-sleeved shirt. His wife hovered behind him, anxious to hear what all this was about. Jo and Mario remained seated on the sofa, and Mario waved to the battered recliner beside them.

"Why don't you have a seat, Pete. I'm sure your wife won't mind giving us a few minutes alone to chat. Save us all going back to the station." Holdman nodded slowly and his wife shrank from the room. "Well, Pete," Mario continued, "it seems your car was spotted again. This time outside one of the victim's houses, on Friday night. Do you mind telling us what you were doing there?" The salesman's face dropped.

"I just drove past, that's all."

"And why would you do that?"

"I don't know. I just wanted to see the house, that's all." Mario leaned closer and lowered his voice.

"Did it bring back memories for you?" The salesman's voice went up a pitch.

"Why should it? It's not a crime, is it, to drive past someone's house? I didn't do anything wrong." Mario leaned into the sofa, and Holdman kept talking. "I looked it up in the phone book."

"Drive by any other houses last night, Pete?"

"No. I was going to, but I didn't. I was just curious, that's all."

"Curious, hey? Did you recognize the house when you saw it?" Holdman was getting agitated.

"Why should I? Why are you doing this to me? What do you want? I don't know anything."

"Pete, you sound like you're getting upset. Perhaps it's not such a great idea to chat here. Maybe we should go down to the station and talk about it there." Mario stood abruptly, and Holdman looked at him in confused panic, unable to comprehend what was happening.

"What? No, there's no need. I told you I don't know anything." Mario reached down and put his hand under Holdman's armpit, pulling him to his feet.

"Come on, Pete, this won't take long." He looked across at Jo, and she rose. Leanne met them in the corridor on their way out and started questioning them, the curiosity burning in her eyes.

"What's happening? Where are you going, Peter?"

"Everything's fine, Mrs. Holdman," Jo responded. "We'll call you if we need you to pick him up." Holdman remained silent, not even looking at his wife.

~ * ~

On their way back to the station Jo called Harry and changed their plans, asking him to meet her at the station.

Twenty-three

Holdman was breaking down. He kept insisting he didn't know why he'd looked up the addresses, but then he'd started to babble about wanting to see what the houses looked like. Julie Morrison knocked on the door and waved Jo over.

"Someone's here to see you." Jo glanced back over at Mario and Holdman.

"You alright here, Mario?"

"Sure. Pete and I can continue our little chat alone, can't we, Pete?" The despondent salesman didn't respond.

~ * ~

Jo showed Harry and his young colleague into another interview room, where she offered them coffee. She left them alone while she went to make it, and Anne-Marie looked eagerly around the room.

"I've never been in a police interview room before. It's pretty grungy. But that's kind of how I thought it would be." Harry had told her Jo's proposal on Friday, and while she'd initially seemed a bit disappointed about missing the chance to go undercover, she'd regained her enthusiasm when Harry told her there could be a link to the Wolfman story. He let her know they'd be working together from now on, along with the Homicide Squad, and all details had to be kept confidential. So now she was enjoying herself. Jo re-entered with the coffees.

"I'm afraid it won't be good. I usually get it from a place down the road, but this was closer—station brand. I'm sorry I had to ask you both to meet me here—I know the ambience isn't great." Harry grinned.

"Hey, we're used to crap coffee: we're reporters." Jo took a seat across from them, and addressed Anne-Marie.

"So, I guess Harry's told you why I wanted to talk to you." She nodded. "Good. So maybe you can tell me what you've already learned about Mountview, and then we can go through what they told you about the studies. Is that okay?"

"Sure."

~ * ~

Billy was only vaguely aware of his hunger. The Man hadn't been for a long time, and he'd only had the bucket of water to try to fill his stomach with. But Billy barely registered the rumblings coming from his stomach. His body was weak and he remained curled in the fetal position. It took more and more effort to move. The worm had continued to grow, and Billy was finding it harder and harder to remember who he was.

~ * ~

Mario was back at his desk when she walked Harry and Anne-Marie out. On her way back she stopped to talk to him.

"So, how'd it go with Holdman?"

"Called his wife to come get him—claimed he had a medical appointment this afternoon. I'm assuming that's his appointment with Doctor Lui, so I let him go. But I thought I was getting close in there—he's really on edge. Bringing him in seemed to push him a bit further. I think we need to keep an eye on this guy. But we'll have to play it carefully—if he wises up and asks for a lawyer we're fucked. We've really got nothing."

"Yeah. Listen, Mario, I've got to take off for the rest of the afternoon. Can you cover for me?"

"You still going through with this Mountview thing?" he asked disapprovingly. "I've got a bad feeling about that."

"Trust me on this—everything will be fine. But I've got a few things I need to do first, okay?"

"You're going to ring me as soon as you're through, right?"

"Yeah, but Harry's friend didn't know how long it would take, so don't worry if I call late. It could go on all afternoon, depending on what happens."

"I'm not happy."

"Thanks, Mario."

~ * ~

Jo cast a critical eye over herself in the full-length mirror in her bedroom. She'd traded in her suit for jeans and a light sweater, and pulled her tight curls up under a skull cap, fixing a wig on top. Luckily, she and Anne-Marie both had green eyes, and some concealer lightened her complexion to a shade closer to Anne-Marie's. Not much she could do about the wrinkles, unfortunately. Hopefully no one would be looking too closely.

Anne-Marie had told her about the 'old battle-axe' on reception, whom Jo guessed was the woman she'd spoken to on the phone. Dorothy Porter. Hopefully Mrs. Porter would take her straight through to Robinson and Jo wouldn't have to see Winton, who was the most likely to recognize Jo as an imposter. Of course, she also had to hope the guys on surveillance duty wouldn't recognize her.

~ * ~

At one p.m. Peter Holdman turned up to his appointment wearing long shorts and a grayish-brown stubble on his bloated cheeks. She was struck by the change in his appearance since last week—he seemed pale and shaken. He sat down heavily.

"Good afternoon, Peter. How are you feeling today?" Rebecca was feeling uncomfortable and trying not to let it show. She'd received a call from Detective Laspina just before lunch, letting her know that Peter had been seen driving past one of the victim's houses on Friday night, after they'd spoken to him.

"I think he's going to crack soon, Doc," the Detective had speculated, and Rebecca had been defensive.

"I hope you're not suggesting I use our therapy sessions to get some kind of confession out of him. I'm his therapist—I'm supposed to be helping him."

"I thought you doctors believed that admitting the problem is the first step to healing. But I'm not suggesting you do anything. I'm sure you'll do whatever you think is right. For the patient. I'm just letting you know what's happened since we talked to you, that's all."

"So, he has no idea I talked to the police?"

"None at all. We picked him up on the pretext that his vehicle was seen near a crime site, and only re-interviewed him today because his vehicle was actually seen. By the way, he was home sick when we spoke to him today. He hasn't been back to work since we picked him up on Friday. Seems a bit shaken by all this."

"Well, thanks for your call, Detective."

"Sure thing, Doc. Keep in touch." Although he hadn't explicitly asked her, she knew he'd want to know how the appointment went, and the thought made her uncomfortable. She'd talked to the police on Friday after they tracked him down—they wanted to let her know her description had helped them find him, and that he'd been posing as one of his more successful colleagues. That information had only reinforced her belief that she was dealing with a vulnerable man who needed help. In light all these conversations between herself and the police, Rebecca couldn't kid herself that the doctor-client relationship wasn't compromised. Once again she found herself hoping he wouldn't show. A few times throughout the morning she'd thought about ringing him and canceling the appointment, even suggesting he see another psychiatrist. But she hadn't, telling herself that a conversation like that shouldn't be sprung on someone over the phone. He trusted her.

"I'm starting to feel like the dreams are real. I've been feeling anxious, worried that they might be real."

"Peter, if these dreams are becoming more vivid, you might want to reconsider hypnosis as a way of trying to understand them. If we can work together to see what's driving them, you may find yourself less overwhelmed by them."

"What would it involve? I mean, would you put me to sleep or something?" Rebecca was taken aback by the about face. Although she'd raised it before as a possibility, she knew he had a lot of reservations about the process, and was only raising it again now to give him something to think about.

"Well, we'd have to get you into a relaxed state, but you wouldn't actually be asleep. You'd still be aware of what's going on. And, of course, you could stop at any time."

"I think I want to do it."

"You do? Well, okay then, maybe we could schedule another appointment for later in the week, so you could start."

"No, I want to start today."

Twenty-four

While Peter met with Rebecca, Jo was being shown down a long stretch of corridor by the stern-faced Mrs. Porter, who hadn't paid much attention to her when she'd checked in as Anne-Marie. Despite being ten minutes early, Jo was taken straight through to a room that looked like a cross between a doctor's office and a medical laboratory. At the far end of the room sat a bulky, vinyl-covered chair like the ones found in dentists' offices. It was flanked on both sides by technical-looking medical equipment. Closer to the entrance two large oak desks were pushed against the wall, and a computer sat on each one. Office chairs faced each desk, and the receptionist pointed to one now.

"Please have a seat," she ordered, "and I'll let Doctor Robinson know you're here." The bustling efficiency with which she'd been dealt had left her little opportunity to get a feel for the layout of the place. She'd seen the large reception area, which was at the front of the building, and had been ushered past a number of closed doors on the way to Robinson's office. The single-story building had seemed quite large from outside, so the rooms must continue further down. Apart from Mrs. Porter, she hadn't seen anyone in the building, which was strangely quiet. The research tests must be one-on-one, she surmised, wondering if she'd get a chance to talk to any other participants. Her thoughts were interrupted by the sound of the door opening. A tall, distinguished-looking man entered, and held out a well-manicured hand.

"Anne-Marie, isn't it? I'm Doctor Robinson."

"Pleased to meet you, Doctor." He pulled out the chair at the desk beside her, swiveling it round so that he was facing her directly.

"Well, Anne-Marie, permit me to tell you something about the tests we'll be running today." His voice was well-modulated and soothing. "As you'll already know, all our participants have to sign a confidentiality agreement because of the commercial nature of our research. We're looking primarily at what stimulates people's desires—what makes them want to buy certain products and not others. So today you'll be exposed to various images and sound recordings, during which time we'll measure electrical activity and other patterns in your brain."

"How will you do that?"

"Do you see those machines over there?" She followed his gaze to the machines flanking the dentist chair and nodded. "One measures data from EEGs—the electrical activity of the brain. The brain produces different brain waves depending on the mental state. The other machine is used to examine patterns of activity in the brain's central cortex. Basically, it tells us whether most activity is occurring in the left or right side of the cortex. The tests are all non-intrusive, and you won't experience any discomfort during the process. A special helmet will be fitted over your head, and is connected to a visual and audio aid. It's like a pair of thick skiing goggles with earphone attached. The sound and visual images will be fed through this device. The helmet will also be connected to the machinery that measures brain activity."

"It all sounds a little daunting." He gave her a reassuring smile.

"Not at all. It's a very safe, comfortable process."

"What exactly are you trying to find? I mean, what are you using the research for?"

"I'm afraid it's difficult to be too specific about that. Researchers don't always get to determine how their work will be used, so I can't tell you precisely what its commercial applications will be. All I can tell you is that I'm looking at how the brain responds to certain stimuli." Jo couldn't really think of anything else to ask. Although there was a lot she wanted to know, she couldn't really ask him what he knew about the Wolfman, and why two of his former participants were dreaming about him. As it became increasingly obvious that she was actually going to have to participate in the research, Jo began to worry that she may have just wasted her entire afternoon.

"I'd like you to take off your shoes and make yourself comfortable on the chair over there," he instructed. Jo reluctantly obeyed, pulling off her sneakers and making her way over to the dentist chair. She felt self-conscious about the whole process, not least of all because she worried her wig might not stay in place. When Robinson wheeled his chair across the room after her, her self-consciousness increased.

"Now, I'm just going to move the chair back a bit," he told her. He pressed something and the chair reclined until she was in a half-sitting, half-lying position, feeling increasingly apprehensive. "It's important we get you into a state of deep relaxation—that's why it's better if you're not sitting upright." His voice was soothing, but Jo was finding it difficult to relax. "Try to relax. I'm not going to hook up any machinery yet. We're just going to concentrate on making you calm. I want you to listen to my voice. Try to block out any other sounds. Think of a calm place, somewhere you feel safe. Imagine yourself in that place, and listen to my voice. You are starting to feel relaxed. You're in your safe place, and all you can hear is my voice. You can feel your muscles relaxing." Despite her efforts to resist, Jo could feel herself responding to the sound of his voice.

"You feel your mind open up, taking in the sound of my voice. You are going deeper, deeper into a state of relaxation." Jo tried to fight the sense of tiredness overcoming her, the sense of letting go, and struggled to remain conscious of what was happening around her. "Okay now, listen to my voice, I want you to tell me your name."

"Anne-Marie Benson." Her mumbled response sounded like it was coming from far away.

"No, tell me your real name." Jo felt the chill rise beneath the calm. His voice remained calm and soothing.

"I'm Anne-Marie Benson," she repeated.

"Surely you don't expect to pass for a twenty-three year old. I read Doctor Winton's notes—now tell me who you are." A hint of impatience had entered his voice.

"Anne-Marie asked me to come. She had to work, so she asked me to fill in. I'm sorry—I didn't think it mattered." His voice was calm again.

"No need to be sorry—just tell me your name." Jo struggled against the inertia that had spread throughout her body, and tried to sit up. Something was holding her down. It took her a few seconds to realize her hands and ankles were strapped to the chair. She hadn't even felt him doing it. Panic broke through the inertia.

"What are you doing? Let me up!"

"Calm down, try to relax. It's all part of the process. Tell me your name." His voice was insistent. It was no longer inspiring calm.

"Jo, my name is Jo. Now let me up."

"Jo," he repeated. "Is that short for Joanne?"

"Josephine. Untie these straps. I don't consent to this."

"Ah, Josephine. A beautiful name. Mind if I call you Josephine?" He drew out the 's' sound in her name, sounding almost reptilian.

"Yes, I mind. Now untie me or—"

"Or what, Josephine? What will you do? Are you a detective, Josephine? I've had a couple here over the past week, asking questions." Jo thought for a minute, unsure whether the truth would help her in this situation or not.

"Yes, I'm a detective. So you'd better untie me immediately, or I'll charge you with unlawful restraint." He laughed, and the sound chilled her.

"Poor Josephine. Now how are you going to charge me with anything?"

"I'm warning you, Robinson."

"And now you're warning me. Aren't you precious." Jo struggled to free herself, yanking on the leather straps binding her wrists. She tried to remember when he had fastened them, but couldn't. Was it possible she'd dozed off without realizing it? She tried to hold back the rising sense of panic as she realized how helpless she was, how exposed.

"Why are you doing this?" He leaned in closer, his dark eyes boring into hers.

"It's all part of the research, Josephine." Staring back at him, Jo felt the air leave her body. What she saw terrified her. She'd looked into the eyes of psychopaths before, and she recognized that look in Robinson's eyes. But there was something more there—something primal. Something evil. Her mind was flooded with hundreds of ugly images witnessed in the line of duty, and Jo felt her world spinning out of control, as she moved into a darker place.

"Who are you?" Her question came out in a frightened whisper.

"I'm what you fear most, Josephine." She tried to look away from him but he reached out and clasped her face, digging his thumb into her left cheek. Through the faint odor of soap she detected a whiff of garlic on his hands. Jo tried to struggle but there was something wrong with her body. He'd done something to her, making her weak. She could feel the darkness wash over her as she slipped into unconsciousness.

Twenty-five

When Harry and Anne-Marie left the precinct they didn't return to the office straight away. After talking to Anne-Marie on Friday, Harry had enlisted her help on some additional research, which he hadn't felt ready to tell Jo about. While he'd been a bit reluctant to ask, Anne-Marie hadn't seemed at all concerned about spending her weekend at the office. She'd already uncovered Robinson's excellent academic record at Harvard, so with a bit more effort they'd persuaded the secretary at Harvard's Admissions Office to reveal where he'd gone to secondary school. After advising Harry of the institution's strict codes of confidentiality, the secretary finally agreed to transfer him through to the Press Officer, Aaron Morrison. Aaron proved less reluctant to talk about a former student, particularly when he heard that Harry was doing an article on Doctor Robinson's contribution to neurological research. He readily agreed that, given his public status, it was probably public knowledge that Doctor Robinson had attended St Mark's Boys' College.

~ * ~

Although the Principal at St Mark's was initially hesitant to talk about a former student, he'd agreed to the interview after Harry

118

offered to have someone from Mountview phone him about it. After explaining that the Daily Courier was contacted by the company sponsoring Doctor Robinson's latest research, Harry managed to convince Principal Skinner to meet him on Monday afternoon. Harry confided that Market Promise was eager to generate publicity prior to announcing what was rumored to be a breakthrough in neurological research. Skinner decided it was unnecessary to have Mountview staff contact him, given the tight time frame.

~ * ~

As he pulled up to the long, gravel driveway that took them to the visitor's car park, right by the main entrance to St Mark's, Harry was hoping that Skinner could shed some light on the kind of man Robinson was. A few minutes later he and Anne-Marie approached the middle-aged woman behind the front desk, who was watching their approach over the top of her glasses.

"Hi, I'm Harry O'Brien from the Daily Courier. And this is Anne-Marie Benson. We have a twelve-thirty appointment with Mr. Skinner." They were actually a few minutes early.

"Yes, he's expecting you. Please follow me." She trotted off ahead of them, stopping before a heavy timber door and knocking tentatively, before opening it a fraction and peering through. "Principal Skinner, Mr. O'Brien and his colleague are here to see you now. Shall I send them through?"

"Thank you, Phyllis," they heard him reply, and Phyllis opened the door wider to let them through. The large room was tastefully decorated with antique furniture, its walls adorned with photographs of people Harry assumed to be former students. He recognized a few politicians and prominent businessman amongst the mix. It was the type of room designed to impress parents of prospective students, and Harry didn't imagine the school would be cheap. Skinner was a distinguished-looking man in his sixties, silver-haired and crisply dressed in a dark suit with gray silk tie. He rose to greet them, extending his hand across the rosewood desk. Harry took it and introduced himself and Anne-Marie.

"Please, have a seat," Skinner offered politely. "Would you like tea or coffee?" Harry looked across at Anne-Marie, who was clutching her notebook tightly. She shook her head.

"We're fine thanks, Mr. Skinner." The Principal looked across at Phyllis, who was still hovering in the doorway.

"Could you bring me a coffee, please? And some cold water for our guests." Phyllis departed silently, and Skinner turned back to Harry.

"So, Mr. O'Brien, what would you like to know?"

"Please, call me Harry. We were hoping you'd be able to give us some background on Terry Robinson. What kind of student he was, that kind of thing."

"Yes, well of course I wasn't the principal in those days, although I do remember Terry from English. I was Head of English at the time. My predecessor was a man named Galvinstone—passed away almost ten years ago now, sad to say. Anyway, I had Phyllis pull his academic record—I'm sure you won't be surprised to learn that Terry was an excellent student. Wonderful grades. Excelled in Science and English. And an invaluable contributor to the school's orchestra and debate team. Helped take the debate team to first place in his last three years with us." Anne-Marie was scribbling furiously.

"Mr. Skinner, we understand that Doctor Robinson was orphaned while he was a student here. Can you recall the impact that had on him?" Skinner squirmed slightly, clearly more comfortable talking about academic records.

"Ah, yes, well, tragic accident. Very tragic. I'm sure it was devastating for him—as it would be for anyone. St Mark's currently employs an excellent counselor, and I'm sure his predecessors have been equally competent. Terry would have received extensive grief counseling to help him cope with the tragedy. The school is very supportive of its students' emotional and psychological needs. You'd be surprised how often we have to provide crisis care." Phyllis returned with a tray bearing coffee and two glasses of water, and moved unobtrusively around them to place it on the table.

"Can you recall his actual response to the tragedy?"

"Well, of course, it's so long ago now. Almost thirty years. And I wasn't actually the one who had to deliver the news. I imagine that unpleasant task fell upon my predecessor. It's not an uncommon responsibility for Principals—delivering bad news to their students."

"No, I imagine that would be difficult."

"Yes, certainly one of the less pleasant responsibilities of the job. Anyway, he must have coped with the whole tragedy—with the support of staff and fellow students. Because his grades never suffered, as they sometimes do under these kind of circumstances."

"Can you remember whether Doctor Robinson had a lot of friends at school?" A look of discomfit flickered across Skinner's face.

"It's difficult to remember. It was so long ago now, and we have so many students. Of course, he must have had friends in the debate team and orchestra." Skinner no longer met Harry's eye, making Harry wonder if there'd been something about the young Robinson that Skinner didn't want to discuss.

"What happened during the holidays? Where did Doctor Robinson go after the accident?"

"Ah, well now, most holidays were spent on school grounds, as far as I can recall?" Skinner seemed to recall more than he was letting on.

"Isn't that unusual—for students to spend their holidays at the school? Weren't there any other relatives who could have taken him in—aunts, uncles, grandparents?"

"It's not as unusual as you might imagine. There's always staff around during the holidays, and some students remain if their parents are overseas, for example. Provisions were made in the boy's trust to cover the additional expenses. As far as I remember, there wasn't anybody else who could take him in. Apart from the family housekeeper, who'd been retained under the trust. The family solicitor was Terry's legal guardian, so he made all the necessary arrangements with the school."

"Do you recall the solicitor's name?"

"I'm sorry, I'm not sure it would be appropriate to delve into Terry's legal affairs, even if I did remember. Is there a reason for asking?"

"Well, we're just trying to give the article a personal slant—you know, the man behind the research, that kind of thing. I thought his solicitor might be someone we might talk to. But I expect you're right—perhaps it would be inappropriate to talk to the family solicitor." If he thought it would be helpful, Harry could always track down the solicitor's name from the documents JP had sent him. "So, just to clarify, Doctor Robinson spent all his holidays at the school, is that right?"

"Well, he may have returned home a few times over the years. The family residence had been left to him, of course, and as I mentioned the family housekeeper had been retained. She would have been responsible for his care at those times."

"Do you recall her name?"

"I'm sorry, no." Harry wondered if it was the same woman the police had spoken to about Robinson's whereabouts. He was struck by the fact that Skinner seemed to remember quite a bit about Robinson's situation, despite the fact that, as he'd already pointed out, he would have had so many students over the decades. Harry wondered if there'd been something memorable about the young Robinson. "Excuse me for saying so, but don't you think this story is taking a morbid focus? I understand you wanting to personalize it, but I gathered from your call that it was still primarily a celebration of his contribution to research."

"Yes, but the story of how a young boy overcame such terrible tragedy to emerge as one of our nation's great thinkers has got a certain appeal, wouldn't you say?"

"I suppose you know best. Still, I wouldn't overestimate the adversity too much. He was, after all, privileged to receive such an excellent education." Skinner smiled slightly, and Harry grinned in response.

"Of course. Well, we don't want to take up too much of your time—I know you must be busy." Getting to his feet, Harry extended his hand. "Thank you for agreeing to talk to us today. I hope you don't mind if we call to check any details." Skinner rose and took his hand, and Anne-Marie stopped scribbling and jumped to her feet.

"Of course not. It's been a pleasure."

Twenty-six

Jo's eyelids felt like heavy weights across her eyes as she struggled to open them. When she did, all she could see was darkness. She blinked but the darkness remained. Her body felt stiff, and as she willed it into a sitting position she realized her wrists and ankles were strapped down. Disorientated, it took her a few moments to remember what had happened. Her head felt like it was stuffed with cotton wool, and she wondered if he had drugged her. He must have given her something to make her pass out. She wondered what time it was, how much time had passed. It must be night-time; it was so dark. But even as she wondered she knew something else had changed—something other than time. Although she couldn't see anything, the room felt different. She was in the same chair, but the room wasn't the same. She felt a sense of space, and smelled the heavy odors that lingered in the air. The smell of dampness, unwashed bodies and a harsher smell, like some kind of cleaning fluid. And something else she couldn't identify.

"Robinson?" Her voice sounded raw and weak, barely audible, and she tried again. "Robinson, are you there?" Straining in the darkness, she listened for a response, but heard nothing. The sound of her voice confirmed that she was in a larger room. "It's okay, Jo", she

124

told herself. "Just think. Where are you?" The complete absence of light and the feeling of damp indicated she was in a basement. Even if it was late, some light should get into an above-ground room. Although she could be in a room without windows. Still, even the tiniest gap under a door should let in some light. Unless there were no lights on outside. She tried to picture the layout of Mountview. They're been no hint of a basement level, but she couldn't say anything for certain.

Her speculations were interrupted by a brief flicker of light, as a door opened and closed. Her chair was facing the doorway, but she'd only caught a glimpse in that brief moment, and her mind struggled to make sense of what she'd seen. A light was flicked on, and suddenly the wall nearest the doorway was bathed in a pale light. Jo pulled against the straps binding her hands as she watched Robinson lead the naked boy forward. She recognized the boy immediately, and tried to yell out to him.

"Billy!" The sound stuck in her throat. Staring straight past her to the back wall, he didn't look up at the garbled sound of his name. Something that looked like a giant fish tank stood near the doorway, filled almost to the top with liquid. The smell that Jo had been unable to identify became clear in one horrible instant: lavender oil. Robinson was leading the boy to the tank.

"Robinson, stop!" She heard the fear in her voice, and tried to control her breathing. Surprisingly, he did stop, turning slowly to face her. As he did so his mouth broke into a wide grin, and Jo had to choke back the scream. The sound that came out of her mouth was a strangled gasp. Robinson's mouth was full of metal. His teeth were steel daggers, each one sharpened to a point. Billy began to whimper, and the sound wrenched at her heart.

"Billy, can you hear me? I'm a detective. My name's Jo. It's okay, Billy, try to be brave." The boy stared blankly ahead, another whimper escaping his lips.

"So, Josephine, you recognize young Billy, do you?" His calm tone sounded sinister. It was the tone you'd expect him to hear from someone discussing the weather or something equally innocuous. It was completely out of place in this hell-hole. "He's looking a little emaciated at the moment, don't you think? You see, I noticed your colleagues following my car over the weekend. Regrettably, I wasn't able to go and feed him with them watching." Something about the comment bothered Jo, but she couldn't quite work it out. Her thoughts were weaving in and out her mind, difficult to grab hold of. But the reference to the surveillance team revived her spirits, as she dared to hope they were still outside. Her spirits plummeted again as she realized they might have been called off by now.

"Other detectives will be looking for me. My partner was expecting me to call—he knows I'm here." Robinson chuckled.

"No one's looking for you, Josephine." She felt another chill pass through her body, wondering what he meant by that. He pushed Billy forward and then, in one smooth rapid movement, scooped the boy up in his arms and dumped him over the top of the tank. Jo watched with alarm as Billy sunk under the water, his face and body fully submerged. At first it looked like he wasn't going to resist, and Jo tugged furiously at her straps. Robinson leaned over and casually put his hand under the boy's arm, lifting him into a standing position. The boy sputtered and gasped for breath. In an upright position, the water almost reached his chin. Robinson flicked the water from his wet shirt sleeve and strode across the concrete floor. The carpet she remembered had been replaced; if she needed any further evidence that they weren't in the same room, that was it. He slithered past her, and she heard the sound of metal wheels rolling across concrete as he pulled his chair up alongside hers.

"So, Josephine, let's talk." The drawn-out 's' sounds whistled through his metal teeth, sending shivers down Jo's spine. His casual tone seemed to belie the mouth full of metal. Jo couldn't look at his mouth, and she couldn't drag her eyes away from Billy. She felt like she'd been caught in a nightmare, where some madman wanted to engage her in polite conversation, as if there wasn't a naked boy soaking in a tank only a few feet away. He followed her gaze.

"Now, don't worry about young Billy over there. He's perfectly safe. I always keep an eye on them when they're in the tank. They can lose their urge to live at this stage, so it pays to be careful." Jo forced herself to remain calm, deciding to look for answers in the hope that he'd reveal something she could use. It took most of her effort not to scream.

"Why is he in there?"

"I'd have thought you could work that one out for yourself, Detective. Smart woman like yourself." Each 's' whistled through his teeth. "One has to clean the meat, after all. It smells positively rancid at the moment."

"What have you been doing to him?"

"Josephine, you do me a disservice. He's been well kept. Well, apart from these last few days. But then, that's hardly my fault, is it?

"Why have you kept him here? I mean, why not just do what you do?"

"Why not just eat him—is that what you mean to say? I can see you're no connoisseur, my dear. You see, human flesh is no different to that of sheep or cows—it's better when it's young and tender. But even young, tender flesh can be improved with careful preparation. Good veal comes from young calves that are kept tied up in the dark. They bind calves' legs, just like I've bound Billy's legs, to promote muscle deterioration. It enhances the tenderness of the flesh."

"He's not a cow," she spat, unable to keep the revulsion from her voice.

"I can see you're no vegetarian, Josephine. You think it's okay to eat cows, but you have to draw the line somewhere. And I respect that—really I do. But you're ignorant about the joys of human flesh. Maybe I can persuade you otherwise. Once you taste the sweet flesh of Billy's buttocks, I know—" She interrupted him.

"You'll have to kill me first." Her voice was a strangled whisper. The effort of keeping down the scream was draining her voice of volume.

"Oh, well, that can be arranged, of course, but I think I'll be able to bring you round to my way of thinking."

"You're fucking insane," she hissed. "I'll—" But she didn't get to finish the sentence. The blow struck her cheek with a force that made her head spin, and her body reeled back in the chair.

"Now, now, no need to be rude," he admonished. "That's not going to do anybody any good. It certainly won't help young Billy over there if I have to kill you, will it? I mean, that will just speed up his own demise." Jo struggled to clear her mind, to devise a plan. But she was completely helpless. For a brief moment the rage had felt good, dulling the panic. But she knew it wasn't going to do her or Billy any good.

Jo knew what was going to happen. She'd known from the moment she saw Billy and the tank. But she also knew she had to stop it somehow—that she couldn't let it happen. Getting herself killed wasn't going to achieve that. She had to keep him talking until someone came to investigate. Even if the surveillance team had left, Mario would be looking for her. She wished she knew what time it was. Hopefully, he would have realized something was wrong by now. The thought that had been weaving around her head before suddenly came back, and struck fear into her heart. Robinson said he wasn't able to feed Billy over the weekend, because of the surveillance. But the surveillance team had followed him to Mountview, so if Billy was there, Robinson should have been able to feed him. Which meant maybe they weren't at Mountview. Was it possible he'd moved her while she'd been drugged? After all, she had no idea how much time had passed. Maybe more than she'd realized. If he'd taken her to another place, maybe he'd lost the surveillance unit. After all, he'd known they were there—he wouldn't lead them right to Billy. Maybe it was even later than she realized, and he'd waited until the surveillance was called off before moving her. If they weren't at Mountview, who knew how long it would take for someone to find them.

Telling herself to calm down, Jo tried to think of what they already knew about Robinson. They knew where he lived. But that was an apartment, so it wouldn't have a basement. Maybe he had a darkroom or something, and that's where they were. In which case, the squad should come looking, once Mario raised the alarm. She had to stay calm. Keep talking to him—give her colleagues time to find them.

"It must have been difficult for you—growing up without your parents."

"Are you trying to understand me, Josephine?"

"Just making conversation. What was it like for you? Did you enjoy boarding school?"

"Why don't we talk about you first, Josephine. What was it like to watch your little sister get attacked while you stood helplessly by?" Jo felt like he'd just delivered another blow to her face.

"How do you know about that?" He gave her a reptilian smile, and she caught another glimpse of the glistening metal. She shuddered at the thought of what those teeth could do. At what she'd seen them do.

"Sweet Josephine, I know all about you. I've been inside your mind. But that doesn't mean I'm not interested in further exploration. Why don't you tell me about your sister? What's her name?" Jo didn't want to talk any more. "Have we finished our conversation already, Josephine? How disappointing."

"Sam."

"Sam. Short for Samantha, I'm guessing. Lovely name. Was she a lovely child, Josephine?" He was watching her with a look of polite interest on his face, awaiting her reply. She nodded. "Tell me about that night, Josephine. What was it like?" Jo had spent years trying to forget it. Not that she'd ever managed to do so. Every time she looked at her sister she remembered that night.

"I was seven. My sister was five. Two men broke into our house in the middle of the night." Her voice sounded robotic.

"Go on," he encouraged.

"I was asleep, but Sam must have heard them come in. I woke up when I heard her call out my name. One of the men put his hand over my mouth and pulled me out of bed. I saw the other man beside my sister's bed. He held a knife to her throat. I tried to break free but the man held me back. He had one hand over my mouth, the other arm across my chest, pinning my arms down. He was so much bigger than me, I couldn't break free."

"What happened next, Josephine?"

"The man with the knife said, 'Make another sound and I'll cut your throat'." Jo could still hear his guttural voice in her head. "Sam was looking at me. Her eyes were pleading with me to help, but there was nothing I could do. She started to cry. So he took the knife and dug it into her neck, dragging it downward. He was telling her to stop, but she was getting more hysterical. I could see the blood on her neck from where he cut her. She was trying to stop crying but she kept making these little noises. She was so scared."

"And then what happened?"

"My mother came in. She was holding a gun. I didn't even know we had one. It was strange to see it in her hands. Everything seemed to be moving in slow motion. Both men were looking at her. She said, 'get away from my daughter', and then she shot him. The man with the knife. Shot him twice. He fell down and the other man ran away, pushing past her." It was all so vivid in her mind, the sound of her mother's voice, the gunshots, the sight of the man falling to the ground in slow motion, blood streaming from his chest. Later Jo would learn that the gun belonged to her father, a businessman who was out that night 'entertaining clients'. There was something about the way her mother said that which made her think her father was doing something wrong. A few weeks later her mother made him move out of the house, and Jo had seen him less and less frequently over the years. Despite the fact that the intruder died in hospital the same night, no charges were brought against Jo's mother. The police had been kind to all of them.

Jo suddenly realized that night had been a pivotal moment in her life. It was what had driven her into the force, and shaped the way she approached detective work. Her ability to identify with the victims had given her insight into countless cases, as she reconstructed scenes from the victim's point of view. But she realized that her greatest strength was also a weakness. At certain times over the past few weeks she'd felt a paralysis that reminded her of that night, years ago. There'd been a time when all she'd wanted to do was look away, not see the victims' suffering. It was as if Robinson had tapped into her greatest fear, as if he knew that watching someone else's fear and suffering was far worse than any fear and suffering she might endure herself. As if, in empathizing with the victim, she felt the suffering magnified to a greater extent than if she herself was the victim. She knew she had to fight that paralysis now. She had to gain time—for Billy as well as herself. Robinson was watching her closely, his dark eyes fixed on her as if he were looking into her mind, following her thoughts.

"Does Billy remind you of Samantha?" Jo fought to keep her voice calm.

"Well, he's a victim, if that's what you mean."

"And it's your job to protect the victim, isn't that right?"

"Yes."

"Tell me, what's your relationship with your sister like these days?"

"We get on fine."

"Do you remember that night when you see her? Do you think of that frightened little girl with the knife at her throat? Perhaps you remember your own helplessness."

"It was a long time ago now—it's over." His eyes bored into hers, until she had to shift her gaze.

"I don't think you're being honest with me, Josephine. Maybe you're not being honest with yourself. Do you ever find yourself avoiding your sister?"

"No. I told you, it was a long time ago." He sounded disappointed with her.

"Josephine, I want you to feel you can tell me the truth. If you don't think you can do that, than there's really no point in us talking, is there?" He rose and moved outside her line of vision, switching on another light. She wriggled her chair around to face him, and suppressed her reaction to the new horrors lit up along the back wall. Long chains hung from the ceiling, and leather handcuffs dangled from the chains.

"Yes, I think of that night when I see her. Sometimes, if she's having difficulties—relationship difficulties—I avoid her. I don't like seeing the pain in her eyes." He moved towards her again, swinging her chair back to its original position, so that it faced the tank. He stood beside her, but his eyes glistened with a madness that didn't see her right now.

"Well, that's interesting, Josephine. But haven't there been times, growing up, when you wanted to hurt her? When you wanted to see the pain in her eyes?" He turned to face her, his attention back now as he waited for her response.

"No, of course not, she's my sister." But that wasn't completely true. "Well, when we were little maybe. After our father moved out. Sometimes I'd wake her up by pinching her." Jo felt a rush of shame as she relived the memory. He sat back down besides her, giving her his full attention again.

"Poor Josephine. But perfectly understandable. I know what it's like to be the older sibling—sometimes you just want to hurt them."

"How old were your brother and sister when they had the accident?" He leaned back into his chair, and for a few minutes she thought he wasn't going to respond.

"My sister was born only a few years after me. But my parents waited longer before producing my brother. I was already in boarding school by then. I can remember coming home for the holidays and seeing him for the first time, so young and tender in his little crib. So vulnerable. I just wanted to eat him up." He grinned wickedly, flashing his metal, and Jo tried to repress the shudder of revulsion that ran through her body.

"I guess that would have upset your parents a little," she observed.

"Well, you can imagine. I mean, I'd taken a few bites of my sister by that time, which is how I came to end up in boarding school at such a young age, but after taking a bite out of little brother I'm afraid I really severed my ties with Father. He came at me with a baseball bat. Lost quite a few teeth over that one. Of course, with the family name to uphold and all that, we told everyone it was a riding accident—that I'd hit my mouth on a rock. I seldom got home for the holidays after that."

"I can understand why your family might want to keep something like that secret."

"Indeed. But that's enough about me. All this talk is making me hungry. How about you, Josephine—have you eaten?"

"I'm fine. I had lunch before coming to Mountview."

"Ah, but that was such a long time ago now."

"How long ago, exactly?" He laughed.

"Time's not important. But Billy's water must be getting cold by now—I really should get him out."

"No, wait—" But Robinson was already moving towards the tank. When he reached it, he turned back to her.

"By the way, Josephine, you haven't mentioned whether or not you like my tank."

"It's very unusual. Like a giant fish tank or something. Did you have it custom-made?"

"Indeed. By someone who specializes in fish-tanks, so your impression is quite right. I was planning to have the largest salt-water fish tank in New York. I'm quite partial to sushi, you know." He grinned again. "But I found another use for it." With one sudden movement he plunged both arms into the water, and pulled the dazed-looking boy out by his armpits, knocking the unresisting body against the glass on the way up. He dragged Billy roughly across the floor, while Jo watched on helplessly. With his ankles bound Billy kept stumbling, and Robinson had to pull him along. As he dragged him past Jo, he reached out and swung her chair round in one vicious movement, so that she faced the back wall.

"Want to make sure you get a good view, Josephine." Positioning Billy under the chains, he left him standing there shivering while he walked off into the unlit corner of the room. The shivering boy stood where he was placed as if he was in some kind of trance, and while Jo wanted to scream at him to run, she knew he wouldn't get far with his bound feet. When Robinson returned he held a large butcher's knife in his right hand, and Jo felt her heart lurch upwards to her mouth. She tried to keep the terror from her voice, struggling to reason with the madman.

"Robinson, wait! You don't have to do this!" Ignoring her he reached for the boy's wrists with his free hand, pulling them out so they were outstretched from Billy's chest. He raised his right hand and seemed to deliberate, perhaps savoring the moment, before plunging the knife down, severing the rope in one rapid movement. Billy's arms fell limply to his side, and Robinson let the knife slip from his hand. Jo jumped at the sound it made as it hit the concrete floor, and was forced to sit helplessly by as Robinson roughly grabbed Billy's right hand and fastened it in the handcuff. He removed a key from his trouser pocket to lock the cuff, and then repeated the process with Billy's left hand. Jo struggled to regulate her breathing as she watched Robinson yank down on one of the chains. Billy's body lifted slowly, until his naked flesh dangled in the air like a carcass in a butcher's shop. Robinson then crouched down to retrieve his knife, and sawed the rope from the boy's ankles. Stretching back up, he pulled once more on the chains, until Billy was hanging about three feet from the floor.

Jo yanked against her arm restraints with all the strength in her body, watching the skin rub off her wrists while the straps held. She fought the growing sense of hopeless despair, of frustrated helplessness, threatening to overwhelm her. She lashed out angrily, kicking against the ankle straps, unable to feel the pain even though she could see the blood seeping from the leather. Breathing became harder.

"Try to relax, Josephine," came the serpentine advice. "Breathe deeply." Framed by the light shining against the back wall, he looked like a silver-haired demon. "If you can relax I'm sure you'll enjoy the show. I know it's not much to look at now, but that often happens when the meat has been kept in the dark for so long. Their little minds seem to slip, and it's only the intense pain that wakes them up again. You won't believe how they scream when they finally realize what's happening. You won't have heard anything like it in your life."

"He's just a boy." she pleaded. "Please don't do this." Deep down she knew there was no use pleading with him, and she detested the weakness she heard in her voice.

"I'm not greedy, Josephine. I'm going to share. I promise you, it's a rare delicacy unlike anything you've ever tasted before. It's one the boy here has already enjoyed, haven't you, Billy?" He cast his eyes up at the dangling boy, and feigned disappointment when Billy failed to respond. Shrugging, he moved back into the shadowy corner, and this time returned with a large metal tray, which he set beneath the hanging body.

"Personally, I enjoy the biting more than the eating. That's just me, of course. That's not to say I don't relish a morsel afterwards. Grilled of course—I'm no fan of raw meat. Sushi's one thing, but fresh boy meat needs to be lightly grilled. Not overdone, but I suppose that goes without saying. How about you, Josephine? How do you like your meat?"

"You fucking animal," she spat, unable to hide her disgust any longer.

"Oh dear. I thought we agreed earlier to refrain from vulgarity. Clearly you need a reminder in civility." He reached down and plucked the butcher's knife from the floor, holding it up to Billy's throat. "Is this how the man held the knife to Samantha's throat, Josephine? Did he hold it here, while you watched?" Jo gaped in horror as he pressed the end of the thick knife into the skin, dragging it down to the boy's chest. Billy started whimpering.

"I'm sorry, Doctor Robinson. Please forgive me," she begged. With the knife still in his hand, he turned slowly to face her.

"So tell me Josephine, how do you like your meat?"

"Well done."

"Tsk-tsk. You disappoint me. I hope you're not one of these people who buys their meat in a little Styrofoam tray and cooks it until it's barely recognizable as meat. The kind of person who won't buy their meat in bulk, because they're too squeamish about where it comes from. They don't want to see the blood. Are you like that, Josephine?"

"Maybe."

"Perhaps I can convince you to try it rare. As I was saying earlier, I only keep a morsel for myself. I'm not like one of those psychopaths you see in the movies, who keep a freezer full of flesh. As far as I'm concerned, that's just vulgar. Human flesh is best eaten fresh. Preferably, on the day of the kill. I only keep a bit back for my boys; the rest goes in the garbage. But enough of this chit-chat." He moved in closer to the swinging body and grabbed it just above the hips, a grasping claw on either side. Jo wanted to press her eyes closed but couldn't, and as he leaned in closer, pressing his wide, wet maw of metal against the boy's shoulder, Jo felt her breathing get more and more labored. Billy's agonized scream filled the room, filling her head. It wasn't until she saw Robinson bending over her, grinning menacingly through the blood-drenched metal, that she realized she was screaming, too. As he leaned over her everything grew dark again, as her mind flooded with bloody images of children dangling from chains like carcasses, writhing and screaming in agonized terror.

Twenty-seven

After returning from their meeting with Skinner, Harry had been going through all the information they'd collected over the weekend. Which wasn't that much. They'd conducted an extensive Internet search, and eventually found a reference to the accident that made Robinson an orphan. They'd then spent hours in the paper's archive section going through microfilm of back issues, and finally found the accident report in an edition dated Tuesday, September 17, 1979:

At approximately 10 p.m. Sunday night, September 15, a local businessman and his family were tragically killed on the Long Island Expressway when they collided with an 18-wheel semi-trailer. It is believed that Doctor James Robinson and his family were returning from a weekend in the Hamptons at the time of the accident. Along with his wife, Mrs. Mary Robinson, Doctor Robinson was traveling with his two children: Katie, aged 9, and James, aged 1.

At this stage police believe Doctor Robinson fell asleep at the wheel, losing control of his vehicle. It swerved into oncoming traffic and collided with the semi-trailer. The driver of the semi-trailer, a Mr. Mack Davies, was unhurt. He told police that 'the car just came out of nowhere.' The car crumpled on impact, and its passengers were killed instantly, with the exception of Katie Robinson. Katie was taken to hospital with severe injuries, and passed away in the middle of the night.

The Robinsons are survived by a 12-year old son, Terry Robinson, who was at boarding school when the accident occurred. After interviewing Mr. Davies and several witnesses present at the scene, the police have determined that Mr. Davies is innocent of any negligence. They have declared the case closed.

Robinson had proven adept at keeping his personal life personal, and they'd struggled to uncover much more about him. Harry had turned once more to JP's services, but when the documents were faxed through they didn't bring them much closer to knowing the neurologist. Robinson still owned the family residence in Sutton Place, but had no other property. He'd sold the house in the Hamptons when he'd turned twenty-one, and the family trust had turned over all its assets to him, including a considerable income. Robinson was respectably wealthy, and didn't need to work for a living. Which seemed lucky, given that he didn't appear to be drawing an income from Mountview.

As he re-read all the information they'd gathered over the weekend, and mentally replayed the conversation they'd just had with Skinner, Harry didn't feel any closer to understanding the connection between Robinson, Pam Grinstone and Peter Holdman. But he was convinced that one existed, and he couldn't shake the sense of unease that had been with him all afternoon. Staring at the notes on his computer screen, he had the strange sensation that the world had just shifted slightly to the left. Became slightly darker. A host of ugly images filled his head—images from crimes scenes he'd covered. And one of a small, naked boy curled up on a dirty mattress. He forced himself to stand and go to the bathroom. It felt like he was walking in slow motion, and the air around him had suddenly become heavier. The faces of his colleagues passed in a slow blur. Everything looked the same, yet different at the same time—as if someone had turned on a dimmer switch and cast the entire office in a different light. In the bathroom he splashed water on his face, and felt another shift, as if reality was slipping back into place. Harry looked at himself in the mirror. He looked like shit. Maybe the acid he'd tried in college was finally catching up with him.

As Harry came out of the bathroom he realized that his strange experience had heightened his sense of unease. Uncertain what else to do, he phoned Mario.

"Detective Laspina."

"Hi, Mario, it's Harry O'Brien. Listen, I'm just ringing because I'm worried about Jo."

"Why? What's happened?"

"Well, nothing that I know of. Not for sure. I've just got this feeling that something's wrong."

"Jesus, everyone I talk to lately is having bad feelings or weird dreams. Nobody's got anything concrete. I'll tell you, Harry, I wasn't happy about Jo going into that place today, but she made the decision. I'll get her to call you when she's through, okay?"

"Mario, I really think something's going on over there."

"Do you know something you're not telling me?"

"No, not really. I mean, I haven't got proof of anything yet, but—" Mario cut him off.

"Listen, there's two officers outside Mountview right now. Nothing's going to happen to her in there."

"Can you get them to go in and check on her?"

"Are you fucking crazy? Hopefully they won't even realize she's there. You know we'd need a warrant to go in. We've got no grounds. What's got into you anyway, is... Hey, can you hold on a sec. I've got to take another call." Harry heard him pick up the other line. "Hello, Doctor Lui, this is Laspina." But Mario must have put his mobile down because Harry couldn't hear anything after that. A few minutes passed and Mario was back on the line, a sense of urgency in his voice.

"Listen, Harry, I've got to go. Don't worry about Jo—I'll get her to give you a call as soon as I talk to her."

"But, Mario—"

"I really gotta go."

"Mario—" But Harry was speaking into empty space. He knew he was being irrational. He understood that the police couldn't barge into the offices of a respected neurologist just because Harry had a bad feeling. What had he been thinking? He was overreacting. Jo was a cop. Besides, she'd only gone in for the afternoon. Mario was right—he should just wait for her to call.

Twenty-eight

It took her a few minutes to work out where she was. The lights had been dimmed, but Jo recognized the office where she'd first met Robinson. Looking around, she realized the room was unoccupied. An excruciating thumping noise was beating in her head, and it wasn't until she raised her hand to her pounding forehead that she realized her hands weren't tied. Looking down, she saw that her ankles had also been unstrapped. She'd been left in the reclining position Robinson had put her in earlier, and it took all her energy to sit up. She saw her sneakers sitting beside the chair. Still disorientated from the effort of sitting up, Jo tried to recall what had happened, and the flood of memories, the piercing screams, threatened to force her back down into the chair.

"Billy," she gasped, wrestling with the onslaught of images that threatened to overwhelm her. It took every ounce of energy she had to climb out of the chair, and she almost collapsed back into it when her legs threatened to give way beneath her. She felt like a coma patient who hasn't used her limbs for a long time, and doesn't realize how much muscle deterioration has taken place. Where was Robinson? Why had he left her alone? It occurred to Jo that whatever drug was causing the fierce thumping in her head might have been expected to keep her unconscious for longer. She had no idea how long she'd been asleep, and felt that if she didn't resist the urge to sit back down to rest she might easily slip back into unconsciousness. She looked down at her wrist-watch, but it wasn't there. Robinson must have removed it when he strapped her down. She didn't know how much time she had—he could return at any moment. She had to make her move now.

Not bothering with her sneakers, Jo crept across the floor in her socks, trying not to make a sound. Her heart was in her mouth when she reached the door, and she was stunned when the handle turned. Peering out cautiously, she looked up and down the empty corridor, wishing she had her gun. There was nowhere to hide if someone came along, but she had no other options. She had to get help, and pray that it wasn't too late for Billy. Emptying her mind of all thoughts, Jo inhaled deeply and ran. She ran faster than she'd ever run before, moving past a wide-eyed Dorothy Porter, who seemed too surprised to stop her. Pushing the front doors with all the strength she had left in her body, Jo stumbled out into the car park, and was temporarily blinded by the light. Confused by the brightness, she forced herself to keep moving, leaving the car park and running down the street. Blinking rapidly at the sight of the white sedan, Jo stopped running and stared, trying to convince herself it was real. The whole scene seemed surreal—the bright light, the car. How many days had she been in there? Why was the surveillance team still here? Flinging herself against the car, Jo struggled with the passenger door. A startled-looking detective opened the door for her.

"Can I help you, Ma'am?"

"Jones, it's me. Hanson." His eyes widened in amazement.

"Jo?"

"Yes." She struggled to catch her breath.

"Are you wearing a wig?"

"What?" She'd completely forgotten about the wig. "Yes, call for backup. We've got to get back inside. Robinson's the Wolfman!" Petersen had climbed out of the driver's seat and was giving her a strange look.

"Calm down, Jo. Tell us what happened."

"It's Robinson. He had Billy Matheson in there. He tied me up—I don't know for how long, but I saw Billy. I don't know if he's okay. I saw Robinson—" She choked on the words. "We've got to get back in there. I think there might be a basement." Petersen had ducked back into the car and was on the radio. Jo could hear him calling for backup, but his voice sounded like it was coming from such a long way away. Jones was watching her with a concerned look on his face.

"Are you sure you're okay, Jo? You don't look so good—maybe you should sit down for a minute."

"No, I'm okay. We've got to get back in there and—" But Jo couldn't finish the sentence. Everything around her was growing hazy, and she felt herself slipping. She heard worried voices asking if she was all right, but they seemed to be coming from far away. The last thing she was aware of was the feeling of arms wrapping around her, easing her down into the back seat of the car.

Part II

Descent Into Darkness

Twenty-nine

When Jo opened her eyes she had no idea where she was. She was in bed, but it wasn't her own. Her eye caught the glimmer of light to her left, where a bedside lamp cast a soft glow on the rose-colored walls. She could make out the thick cream carpet at the base of the bedside table, but beyond that the room was swallowed in darkness. Still, there was something familiar about the room, even if she couldn't quite figure it out. Before she'd had time to look around, a soft voice came out of the darkness, making her jump.

"Jo?" Swiveling her head to the right, she pinpointed the source of the voice. "Jo, it's me. Mario. You're okay. You're in our guest-room." She could see his silhouette now, sitting in the corner, just behind her head. He fumbled for the other bedside lamp and the silhouette became Mario. He looked tired and rumpled, as if he'd been sleeping in his clothes, and the sight of him almost moved Jo to tears.

"Mario, what happened? How did I get here?" The images of Mountview and Robinson began flooding through her mind before she'd even finished the sentence, and she reeled back under their onslaught. The images hit her like a physical blow, and she felt too weak to defend herself.

"Everything's okay. Petersen brought you over, after you passed out in the car. Do you remember?" He paused for a response, but when he didn't get one he pushed on. "He wanted to take you to hospital and I told him to bring you here instead. Maria sat with you until I got home." The memory of seeing Jones and Petersen returned, dispersing some of the more horrific images in her mind.

"What about Robinson? And Billy? Is he dead?" Responding to the agitation in her voice, Mario's voice was gently reassuring.

"Take it easy, Jo. Everything's okay. Billy's going to be okay. You need to relax now. You want me to get you some coffee?" Although she wanted the coffee, she needed to hear about Billy first.

"In a while. Tell me what happened. Is Billy badly injured? What about Robinson? Is he in custody?"

"Billy's safe at home with his parents. And we got the killer."

"Billy's gone home already? What about his injuries?"

"We made sure he got medical attention. For the most part it seems the damage was psychological rather than physical. He was very shaken up. Not talking to anyone. Hasn't said a word since we brought him out. We got his folks to take him home for the night. They're bringing him in for questioning tomorrow—we'll see if Doctor King can get through to him. Get him to talk."

"So Robinson's in custody? What happened after I... passed out." Even in the dim light she could see Mario's discomfort.

"Petersen and Jones called for backup. When it came, they left you in the back seat of the car and went in. They checked the place out thoroughly. Jo, there weren't any underground rooms, no evidence Robinson was keeping Billy, or any other kid, in there."

"Robinson must have driven me to wherever he was keeping Billy. I'd already thought about that. But then how did you find him? Did Robinson talk?"

"Jo, listen." Mario's voice was patient and kind, as if he was explaining something to one of his daughters. "We got a tip about the place from Doctor Lui. That's how we found Billy."

"Doctor Lui?" He nodded. "I don't understand. How did she know about Robinson?" Mario reached out and placed a large hand on Jo's arm.

"I don't really know what went on in there, but we haven't charged Robinson with the murders. We brought him in for questioning, but we had to let him go. We've got Peter Holdman in custody for the killings."

"Holdman? But, Mario, I actually saw Robinson do it. He must have driven me to wherever he keeps the kids, and then brought me back to Mountview. I was there; I know it." Mario shook his head.

"He can't have. Petersen and Jones were there the whole time. They didn't see him leave."

"But he knew they were there. He's clever. He must have lost them." Mario was silent for a while.

"Jo, the house was on the other side of the city, in the Bronx. He can't have taken you there and got you back in time. You weren't in there long enough."

"That's not possible. It seemed like days."

"It's still Monday, Jo. Well, technically Tuesday morning now, but you've been here all night. You've been asleep for hours." Jo's mind rebelled at what he was telling her. She felt like she was stuck in some kind of twilight zone.

"I saw him rip into Billy's shoulder." She heard the uncertainty in her own voice.

"Jo, I saw Billy—he's all right. Holdman hadn't started on him— we got him in time. I mean, he's very shaken up. He'd been kept in the dark for weeks, naked and tied up, so he's not doing too well psychologically. But physically he's okay. There was nothing wrong with his shoulder." Jo felt like she was losing her mind. "Look, why don't I fix that coffee now. It'll make you feel better." She nodded weakly, and while Mario left to make the coffee Jo wrestled with what she'd just heard. She couldn't make sense of what had happened, and trying to seemed to suck what little energy she had left. When Mario returned with the coffee the concern was etched deeply into his face.

"You hungry? You want me to fix you something to eat? Maria made some lasagna tonight. I could heat some up if you'd like. Or there's some left-over roast beef there if you'd rather have a sandwich. I could—" She cut him off.

"It's okay, Mario, I'm not hungry. Coffee's fine."

"Yeah, right." He held out the mug. "Hey, by the way, Harry's been real worried about you."

"Harry?"

"Yeah. He rang earlier today, really freaking out. Insisting that something was wrong over at Mountview. He called back last night, before I had a chance to let him know you were okay. I know he'd really appreciate hearing from you. When you're feeling up to it, I mean, not right now."

"Yeah, thanks, Mario. I'll give him a call in the morning." Harry's face had been among the many painful images that had flashed through her mind at Mountview. Along with her father's. She wasn't really sure she could face him right now. She felt like an open wound: raw and vulnerable. More than anything else, she wanted to curl up in a ball and sleep for days, forgetting everything that had happened. Or imagined, as the case may be. Yet there was another part of her that wanted to pick at the scab that was already forming, and confront her raw, vulnerable self with what she'd experienced.

"I don't understand what happened today. Why did you charge Holdman?" She didn't like the weakness she heard in her voice.

"Doctor Lui called. She did some kind of hypnosis with him and he told her where Billy was being kept. Well, not exactly where—he didn't give specific directions or anything. But it was enough for us to track it down. I've been thinking about that hypnosis stuff since I've been sitting here. Do you think Robinson could have put you into some kind of trance? Like Doctor Lui did to Holdman? I mean, she used hypnosis to get him to talk; maybe Robinson did the same."

"I don't know. It all seemed so real at the time. I guess he must have done something—I'm pretty sure he drugged me. But tell me about this place."

"Okay. Maybe we should do a blood test—check if Robinson gave you anything." Noticing her impatience, he continued. "So, I got the call from Doctor Lui after her appointment with Holdman today. He told her about the place where the kids were kept, and from the description she gave us we figured it was in the Bronx. So we just rang every real-estate agent in the borough until we found one who'd rented a place to a Mr. Peter Holdman. He recognized the place from our description, and as soon as we get there I knew it was the place. It was just like the Doc described it."

"So you actually saw it?"

"Yeah, there were these two big basement rooms, just like Holdman said. Completely soundproofed—ain't nobody was going to hear what went on down there. Besides, there was a vacant lot on either side, so it was pretty deserted. The nearest residence was a tenement block, where everyone minded their own business. The house was pretty run down. Anyway, there's these two big basement rooms, and we found Billy in one, tied up and lying on a stinking mattress. There was this huge tank in the other one, like a gigantic fish-tank." Noticing the horrified expression on her face, he paused. "You okay?"

"Yeah, keep going."

"And there were chains hanging from the ceiling." He shivered involuntarily at the memory. "The smell was terrible. Anyway, we've had the forensic guys all over the place—DNA everywhere. They're going to be working on it all night—hopefully we'll have something back by morning."

"Why would Holdman rent the place in his own name?" Mario shrugged.

"I don't reckon he's all that bright. Evans and Mackerson went and picked him up as soon as we found the place, and Holdman completely freaked out. Finally decided to get himself a lawyer. The lawyer's advised him not to talk, so we haven't got a confession yet. But I reckon he wants to talk—I'm going to try again this morning. I wanted to come home and check on you first."

"I want to come in with you when you talk to him." He looked down at his big hands, an embarrassed expression on his face.

"Yeah, well, the thing is, Jo, Alton was pretty pissed at how things went down, you know? Wanted to know what the hell you were doing in there. Why our guys had stormed the place without a warrant. Might have been different if there was something to find, but there wasn't. And that Robinson's a real arrogant bastard, talking to the detectives real snotty like they'd violated his rights. Had his lawyer in there in no time. We had him down at the precinct without grounds. I mean, I didn't even know he was coming in. It was pretty chaotic in there this afternoon. Yesterday afternoon. We were out looking for the house when Petersen called for backup over at Mountview. They only sent one car on account of everyone being out. And then they brought Robinson in, and Evans and Mackerson came in soon after with Holdman. So there we are with two guys in for the same crimes. It was crazy." He took a breath and continued.

"Robinson was cool as a cucumber too, saying he didn't know what was going on. Claimed you'd been participating in some studies. Anyway, Alton calls me into his office, and I reckon it's only because I was in the middle of interviewing Holdman that he didn't suspend me on the spot. This was about ten o'clock last night. Holdman had been in for hours and was breaking down. We left him in the interview room after the lawyer advised him not to talk, not taking him to the holding cells straight away. Letting him sweat—wondering if we were coming back."

"Anyway," Mario continued, "Alton's demanding to know what you were doing. Wants to know why we had Robinson in there. I mean, he could see trouble—Robinson's no fool. He's already making claims about police interfering with his research. He knows we've got nothing. Except, you know, what you told Petersen and Jones. And that would have been enough, if there'd been something to find, but—

" He left the sentence unfinished, an embarrassed look on his face. "Anyway, the only other thing we've got is that connection with Holdman. If Robinson gets too heavy we could always use that—bluff it out by saying Holdman's story led us to Mountview. It's a stretch, but it's something." He inhaled again and kept going.

"But Alton's unhappy. Except for that fact we've got Holdman and he's looking good for the killings—and of course, there's Billy— I think he might have thrown the book at both of us tonight." Seeing her despair, and misinterpreting its source, he rushed on. "But don't worry. As it stands he just said maybe you should take a few days off. Have a break from the case—maybe it's getting to you." The despair had almost overcome her as she listened to Mario talk, and she'd been left feeling numb. It was too much to get her head around.

"But Robinson tied me up," she insisted. There was a plaintive note there, but as she continued the emotion drained from her voice. "My wrists and ankles were strapped to that chair." She looked down at her wrists, remembering how she'd rubbed at the skin in her attempts to get free. There were no marks. She felt the rising panic as she peered down at her ankles, but it was soon enveloped by the numbness. There were no marks on her ankles. Maybe she really was losing her mind. Jo would have been scared if she wasn't so numb. Maybe the numbness was a coping mechanism, she thought, and as soon as she thought it she wondered at the detachment with which she'd analyzed the situation. There seemed to be a struggle going on in her mind right now, between panic, self-doubt and fear on one side, and detached numbness on the other. She wasn't sure which side she wanted to win.

"How'd you get free then?" Mario's voice sounded like it was coming from far away.

"I... I wasn't tied up when I regained consciousness."

"But why would he have untied you if he wanted to keep you there?" Mario prompted her gently, but she could tell from his tone he was worried about her state of mind, and was trying to lead her towards his own conclusions. She realized he didn't believe her, and couldn't remember that ever happening before. It made her feel even more alone. "You just ran out of there, right? Nobody tried to stop you?" She shook her head. He was right—it didn't make any sense. Robinson had let her go—he'd wanted her to run.

"Listen," he told her gently, "we'll get Marcy to do a blood test in the morning. Maybe he did drug you—messed with your mind or something." He paused. "Maybe she can come here and do it. I mean, it's probably better if you stay the night, right? You can go back to your place tomorrow. If you want to take a shower I can get you some of Maria's clothes." Lacking the energy to go anywhere, Jo submitted, happy to let Mario take charge.

~ * ~

Harry couldn't sleep. He'd been self-medicating with bourbon for the last couple of hours, but as he watched the time move towards three a.m. he felt like he'd started to drink himself sober. When Mario told him Jo was staying at his place tonight, his first instinct had been to rush right over. But Mario had warned him off, telling him Jo was asleep and needed to rest, and that Maria was keeping an eye on her until Mario got home. Harry knew something had gone wrong at Mountview, but Mario wasn't giving too much away.

"We don't think it's Robinson," he'd told him. "We've got someone else for the homicides." At least they'd found Billy alive, which was a huge consolation. But Mario wouldn't give him any details, insisting he'd have to wait until the police knew more. He promised to give Jo the message to call him, but warned she was pretty out of it and might not get the message until tomorrow. Which was now today. Harry had spent the entire night sitting on the sofa willing the phone to ring. It had been a long night, and Jo had been the only thing on his mind. Despite Mario's assurances that she was fine, Harry knew something was up. He'd heard it in Mario's voice, which had only confirmed what he already knew. Something had happened.

Harry had lived with Jo for two years, and she wasn't the type to have a sleepover at someone's house. She was too self-protected to

154

admit she needed help from anyone. In the time they'd been together, Harry had learned to guess what she was thinking without waiting for her to say it, because too often she wouldn't say it. Not if she was really upset with him. She'd first stew over things for a while, thinking it all through in her own mind before agreeing to talk. Even before he'd told her about Kelly he'd known it would break them up. He'd known it as soon as he'd done it. Jo's father had cheated on her mother, and she'd never forgiven him for it. She still refused to talk to her father. In the week following his infidelity Harry said nothing. He'd avoided Kelly at work, and Jo at home. When he couldn't avoid Jo in their shared apartment he'd picked ridiculous fights with her, fights over nothing, trying to arouse enough rage in her to make her stay away. Or turn on him severely enough that he'd tell her out of spite. The guilt of keeping it in had kept him down at the Exchange every night, until one night he'd come home late, completely shit-faced, and started accusing her of being a dominating, controlling bitch because she'd asked where he'd been, and why he was drinking so much lately. It hadn't been one of his proudest moments.

Instead of raging at him, like he'd expected, Jo had been disturbingly calm, but she'd had her bags packed by the following morning. He'd nursed a crippling hangover as he'd watched her leave, and as soon as she was gone he'd headed for the bathroom and spewed up everything in his guts. He'd felt like dying. A few weeks later he'd found a new apartment.

Thirty

When Jo didn't answer her mobile the next morning Harry rang Mario's place and got Maria.

"Oh, hi, Harry," she greeted him cheerfully. "Mario dropped her home on his way to work. They left about twenty minutes ago." Harry hadn't really stopped to consider whether she'd want him coming over. He was in his car minutes after Maria agreed to give him the address. Now, as he stood at the door, preparing to knock, he hoped she wouldn't mind. It took her a few minutes to answer, and when she did she was wearing a dressing gown, and looked like she'd just stepped out of the shower. Her dark ringlets hung damp around her shoulders. Harry was immediately struck by how drawn and fragile she looked, and for a few seconds both of them just stood there looking at each other.

"Come in." She didn't ask him how he knew the address. He followed her into a tastefully furnished sitting room, recognizing some of the furniture from their old apartment.

"Have a seat. I'll just change." Her voice sounded flat. As Harry settled himself into the newly-acquired cream lounge he looked around, taking note of the other new acquisitions. Jo liked to shop, but she'd always hold off until she could afford exactly what she wanted.

So that each piece was carefully selected and blended perfectly with the other furniture. Jo returned in jeans and a loose tee shirt.

"Aren't you going to work today?"

"No, I'm taking a few days off." She flopped into the chair across from him and gave him a weak smile. "Not really my choice."

"Something go wrong yesterday?"

"You could say that. Apparently I got the wrong guy, and the Chief wasn't too impressed with my undercover job."

"Is there going to be an investigation?"

"I don't know." She sounded like she didn't really care, which wasn't like her.

"What happened yesterday?"

"To be perfectly honest, I'm not really sure. Robinson put me in some kind of dentist chair and after that—I really don't know. I must have been hallucinating or something, because I saw him attack Billy Williamson."

"But it didn't happen? Billy's okay?" She nodded.

"They found Billy yesterday."

"Yeah, Mario told me. That's something then, hey?" Her smile brightened for a few seconds.

"Yes, I mean, I'm really relieved about that. It's just that, whatever went on yesterday has really fucked with my head. They think Holdman's the killer. They've got him in custody. Mario's going to ring if they get anything out of him, seeing that I'm on temporary leave." She smiled wryly, and Harry watched as the smile died on her face.

"Holdman? But you still think Robinson's involved in this?"

"I'm not sure of anything. The place where they found Billy was rented out to Holdman. He must have paid cash—there were no records on his bank statements."

"Did Billy identify Holdman as the killer?"

"Billy's not talking. Post-traumatic shock."

"Poor kid." Harry paused for a moment. "So, when you were... seeing the attack—"

"Hallucinating," she corrected.

"Well, whatever it was, you saw Robinson as the killer? Not Holdman?"

"The way Mario described the room—it was exactly how I saw it." She spoke quietly, as if she were talking to herself. "Although, I guess that could just be Pam Grinstone's description, maybe even some of Holdman's. You know—the big tank, the chains from the ceiling. I even saw Robinson's Wolfman teeth, and they were just like Holdman described them: a bear-trap." She shivered involuntarily at the memory. "Robinson even told me a story about the teeth. Claimed his father knocked out his teeth when he was a kid, for biting his baby brother."

"Robinson told you that?" She nodded, coming out of her reverie long enough to meet Harry's gaze. "Jesus, Jo, that must be some experiment he's conducting down there. I mean, first Pam, then Holdman, now you. You all saw the same type of thing. He's involved somehow—he's got to be." The phone interrupted them, and Jo moved slowly to answer it. Harry could hear her talking to Mario, but couldn't catch the words. Harry's concern grew as he watched her mounting agitation. Five minutes later she hung up the phone and slumped back into her chair.

"That was Mario. Holdman confessed. They found a hair with his DNA at the house. They're charging him."

"Jesus." Harry couldn't think of anything else to say.

"So, shouldn't you ring your office?"

"Come on, Jo, I didn't come for a story." She arched an eyebrow, a shadow of her former self returning. He grinned. "Besides, we don't go to print until seven p.m.—plenty of time." But she wasn't in a joking mood. "Really, Jo, I'm worried about you."

"Well, do me a favor and don't be, okay? I'll be fine." Harry felt like he was being dismissed, but didn't want to go. After sitting in silence for a few more minutes, he realized he didn't have a choice.

Thirty-one

Harry went to the office and wrote up the story: Police Arrest Man for Wolfman Murders—Latest Victim Found Alive. The police still hadn't released Holdman's name, so he had to refer to 'the suspect'. But he couldn't stop thinking about Robinson, and by two o'clock he was back knocking at Jo's door. She opened it looking like she'd just woken up.

"Twice in one day, Harry? What's up?" She wandered off into the apartment, leaving him to follow.

"I was thinking about what you said. About Robinson's teeth. I've got the name of his dentist, but I need you to come with me. Flash the badge, you know the routine. He probably won't talk to me."

"What are you talking about? And how the hell did you get the name of his dentist?"

"Bank records. But listen, if—" She interrupted him.

"And how did you get his bank records?"

"Come on, Jo. It's not like you guys had enough for a warrant. I was just eliminating a bit of red tape. Doing my own research. The point is, if Robinson was telling the truth about that accident as a child, he must have false teeth, right? I mean, I'm assuming he doesn't go about his normal life with steel teeth, am I right?" Without waiting for her response, he continued. "They can't all be capped with

159

steel, or he'd have to wear something over them. What if he's got a set of false teeth like the ones you described? A metal trap."

"And what if I was hallucinating the whole thing?"

"Well, you said Holdman said the same thing."

"Maybe that's because he's the killer. Maybe we should be talking to his dentist."

"Have the police found any metal teeth traceable to Holdman?"

"Mario hasn't mentioned it. But then, I'm not completely in the loop at the moment."

"So, give him a call. If they have, we can forget about it."

"I don't feel like calling Mario. He's busy." She sounded defeated. He couldn't remember seeing her like this before. Not since that night just before she'd moved out.

"Okay," he replied. "I'll ring." She shrugged.

~ * ~

Mario sounded tired and harassed when Harry got through to his mobile, and seemed anxious to get Harry off the phone as quickly as possible. But Harry pushed on and got the information he needed, along with a warning not to print any of it.

"They haven't worked out how Holdman could have caused the damage to the victims' bodies. Because there's no ordinary teeth marks on the bodies, they can't conclusively prove he did it. All they've got is that hair. Along with the confession and his link to the house."

"Well, DNA evidence and a confession are pretty good evidence, don't you think? I'd say that's about as close to proof as they're going to need to put him away for this."

"Yeah, but we know he participated in Robinson's research—it would have been easy for Robinson to get one of his hairs. You said his bank records didn't show him paying any rent. So what if Robinson just leased the place in his name? Maybe Holdman just saw the killings, like you saw him kill Billy, and Pam saw him kill the others. It could have messed him up bad enough to confess to something he didn't do. Hell, it messed Pam up bad enough to kill herself." As soon as he'd said it, after drawing the parallels between them, the implication that Jo herself might be messed up hung in the air like a bad stench. Neither of them said anything for a few moments, and then Jo broke the silence.

"Okay, let's say, just for argument's sake, that Robinson leased the place in Holdman's name. That explains how the rent got paid, seeing that Holdman was barely managing to make the mortgage payments on his own place. But the guy's already confessed. And Alton's warned me away from anything to do with Robinson. And I'm not really sure I'm feeling up to it anyway." She sounded like she was finding a lot of reasons not to go.

"Come on, Jo. I've got the address. I'll drive. If it turns out to be nothing, we'll drop it." He watched the struggle between her desire to investigate Robinson and the inertia that had befallen her. There was something else at play too, some nervous caution that Harry considered totally uncharacteristic. Robinson must have really spooked her. Jo sighed, the struggle finally over.

"Okay, let's do it. If the Chief finds out about this I'm really screwed, you know that don't you, Harry? I'll be under investigation. I'm lucky I'm not already. Hold on a minute and I'll go and change my shirt." She reappeared five minutes later in a long-sleeved, button-up shirt. She was wearing the same jeans, but had traded in her bare feet for a pair of Docs. "Come on then, let's do this before I change my mind."

Thirty-two

The young girl at the counter was talking on the phone when they approached the reception desk, and from the sound of it, it wasn't a professional call.

"Cool," she enthused into the mouthpiece, not looking up at them. "So can you pick me up or will we get a cab? Have you asked Sharon what she wants to do?" Harry cleared his throat and she rolled her eyes at the phone. "Listen, I gotta go. There's someone here. I'll call you back later, okay? Yeah, okay, bye." She looked at them with a bored expression on her face.

"Do you have an appointment?" Jo flashed her badge.

"I'm Detective Hanson and this is my partner, Harry. We need to speak to Doctor McQueen."

"Doctor McQueen is with a patient at the moment."

"Well, can you tell him we're here so he can finish what he's doing?" The girl hesitated for a moment, as she considered their request.

"Well, okay then." She trudged off reluctantly, disappearing into one of the back rooms and reappearing a few minutes later.

"Doctor McQueen said he'll be with you in a few minutes, if you'd like to wait. You can have a seat in the waiting room if you

162

want." Harry followed Jo into an area decorated with a U-formation of mismatched chairs. A long, low coffee table littered with magazines sat in the middle of the formation. Jo and Harry took a seat down from an elderly couple. Across from them sat a harassed-looking mother of two boys under five, who was trying to look the other way as her sons raucously chased each other under the coffee table. The elderly woman caught Harry's eye and smiled, while the mother studiously avoided everybody's eye. Unable to ignore the sounds coming from beneath the table any longer, she shifted her weary gaze to the floor, where they were now rolling on top of each other.

"Joseph, get off your brother right now. I'm counting to ten. Can you hear me? One, two, three—" Harry smiled back at the elderly woman. A pale man in a white coat and black-rimmed glasses stepped into the room and all eyes turned to him.

"Detectives?" He looked in their direction, and Jo jumped to her feet. They followed the pale man into a tiny office, where he waved them towards two lime-colored vinyl chairs, while he took a seat at the plush, executive chair facing the small desk. The dentist was in his early forties, Harry guessed, which meant he couldn't possibly be Robinson's original childhood dentist. As he crossed his arms across his chest Harry noticed the dark hairs springing from the cuffs of his white coat. The thick, black coils contrasted starkly with the white skin.

"So, what can I do for you?"

"Thanks for seeing us, Doctor McQueen." Jo flashed her badge again. "I'm Detective Hanson, and this is O'Brien. We've come about a client of yours: Doctor Terry Robinson." Beneath the thick, black frames the pale blue eyes registered curiosity.

"Oh?"

"We understand Doctor Robinson lost a number of teeth in a childhood accident, and now wears dentures. We need to know whether he ordered his dentures through you, and, if so, whether you have a copy of his dental records, and of the mould used to make his dentures."

"That seems a rather unusual request, if you don't mind me saying so. Can I ask what all this is about?"

"Unfortunately, we can't go into any great detail. We're investigating a homicide, and believe Doctor Robinson's dental records may assist in these investigations."

"A homicide? I can't imagine Terry being involved in—" Jo interrupted him.

"No one is accusing Doctor Robinson of anything, Doctor McQueen. But this is a very delicate situation, and we would ask for your cooperation and discretion in this matter."

"Yes, well, shouldn't you have a warrant or something to obtain a copy of someone's dental records?" Jo stood up.

"If we need to, we'll get the warrant. We were actually hoping to clear this matter up quickly and discreetly, but—"

"No, no," he interrupted. "I agree it would be better to clear this up quickly and discreetly, as you say. I guess everything's in order. I did take X-rays of Terry's mouth and fit dentures. It was actually a rather unusual case. As you mentioned earlier, Terry suffered a childhood accident—the details of which I'm not privy to—which left him with caps on twelve of his teeth. In some cases only small fragments of the original teeth remained, which would have made it difficult to attach the caps. The procedure struck me as very well done, and I saw no need for those teeth, or the remaining undamaged teeth, to be extracted. But Terry insisted on extracting all teeth, so he could be fitted for complete dentures. It was a considerable undertaking, as you could imagine. And I couldn't help feeling what a shame it was—the undamaged teeth were quite healthy. I did suggest a partial denture, which would involve extracting the damaged teeth, and bridging the gap between those and his healthy teeth. But I'm afraid he insisted on the complete dentures."

"So, after you pulled all his teeth, you made up his dentures?"

"Well, not me personally," he smiled. "The dental technician. I took an impression of the mouth—a reverse mould, if you like. The technician used that to construct the plaster mould."

"What happens next?" Jo asked, and McQueen beamed, clearly pleased to have an interested audience. Harry leaned back in his vinyl chair, happy to leave the questioning to Jo.

"The technician then pours an acrylic resin into the mould, to make the actual dentures. The whole process can take anywhere from four to eight weeks—that gives the mouth time to heal after the extraction of the teeth. We did discuss immediate dentures, which don't require a healing period. But Terry was quite content to wait. Apparently he wasn't planning to be seen in public during that time. Although he didn't have to wait the full eight weeks: we fitted new dentures within the month, and as far as I know he's never had any trouble with them."

"So this plaster mould that was used to make the dentures—do you still have it? Or would the dental technician have it?"

"Well, there's a rather unusual story there. You see, when I first had the dentures made up, about three years ago, Terry was traveling extensively. He wanted to keep the mould, in case he had to see another dentist while overseas. Of course, we offered to have a spare set made up for him, and he agreed to that suggestion, but he still insisted on keeping the original mould. Which was his right, of course—he'd already paid for it. I suppose he was just being careful—it wouldn't do for such a public speaker to be missing teeth. And he insisted that the dentures we'd made up fitted his mouth perfectly, so he wanted to ensure he got the same ones again, if ever the need arose when he couldn't get into the office.

"So you don't have another copy of the mould?"

"I'm afraid not. Only copies of the original x-rays I took, before and after I extracted his teeth. Terry was quite adamant that he receive the original mould; he didn't want us to make another copy." He smiled. "Perhaps he was concerned about someone else getting the same teeth as him." Seeing that he was the only one smiling, he added, "that's just a little orthodontic humor. Of course, everyone's dentures are individually made for their mouths." Jo smiled briefly and rose, and Harry quickly followed her cue.

"Well, thanks for your time, Doctor McQueen. You've been very helpful."

"Have I? Well, that's it then, is it?"

"For now, yes. We'll be in contact if we need any additional information."

"All right then. Guess it's back to my patient then, before his anesthetic wears off completely." He gave them both a watery smile.

Thirty-three

Harry was parking his car in his allocated space when he caught sight of the figure walking towards him. His heart sank.

"Afternoon, Harry."

"Hey, Gavin. What's up?" He wound his window down to speak and Gavin shoved his face into the car, giving Harry a good whiff of stale beer fumes and nicotine breath. From a distance, Gavin's face wasn't too pretty. Its deeply tanned, leathery hide was full of cracks and craters. But up close it was worse. Up close, the lines were like angry gashes, as if they'd been gouged into his face with a blunt knife. Angry purple splotches of broken capillaries spread out from the lines like bruises from wounds. Up close you saw the too-deep pores which punctured his face, the red veins in his watery eyes, the profusion of hairs that seemed to spring like thin pieces of tightly coiled wire from the swollen alcoholic nose. The nicotine stains on his teeth, which were noticeable from a distance, seemed bigger when he moved in closer, because Gavin always talked with his mouth wide open, letting you see inside even though you didn't want to. You saw the backs of his teeth, streaked with the same yellow-brown stains that spread out over the fingers of his left hand, which permanently held the stub of a roll-your-own cigarette.

167

Because Gavin talked so much, and never seemed to mind much if you responded verbally to anything he said, as long as a nod was given every so often, Harry usually blocked the sound of Gavin's words and watched the flapping hole instead. Which was better, but still far from pleasant, because the open-close, open-close of the flapping hole was inevitably punctuated by projectile spurts of spittle, and accompanying hand and arm gestures that could strike you if you weren't paying attention. Harry never understood how Jillian, his wife, managed to put up with all the words, and wondered if she blocked them, too. She never had many herself. Always too weary. No doubt living with Gavin did that to you, along with the burden of supporting them both by cleaning houses, while he skulked around all day guarding the place, drinking himself into crazier and crazier bouts of paranoia. Vietnam Vet, she explained sometimes, as they both watched the gaping brown hole.

But she was never too tired to put up a good fight, and Harry could usually hear them going for it through the thin walls dividing their apartments. She left constantly, but just as constantly returned. She must keep the small overnight bag packed at all times. Harry couldn't work out why she kept coming back. What he could possibly give her. He certainly didn't look like he'd be good in bed. It was a mental image Harry didn't want, but one now reinforced by the sight of Gavin rubbing himself against Harry's car, as he squeezed himself around the bonnet to the other side. For a minute he disappeared from view, crouching down to look at something under Harry's car. Wondering what he'd missed by ignoring Gavin's words, and trying to guess what he could possibly be looking at, Harry realized too late he'd missed his chance to flee the car. He watched as Gavin started to squeeze his way back, grimacing as he faced the ugly spectacle of Gavin's hairy belly button staring at him through the window. Spurred into action by the ugly sight, he opened his door as far as he could, which was only a fraction. He pushed against the weight of Gavin's body until Gavin got the message, and stepped back to let

Harry open his door a bit wider. But not wide enough for Harry to get out, which left him sitting there, trapped in his car, a captive audience.

Gavin was saying something about kids hanging out around the apartments, but Harry hadn't been listening, so when Gavin paused Harry just nodded. There was always kids hanging around, according to Gavin. And maybe there were. Who cared—they couldn't get in to the apartments. Gavin always seemed to believe they'd find a way. He seemed to have more faith in them than anyone else. Once when Harry was leaving his apartment for the day, he'd seen Gavin threading a piece of wire under his door. "Petrol bomb", he'd explained as Harry walked past, and Harry had shuddered, wondering how safe they all were when one of their neighbors was hooking up a petrol bomb in his own apartment. Maybe it had a very limited range—just enough petrol to create a small bang and not much else. Sometimes Harry wondered if he should listen more closely to what Gavin was saying.

"Listen, Gavin, I really got to get upstairs." He forced the door open a bit more to emphasize his point. "I've got a couple of phone calls I have to make before 5:30." Gavin looked at his own wristwatch suspiciously, and relented, allowing Harry to pass, still muttering something about homeless kids.

~ * ~

Harry grabbed himself a beer and flopped on to the couch, images of the toothless Robinson flooding his mind. Somehow the image of a mouth without teeth always made him shudder. Not long after he'd moved in, and before he'd learned to properly defend himself against Gavin, he'd woken up to the sound of heavy thumping. He'd been hung over at the time, and at first he'd thought the noise was coming from inside his head. The thumping continued, growing louder and louder, threatening to pop the blood vessels behind Harry's eyes. He could still remember the feeling of the blood vessels, swelling in sympathy with the knocks, banging on the inside of his eyes like a hammer.

Finally, using every ounce of energy he had, he'd struggled out of bed and answered the door, and had been confronted by a face that wasn't quite right. He'd thought he might dreaming. It wasn't just the usual ugliness of the face that seemed wrong; there'd been something he'd couldn't put his finger on straight away. It was almost the same—the cracks, the craters, the burst blood vessels and swollen nose—but there was something else. It had taken him a few minutes of watching the hole flap, as Gavin chatted on about something he couldn't remember—maybe hadn't even heard in the first place— before Harry had worked out that the lower lip had fallen in, and he'd been watching a flapping gum. It turned out Gavin had 'had a bit of a row with the wife', and broken his dentures. Harry traced the source of his unease to some show on television—Jerry Springer or something—where this old couple had come on and described how they took their dentures out before they went down on each other. He'd never been able to lose the image. It had haunted him ever since, and Gavin's visit that morning had added another repulsive element to the story. Gavin had gone around for weeks without fixing the dentures, making Harry shudder every time he saw him.

Back then, Harry hadn't known how to respond to Gavin, who seemed to break every neighborly and even human rule about boundaries, knocking at his door at all hours of the day to see if Harry wanted to join him for a beer. Harry's biggest mistake had been saying yes the first few times, before he knew what he was letting himself in for. When he just thought Gavin was being unusually neighborly. Some nights, when he was pissed, Gavin would come down and knock on Harry's door, a beer in his hand, and Harry would have to either invite him in or talk to him at the door. The other option was simply closing the door in his face, which, while tempting, seemed overly rude. Although he was annoying, the guy seemed harmless enough, and Harry didn't have the heart to offend him—not back then. When it seemed he just wanted a friend.

After a while he'd started to develop strategies to try to get rid of Gavin. Got into the habit of saying he was just on the way out when he came to the door. Which was a hassle, because then he'd have to go somewhere. Or he'd turn out the lights and pretend he was asleep—which was just as inconvenient. Gavin would catch him out too, with all his questions, so Harry had to be careful. He had to say he slept with the TV on, because Gavin had heard it on one night when Harry was supposed to be asleep. Sometimes Harry thought about moving to a different apartment, further away from him, and he often dreamt about Gavin moving out. But both were unlikely. He wasn't going to expend that much effort just to avoid being rude, and Gavin always boasted how he'd 'been in the same place fifteen years.' Eventually he'd learned to live with him, by just being very busy whenever he happened to see him.

Given what a pain his neighbor was, Harry's immediate reaction to the sound of someone knocking on his front door, just five minutes after he'd entered his apartment, was to groan loudly. He immediately concluded that Gavin had followed him upstairs, and had somehow sniffed out the fact that he was enjoying a beer. So at first he continued to lie where he was, dreaming about ignoring the door. But when the banging started up again, he knew he wouldn't be able to go through with it.

"Hold on, I'm coming," Harry called, a note of irritation in his voice. But when he begrudgingly opened his front door a few moments later, the irritation was replaced with disbelief, and for several seconds he could do nothing more than stand and stare.

Thirty-four

The couple on Harry's doorstep looked like they'd just stepped out of a movie set. Nothing recent—more like something from the golden era of Hollywood. Both had a timeless look to them, although if he had to guess Harry would have said they were in their late twenties, early thirties. There was something vaguely familiar about both of them, even though Harry couldn't quite place either of them. The woman was breathtaking, and bore a resemblance to the young Elizabeth Taylor. Like she was in Cleopatra. She even had Elizabeth Taylor's large violet eyes. She stood in Harry's doorway dressed like she was off to the Oscars or some Hollywood premiere, in a gown that matched the eyes, and had the same sparkle. The guy was like some amalgam of every Hollywood hero Harry saw as a child, and he stood beside his leading lady in a dark, old-fashioned suit, wearing a slick, black moustache. He regarded Harry with intelligent blue eyes and broke into a warm smile. At that point every cliché about some people seeming 'larger than life' struck Harry as true.

"Hello, Harry, I'm Alexander. And this is my wife Evelyn." He spoke to Harry in a tone that hinted at some long-standing friendship, and, despite himself, Harry found himself smiling back, warming to the man immediately. "We wondered if we might speak to you about a matter of grave concern to us all." Harry continued to stare, unable to think of any words. Evelyn smiled encouragingly, and it took his breath away.

"Yes, I'm sorry—please, come in." He ushered them into his small apartment and through to the sitting room, where they both looked as out of place as one would expect Hollywood stars to look in such unglamorous surroundings. "Please, sit down. Can I get you something to drink?" Harry felt like he should be offering them a martini or something, but all he had was bourbon and beer.

"We're fine, thank you, Harry," Alexander replied formally. Won't you sit down and join us." Alexander moved down on the couch as he spoke, vacating the end nearest Evelyn, who had eased back into the adjoining armchair as if she was perfectly at home.

"Can I ask what this is about?" Harry found himself talking as formally as his visitor, and realized the question should have been asked before he'd let two strangers into his apartment. But at no stage had it occurred to him to turn them away. As an afterthought he asked: "how do you know my name and address?"

"We've been following your progress on this Robinson case. And we have reason to believe that Robinson is being helped by someone we know. Someone very powerful and dangerous." Although he had no idea who they were, or what they wanted, Harry was surprised that they could be in any way related to the Robinson case.

"Who?"

"We're not completely sure of his identity, but he's known as the Storyteller. Much as you knew Robinson as the Wolfman before you knew him as Robinson. In other words, according to his actions, rather than his true identity."

"So you're saying Robinson is the Wolfman? Not this other man the police have in custody? Holdman." Alexander nodded.

"Holdman's role in all this is only a minor one. The police have the wrong man."

"Do you have any proof? Some evidence I could take to the police?"

"That's not why we're here. We're here about the Storyteller. He's far more dangerous than Robinson will ever be."

"I don't get it. Robinson eats young children—what could be worse?" Alexander shook his head sadly.

"There is worse," he relied gravely. "Unfortunately, you may find that out very soon. I know this might be difficult for you to grasp, but the Storyteller operates in a different dimension. Robinson is simply one of his puppets. Somehow Robinson has found a way to communicate with him, and has entered the Storyteller's world. Even worse, he's brought the Storyteller back into your world. It seems they're working together, and while we're not entirely sure of the ultimate aim of this union, we are starting to feel some of the repercussions." Harry was now staring at his guest in wonder, trying to determine whether he might be deranged in some way.

"Is this some kind of joke?"

"It's no joke, Harry. We realize that this is going to be difficult for you to accept. But we understand that you visited the Storyteller's world yesterday, for a very brief period."

"You're crazy. I never went into any other world." But the memory of his experience at the office yesterday came back to him, and brought with it that feeling of unease he'd finally managed to shake off.

"Harry, it's perfectly human to want to deny what happened to you yesterday. You were concerned about your friend, for whom you still have deep feelings. Those deep feelings enabled you to reach out to her, however briefly, and go to her. You went to the place that Robinson had taken her." Harry started to fear what he was hearing. How could they possibly know what he was feeling yesterday? Harry's usual response to fear was to fight.

"Who the hell are you people? Are you kidding me with this shit?" It was Evelyn who responded, and the kind patience in her voice melted his fear-driven anger.

"We're your friends, Harry." Despite what they were telling him, Harry could believe that this, at least, was true. "We're not here to kid you—we're here to help. And to ask you to help us. What Alexander is trying to explain to you is that the world is not a three-dimensional place. You have already witnessed another possibility, so you're better positioned than most people to hear what we have to tell you."

"Are you talking about parallel universes or something?" She smiled, and he found himself more receptive to what they were saying.

"Something like that. Our world occupies the same space as yours, but I was referring to the dimension of time. That dimension works differently in our world. You experience time as a flow because that's how your world understands it. Especially at this point in your history, when you see more changes in a year than medieval citizens would have seen in centuries. But we experience time differently—the past, present and future are all present in our world." Harry grappled with the concept. Seeing his struggle, she explained.

"I'm not saying time is static. Things do change in our world. They develop. But the form those changes take depends on what happens here, in your world." As Harry struggled to get his mind around what she was saying, his thoughts were interrupted by a heavy banging. It took him a few minutes to realize it was the front door.

"Fuck," he muttered, unwilling to disrupt the conversation, and unwilling to have anyone else join it. "I better get that," he told them, and Alexander nodded. Gavin was holding a beer in one hand.

"Hey, Harry. Thought ya mighta finished with those phone calls by now. Fancy a beer?"

"Sorry, Gavin, now's not a good time. I've got visitors." He closed the door firmly on his unwelcome visitor, and hurried back to the sitting room. His guests had disappeared. He called their names as he peered into the kitchen, and finding that empty as well he rushed to open the doors to his bedroom and bathroom. The apartment was empty. Racing back to the front door, he opened it and peered out into the corridor, where Gavin was still loitering.

"Gavin, did you just see a man and a woman leave?" Gavin looked at him like he was going mad.

"No. Lose your visitors did you, Harry?" Harry closed the door without answering, feeling an inexplicable sense of loss.

~ * ~

While Harry was searching for his missing guests, Mario was raging at the unfortunate young officer who'd been unlucky enough to deliver the bad news.

"What do you mean he cut his wrists? What the fuck with?"

"A razor blade, Detective."

"How the fuck did he get a razor blade in one of our holding cells? Wasn't he searched?"

"Yes, Detective. All his belongings were confiscated. No one found a razor blade."

"Has he had any visitors?"

"Only his lawyer. She swears she didn't pass anything, and no one saw anything."

"Fucking hell, I don't believe this. Go back and tell Pulverenti I'll have someone's balls over this." The young officer scuttled off, and Mario sank back down into his chair. Alton wasn't going to be happy. Although they had Holdman's confession and a detailed description of the killings, there were still a lot of details left unexplained. Like how Holdman had paid the rental on the place in the Bronx. How he'd targeted the kids. What the hell he'd been wearing in his mouth to leave those marks on the kids' flesh. They'd had a couple of breakthroughs. He'd admitted his wife lied about him being home all those nights, pretending she didn't know he'd snuck out of the house. And while he hadn't been forthcoming about his tank supplier, they'd rung every glass and fish-tank manufacturer in the city until they'd found one who'd remembered making something that big. Although the order had been placed over the phone, and the money sent prior to delivery at the murder scene, the supplier did confirm that Peter Holdman placed the order. It bothered Mario that someone would send money beforehand and still leave their name. And there were other things about the crime that bothered him, including all the details they hadn't gotten out of Holdman. But he kept working his way methodically through all the details they did have, trying to make them fit.

King had spent three hours with Billy this morning, and they still couldn't get him to talk. His parents were understandably distraught, their initial joy at having their son home alive soon giving way to anguish over the severe trauma he'd suffered, and the state he'd been left in. Knowing that the killer was now in custody, they were growing reluctant to subject Billy to any more interviews. It was only the hope that King might get through to him that convinced them to allow the session. King had agreed to continue working with the boy, and had suggested that Billy might need additional, long-term treatment. Not that Dan or Shelly were ready to let Billy out of their sight for a single moment, so it wasn't like hospitalization was an option. Still, Mario knew King was worried. Apparently Billy wasn't eating either. Mario would have felt a lot happier about things if Billy could identify Holdman. And on top of everything else, Mario couldn't stop worrying about his partner.

Thirty-five

By the time Harry got into the office that morning he'd almost convinced himself that he'd dreamed last night's visit. He'd gotten way too involved in this case, and his concerns over Jo's safety had prompted his subconscious to develop some elaborate 'other-worldly' explanation for what had happened. He'd simply fallen asleep on the couch after their visit to McQueen, and had dreamed he'd woken up when in fact he was still asleep. Maybe Gavin had knocked earlier, and the sound had filtered through to his dreams. And he'd only woken up when he heard Gavin knocking the second time.

~ * ~

As soon as he saw the large yellow envelope on his chair, Harry knew his rationalizations were about to be challenged. While apparently innocuous, he knew the envelope was some kind of sign. He sat down and took a few deep breaths before emptying the contents onto his desk. What fell out were six typed pages of names and addresses.

"Hey, Paul, did you see who left this envelope?"

"Sorry, I got in just before you. Ask Gina—someone must have given it to her." Harry rose and walked over to Gina's desk, trying to act casual.

178

"Hey, Gina. Did you leave an envelope on my chair yesterday afternoon or this morning? I'm trying to work out where it came from."

"No, the couriers haven't been yet today, and I didn't leave anything yesterday. What's in it?"

"Just something about this story I'm working on. Never mind." Harry returned to his desk, running his eye over the list and wondering what to do it. A couple of the names were familiar: Grinstone, Pam and Holdman, Peter.

As he sat there wondering what to do next, Harry's mind kept returning to the strange couple who'd visited last night. He kept telling himself they'd only visited in his dreams, but he couldn't help thinking they had something to do with this. That in fact it was them who'd delivered this information. They'd said they wanted to help him, so maybe this was their help. After they'd left, and even as he'd started to convince himself that they'd never really been there, Harry had spent a couple of hours doing an Internet search for any references to the Storyteller. He hadn't turned up much, although he had found a reference to Satan as Storyteller in some article about an obscure cult called The Dark Force. Apparently the cult, whose membership was apparently limited to twenty or thirty people, was a breakaway group from LaVey's Church of Satan. They'd started their own cult because they believed Satan was more than a symbol. They cited the Genesis story of the Serpent's advice to Eve as evidence that Satan was the true creator of humanity:

Ye shall not surely die. For God doth know that in the day ye eat thereof, then your eyes shall be opened, and ye shall be as gods, knowing good and evil.

According to the Dark Force, humans know what is good for them better than some God which would deny them knowledge and the right to make their own decisions. They saw the serpent as a liberating force, freeing humanity and breathing stories into a life of endless sameness and nothingness. According to the Dark Force, Satan lives in a dimension outside our own, in a world which can only be accessed through secret rituals and meditation.

Although it was easy for Harry to dismiss some obscure Satanic cult, his attempts to convince himself that there'd been no strange couple was a lot harder. What if there were people, like members of the Dark Force, who could access demons from other dimensions? What if evil really did exist, in some universe parallel to our own? And some greater good, as well? Maybe if he continued searching, he'd find lots of obscure little cults with strange beliefs, and even if most of their beliefs were far-fetched, maybe they were right in sensing that there was something else out there, something besides our normal everyday lives.

As a reporter, Harry had never shied away from the search for truth, no matter how far-fetched it might seem. He'd never been afraid to follow any lead. But the leads he'd followed in the past, and the far-fetched truths he'd uncovered, all had a distinctly earthly basis, and what he'd glimpsed in the last couple of days was distinctly unearthly. Maybe Alexander had been right—it was a perfectly human tendency to deny what was difficult to understand. But Alexander was the product of Harry's subconscious, wasn't he? As much as Harry told himself that what he'd experienced was simply the combined product of this story and his over-active subconscious, he still felt decidedly... unsettled. As if the boundaries of his reality had shifted slightly, and he couldn't quite see things in the same way anymore.

Harry made his decision. He strode purposefully across the office floor, stopping at Anne-Marie's desk.

"Can we talk about the Robinson story? Outside if that's okay—I need a cigarette."

"Sure, Harry—we're still doing it then?" He nodded decisively, and she followed him outside. Out on the balcony, he outlined the latest direction he'd planned for the story.

"Now that the police have Holdman in custody for these killings, we should follow-up on Holdman's involvement in the Mountview studies, and the possible connection between Mountview and the killings. At least one other person who participated in the studies—Pam Grinstone—had visions very similar to the ones Holdman described to the police." He'd briefly mentioned Jo's experience when he came in yesterday to write up the story, telling her that Jo was put into some kind of hypnotic trance.

"What we need to do is find out how other participants were affected. There could be some link here—Robinson could be messing with people's minds in some way." He handed over three of the six sheets of paper he'd just received, and her eyes widened as they ran over all the names.

"Where did you get this?"

"Someone sent it over. They didn't leave their name."

"What makes you think these people will talk to us?" Harry had already thought of that.

"We'll tell them we've been employed by Mountview to conduct follow-up interviews. We can say we're primarily interested in memory retention, and ask them to recall anything they can about the tests. I'll get Darren to make up some ID cards for us." Darren, their security guy, was responsible for printing up their press cards, and already had all their photographs on file. It wouldn't take him long to produce something for them. Harry took out his wallet and handed her two hundred dollar bills.

"See if you can get that changed into twenties before you start talking to people. In case they ask about remuneration for their time."

"You're not planning to talk to all of these people, are you?" She was frowning at the first page of her little pile. "I mean, there must be at least two hundred names here."

"Some of them won't be home. If we just start at the top and work our way down, maybe we'll only need to talk to a few before we have enough for a story. Or group them according to addresses—that will probably be easier. It doesn't really matter where you start on the list. Just tick them off as you see them, so we know who's been done." As they walked back into the office, Lou Burrows was walking out.

"Okay everybody, listen up. The police are holding a press conference about the Wolfman at noon today." He turned to Harry. "O'Brien, you've been covering this—are they ready to release the suspect's name?"

"I'd say so, but I already have the name. I'm kind of working on something else at the moment, so if someone else wants to cover the conference, that's fine with me." Burrows turned back to the rest of the staff.

"Right, Preston and Sloane, I want both of you there. And, Slater, get some pictures." He turned back to Harry. "O'Brien, I'm intrigued to hear what's replacing the Wolfman in your current list of priorities. You can brief me this afternoon." Burrows marched back to his office.

Thirty-six

"Thanks for seeing me, Doctor Lui."

"I'm surprised to see you here alone."

"Mario's kind of busy at the moment. Did he tell you Holdman confessed?" Rebecca nodded, her face grave. "Besides, what I wanted to discuss is as much about clearing things up in my own mind as it is about clearing up this case."

"I'm intrigued. Go on."

"Mario said you used hypnosis to induce Holdman's memories."

"That's correct."

"Well, I wondered if you could tell me more about the procedure. You see, Holdman was involved in some studies conducted at a private neurological clinic, where hypnosis was used. We'd actually started investigating this clinic, after another research participant experienced some very disturbing images. So I'm interested to learn more about the way hypnosis works, to try to get a better picture of what was going on in there."

"To be perfectly honest, Detective, medical science can't really explain why hypnosis works. We still don't know enough about the human mind. But psychiatry has developed a general model of its functioning, and ways to induce it. Essentially, hypnotized subjects are in trance states where they're very relaxed, very open to suggestion, and have heightened imaginations."

"Are they asleep?"

"No, they're alert the whole time. It's more like daydreaming, or the relaxed state between sleeping and waking. They're still fully conscious, but able to tune out all external stimuli, and focus solely on whatever subject is being explored."

"You said that they're highly suggestible. Does that mean the hypnotist can plant ideas into their minds? Things that aren't real?"

"It's possible. That's why psychiatrists who use hypnotic techniques to access the patient's subconscious have to be very careful. There's been a lot of debate over the ethical nature of certain practices. The recovery of repressed memories, for example, has been challenged in court. There's been cases involving sexual abuse, even satanic rituals, where the therapists were accused of planting memories that weren't real. In a state of deep relaxation, the patient takes on the therapist's suggestions as if they were real. They can even have physical responses to the suggestions."

"What do you mean?"

"Well, if the hypnotist describes a frightening situation, for example, the patient can start sweating, the heart rate can increase—things like that."

"So could you use hypnosis to force someone to do things they didn't want to do? Like those hypnotists on television?"

"Well, that's a little more difficult. Even though the subject is reacting to the suggestions as if they are real, they're still aware, on some level, that they're not. It's a very intense form of playing. The subject is very uninhibited, more like a child than an adult, but they still have some control. Really, the people you see in those entertainment shows are going along with the whole thing. You can't force someone to do what they don't want to do."

"Couldn't you make them think they wanted to do it? Maybe at some subconscious level. Perhaps even override what the conscious mind wants, or thinks."

"That's a difficult question to answer, Detective. Hypnosis is in fact used to override the conscious mind, like you say. It's a way to access the subconscious directly. But I don't know that anyone could implant desires in the subconscious mind without the subject knowing. It's more likely that the therapist might access subconscious desires that the patient doesn't really know about."

"I'm not sure I follow."

"Well, it's the subconscious mind that does most of our thinking, but when we're awake we're not really aware of what's in it. We're more aware of the conscious mind, which evaluates all the thoughts that the subconscious has, processing all the information and relaying it back to the subconscious. In other words, the subconscious is like a big warehouse for all our memories, but its actual role in our thinking can go unacknowledged by our consciousness. This warehouse can contain desires and images that the conscious subject is not aware of—or has even blocked. That's why patients can access events they've completely forgotten under hypnosis."

"So perhaps the hypnotist could access these unknown thoughts without the subject's awareness."

"But the subject is aware of what's going on during the hypnotic process itself."

"Can't you hypnotize someone without them knowing?"

"No. The notion of someone being hypnotized against their will is a Hollywood myth. Subjects have to want to be hypnotized, and they must believe they can be. That's why some people can't be hypnotized. The therapist has to assess a patient's willingness to be hypnotized, or the process is a waste of time. You can't force someone to feel relaxed and comfortable—the preconditions for inducing a hypnotic state."

"So that's the only way to hypnotize someone—to get them relaxed?"

"Yes. Psychiatrists use relaxation and focusing exercises to induce the trance. It's common to use progressive relaxation and imagery. Some therapists still use the fixed gaze induction or eye fixation—where you get the subject to focus on an object so intensely they tune out all other stimuli. As they focus, the hypnotist talks to them in a low tone, drawing them into relaxation."

"What about the entertainment hypnotists? Don't they induce the trance a lot more quickly?"

"Not really. They usually work with the subjects off stage beforehand. They do use different techniques. Mostly a series of rapid, forceful commands, which overload the mind more quickly. Some people believe you can also induce hypnosis by disorientating the subject. But in my professional experience, relaxation and focusing exercises are the most effective means of inducing a hypnotic trance."

"How long does it take?"

"Anywhere from a few minutes to half an hour. It depends on the subject, and the skill of the therapist." Jo thought for a few more moments.

"Could someone use drugs to induce a hypnotic trance on an unwilling patient, or to make the process more effective?" Rebecca paused to consider the question.

"Well, there are a number of barbiturates that have been classified as hypnotic drugs. Even those drugs commonly used for anesthesia can have a hypnotic effect. Pentothal, for example, is commonly used as a general anesthetic, and has been referred to as a truth drug. But the effect of such drugs in inducing hypnotic states has not really been fully explored in medical science. There are too many ethical issues surrounding their use in general practice—particularly when the skilled therapist can induce hypnosis without them." Jo thought for a few more moments.

"The clinic that I mentioned used special equipment to measure brain activity. Do you think they could be experimenting with new ways of altering brain activity?" Rebecca gave her an inquisitive look before answering, her curiosity clearly evoked now.

"I can't really answer that. As I said, there is simply far too much we still don't know about the human mind. But if this clinic is looking at hypnotic states, then there are standard tests for measuring brain activity in the hypnotized subject. Do you happen to know what the equipment was, or what tests were being conducted?"

"I'm not really sure. There was an EEG machine." Rebecca nodded.

"Yes, that's quite orthodox. EEGs measure the electrical activity in the brain. The brain produces different brainwaves and rhythms of electrical voltage depending on the mental state, and EEG can measure this. A state of deep relaxation produces different rhythms to full alertness. EEGs from subjects under hypnosis show a boost in the lower frequency waves associated with daydreaming and sleep, and a drop in the higher frequency waves associated with full alertness. In other words, the subconscious is taking a more active role in brain behavior."

"The neurologist conducting the tests also mentioned something about the central cortex."

"Yes, other studies have shown that hypnotic subjects exhibit reduced activity in the left hemisphere of the cerebral cortex, and increased activity in the right hemisphere. Neurologists believe that the left hemisphere of the cortex is responsible for deduction and reasoning, and the right hemisphere is responsible for creativity and imagination. The decreased activity in the left hemisphere indicates how hypnosis can dampen the conscious mind's inhibitive influences." Rebecca gave Jo a troubled look, as she realized where Jo was going with all her questions.

"Do you mind telling me what all this has to do with Peter Holdman?" Jo hesitated, unsure of how much to say.

"Well, I was just concerned that this clinic might be planting images in people's minds. That other person I mentioned—she also had visions of the killings." Rebecca's eyes clouded with horror as she realized what Jo was getting at.

"Are you saying you think Peter confessed to some type of false memory?"

"I don't know. I need to investigate the clinic further. But I'll keep you informed of anything I find out."

Thirty-seven

Harry's first stop was a trailer park in New Jersey. Apparently the clinic's participant list crossed the state line. After wandering through the seemingly random distribution of trailers, he found Number Nineteen, and was greeted by an overweight woman with acne-scarred skin, a bad perm, and stretchy pants. It was difficult to guess her age.

"Sharon Macy?" She eyed him suspiciously, kicking away a mangy little terrier that had rushed out to see who was there.

"Who wants to know?"

"My name's Harry. I've been employed by the Mountview Research Clinic to ask research participants a few follow-up questions."

"That right? Guess you'd better come on in then." He followed her into the too-small kitchen, squashing himself into the chair nearest the wall, leaving her to take the one with a little more room. She lit a cigarette and eyed him carefully.

"Ms. Macy, I wonder if you could tell me what you remember about the tests you participated in. We're interested in testing people's memories."

"Call me Sharon. That was over a year ago now... can't say I remember too much." She took a deep drag on her cigarette. "The doctor there used to put up a screen and show pictures. There was sound, too. Sometimes he put this little helmet thing over my head, and the pictures and sound come through that."

"What kind of pictures? Do you remember any?"

"Can't say I do, really. It wasn't like a movie or nothing like that. Didn't make much sense. Just pictures of different stuff, going real fast. The sound didn't really match the pictures. It was just his own voice mostly. Sometimes he didn't even bother with the tape or nothing—just spoke straight to ya. Even right after I don't think I remembered much of the pictures or words. He'd always ask a bunch of questions afterwards, and there'd be a few things I'd remember. Not much. Not that the questions were always about the pictures. They were about all sorts of stuff. You know, like whether I was hungry, or thirsty, whether there was anything I felt like doing. Funny thing was, I was always hungry and thirsty after I'd been there." She paused for a few moments to stub out her cigarette and went to light another one. He took out his packet and handed her one of his. She took it and eyed him admiringly when he lit one for himself. "Tell ya what I do remember about that place—the money was real good. Had some pretty good shopping trips with that cash, let me tell ya. Hal was going crazy about it at the time."

"Is Hal your husband?"

"Boyfriend. Tell ya what else was strange about that time. I had this real craving for fruit. Couldn't get enough of it. Never bothered much with it before then. Or since then. Thought Hal musta got me knocked up or something the way I was going through it. Turned out I wasn't but, which was good, 'cos I already got two and Hal's not much use at fathering. Me Mum's practically had to raise them kids herself, he's such a useless prick." She took another long drag on her cigarette as she considered Hal's shortcomings. "Hasn't worked a day in his life the lazy bastard—not since I've known him, anyway. Still, don't s'pose you want to know all about that. The point is, once I stopped going to that place, I stopped buying fruit." Poor kids, thought Harry.

"Have you had any unusual dreams since that time?"

"What, ya mean like nightmares or somethin'?"

"Anything at all—unusual dreams, thoughts, feelings. Anything that strikes you as different."

"Well, can't say I dream all that much. If I do, don't remember it. Don't hold with all that crap about working out what ya dreams mean. Don't reckon they mean anything. Still, there has been a few nights when I've woken up and thought I musta been dreaming, because I've been real mad at Hal. Madder than usual. I got to thinking he might be banging that little skank Julie Coven down in Number Three. 'Course, Hal reckons it's all in my mind, but I've got me suspicions. Done half the trailer park that one has. That the sorta thing you talking about?" Before Harry had time to respond the trailer door flew open to reveal a thin man in filthy jeans, sporting a few tufts of yellow hair on his chin.

"What's going on in here?" He sounded belligerent.

"Ah, calm down, Hal. It's just some fella from that place I was workin' at last year. Come to ask a few questions." A sly look fell over his face.

"Oh yeah? He paying you for ya time then, Sharon?" Harry rose with some difficulty and reached for his wallet, handing over a twenty dollar bill.

"Well, Sharon," he said, as he squeezed round the table, "you've been very helpful. Thanks for your time."

"Anytime you got any questions, you know where to find me." Hal glared at her, and Harry let himself out.

~ * ~

Harry spent the next few hours listening to different versions of the same story. Mountview seemed to have drawn most of its participants from a pool of college students and housewives supplementing their income. All described similar cravings to Sharon's. One of the students, a fitness fanatic who ate nothing but organic food and regarded sugar as a dangerous drug, described his cravings for Coca-Cola during the experiments. A mother of three told how she would sneak out of the house in the middle of the night to gorge on burgers while her family slept. None had experienced anything like Pam or Holdman had described. Not that they remembered anyway. Harry hoped Anne-Marie was having more luck then him. They'd agreed to meet back at the office, deciding on coffee at four, rather than breaking for lunch.

His next stop was a two-story house in Queens. The door was answered by an athletic-looking young woman in a tracksuit.

"Hi. I'm looking for Tonia Silverman." The woman turned and yelled in the direction of the staircase, impressing Harry with her vocal chords.

"Tonia! Visitor!" They both watched the stairway for a few minutes, and were eventually rewarded with the appearance of another young woman, this one in jeans, coming down the stairs. Her dark ponytail bounced behind her. The first woman drifted off as Tonia reached the bottom of the stairs, where she regarded Harry with a quizzical look.

"Hi, Tonia. I'm Harry from Mountview Research Clinic. I wondered if I could ask you a few questions?"

"Do you have some ID?" He pulled out the phony card Darren had printed up for him, and flashed it in her direction.

"All right then, come on through." He followed her into a large kitchen cluttered with dirty plates and pans, and took a seat at the large, laminated table.

"Sorry about the mess. I share with three other students."

"No problem. We've been doing some follow-up questions with the earlier participants, looking primarily at memory retention."

"You look like a nice guy and all, Harry, but to be perfectly frank I've had some misgivings about that research."

"You have?"

"Yes. Doctor Robinson didn't fully explain the purpose of the research, but I got the impression it was some type of market research. I know I experienced some cravings while I was there, which I talked to Doctor Winton about. He told me not to worry about it, and that any desires would be temporary, but I'm concerned that some company might be looking for ways to exploit our desires. I mean, what Robinson does—it's some kind of hypnosis, isn't it?" Harry gave a non-committal shrug. "That's what I figure anyway. I'd try to remember what had gone on afterwards, and there were all these gaps in my memory. It's really uncool to mess around with people's heads like that."

"Tonia, I completely understand your concerns. Do you mind telling me why you discussed your concerns with Doctor Winton, rather than Doctor Robinson?"

"Well, he did the initial interview, and said I could discuss any concerns I had with him, so I decided to take him up on it. He seemed more approachable than Robinson. Quite frankly, I didn't really like Robinson. I didn't feel like discussing anything with him." Tonia had Harry's complete attention now.

"Why didn't you like him?"

"I don't know. He always seemed a bit too... smug. Arrogant. And there was something else about him that I couldn't put my finger on. Something that just... gave me the creeps." She shuddered involuntarily as she spoke. "Ever since I started going to that place I've been having these really weird dreams. Kind of freaked me, you know? The thought of that guy messing around with my subconscious in some way." Noticing Harry's look, she added: "I'm a psychology major. First year. But I've done enough to know he was tapping into my subconscious. I've been trying to analyze my dreams, but they're really weird. I hope you're going to do something with this feedback, because I've got some concerns about the ethical nature of that research. If I hadn't signed that confidentiality agreement I'd be tempted to raise my concerns with someone else—like my psychology Professor."

"Tonia, I think you have every reason to be concerned. Can you tell me about your dreams?" She regarded him closely for a minute, as if assessing his sincerity. She must have decided he was okay.

"There's this woman. I can't see her face. She's naked and spread-eagled on a bed. Her arms and legs are handcuffed to the bedposts."

"Why can't you see her face? Is she face down?"

"No, but when I try to look closer everything becomes blurred. She's got dark hair, shoulder length, but I can't really see her features. She's being punished."

"Why? What has she done?"

"I'm not sure, but she feels guilty."

"Can you see who handcuffed her?"

"Yes, but I don't know him. I mean, I've never seen him before. He's tall, and he's got a beard and moustache. Not a big beard—it's trimmed." After every thing that had happened, Harry had been wondering if she'd describe Robinson. But it didn't sound like him—he didn't have a beard or moustache.

"How old is the man? Can you tell?"

"About your age I guess. He's kind of athletic looking, with dark hair. He's wearing a gold ring."

"A wedding ring?"

"No, it's on his little finger."

"What happens next?" he prompted.

"Well, nothing at first. She's just lying there. I keep seeing her spread out like that and I want to help her, but I can't. She kind of fades away if I try to get close. Sometimes I wake up with the image of her just lying there. But I have this other dream, and Robinson's there. Not in the bedroom, but in some weird place—like a forest or something. I don't know. It's all dark and creepy and I'm too afraid to look around. There's weird noises coming from the trees. Anyway, he's got the naked woman and he's trying to drag her towards some huge building. It's a really ugly building—like some giant toilet block or something. Anyway, she's struggling. She doesn't want to go in there. I don't blame her, there's something really creepy about this place. But he drags her inside. Then there's this other man. At first I thought he must have been watching them, but I don't think he saw them go in. He's looking for her." Harry was completely absorbed by her dream, wondering what it meant.

"Is it the man with the beard?"

"No, I don't think so. I think he's there to help. I can't see him clearly, because he's standing in the shadows."

"Think hard, Tonia. Is there anything at all that would help identify him?" She was looking at him strangely.

"Well, I don't really think he's a real person, Harry. It's just a dream. I don't think he's anybody I know. Why are you so interested in all this stuff anyway? It can't be for Mountview—surely they don't want to know all about my dreams. If they did, I might be a little worried." Harry knew he had to win her trust if he wanted to keep her talking.

"Look, Tonia, I'm going to level with you here. I think something strange is going on at Mountview. Two of the people who participated in that research started having very disturbing dreams. One of them killed herself. Like you said, I think Robinson's messing with people's minds."

"That's terrible," she exclaimed, the alarm evident in her voice. "How can you work for people like that?"

"I'm not trying to scare you or anything. What happened to them—it started happening straight away. That's not going to happen to you. I'm just trying to find out what happened there. Maybe your subconscious is offering some clues as to what's going on. Maybe you know more than you realize. More than you're consciously aware of."

"You mean like some kind of repressed memory?" Harry didn't think she'd want the full story, so he nodded.

"Maybe. So, try to remember—what did this guy look like?"

"It was so dark. But he seemed to have a limp. Wait, there is something else." She paused, and Harry realized he was holding his breath in anticipation. "When the moonlight hits his right hand I can see a mark there, above his thumb and forefinger. It's like a new moon—a crescent shape."

"Is it a tattoo?"

"I don't think so. Maybe it's a birthmark. I guess it could have been a tattoo that he'd had lasered off, so it's left a red mark."

"Is there anyone else with him?"

"Not that I can see. You don't think this dream is going to come real or anything, do you?" She sounded worried, and Harry tried to reassure her.

"No, I don't think you have anything to worry about. These are probably just dreams. You don't know anyone who looks like these guys, do you, Tonia? Besides Robinson I mean. The guy with the beard and the ring, or the one with the limp and the birthmark?"

"No."

"Is there anything in your past that you feel guilty about?"

"You think I might be the woman? Well, to be honest, I thought about that, too—you know, as maybe a subconscious image of myself all tied up and restricted. I tried to think of anything that might be bothering me. The only thing I could come up with was... well, there was this fat girl at my middle school. Penny something. I can't remember her last name. All the kids used to call her Penny the Porker, on account of her weight. No one played with her. I used to watch her in the playground sometimes, and feel sorry for her. But I never spoke to her. Not at school. But one night I was down at this church BBQ with my parents—I was only ten or eleven at the time. And Penny was there with her grandmother. I didn't see anyone else from my school there, so I went over to her, and asked her if she wanted to play. She seemed so happy to play with me." A cloud fell over Tonia's eyes as she went back to that time.

"We decided to play hide-and-seek. There was this community hall beside the church, and all the adults were outside. Standing around eating. So I was it, and I took off to hide in the empty hall. There was this kitchen off from the main hall, where the women used to cook sometimes for church events, and there were steps leading out of the kitchen into this downstairs area. They used to hold Youth Group meetings down there— for the older kids. So I go downstairs to hide and there's these three girls there from my school. Not from my class—they were older then me. So they ask me what I'm doing, and I tell them I'm playing hide and seek. Then they ask me who with, and I say 'Penny the Porker'. I didn't mean to say it—I'm ashamed as soon as it comes out of my mouth, but it's too late. These older girls pull me off into the shadows and tell me to be quiet. When Penny comes down looking for me they all jump out at once and start going 'oink, oink, oink', and they push me forward. I don't know why I do it but I start going 'oink, oink, oink' too, only I'm so ashamed. I've still got the image of her face crumpling up with tears before she runs off. I didn't ever speak to her again, but I always felt like I should have gone over to her at school and told her it wasn't my idea, that I didn't want to do it. But I was too ashamed, and too much time passed, so I just ignored her." Tonia had been looking down at the floor as she told her story, but as she came to the end she met Harry's gaze, and he could see the shame still there. She shook her head slightly, as if she was shaking off the past.

"But that was such a long time ago. I guess the woman could be me—I've got some guilt—but I don't know."

"I guess most people are guilty about something," Harry consoled. "It could mean anything."

"What do you think is going on at that place?" she asked earnestly. "I mean, what do you think the connection is—between those experiments and the dreams? What if I start having more dreams?"

"I'm still trying to find out what's going on. I'll give you my number if you like—you can call me any time you want to talk. And when I learn something, I'll let you know."

"Do you promise?" Her face wore a serious expression, and there was an intensity there. Harry could hear it in her voice.

"Yes."

"You're not really employed by Mountview, are you, Harry?" Harry hesitated briefly. "You don't have to worry about me reporting you to Mountview or anything." He smiled.

"No, I'm a reporter. Here's my card. Please call me if you have any more dreams. Or if you just want to talk."

Thirty-eight

Harry had stayed too long at Tonia's to make his next appointment and still get back to the office in time to meet Anne-Marie. He decided to put it off till the morning, and pick up some coffee and donuts on the way back. Anne-Marie would hopefully be on time, and the coffee wouldn't go cold waiting for her. He didn't have to worry—she was already there when he got back. But before he got the chance to talk to her Preston was coming across the room to intercept him.

"Hey, Harry, you missed an exciting press conference today. Their suspect slit his wrists in a holding cell last night. He's dead."

"You're kidding? Holdman?" The news shook him.

"Yeah." Paul raised an eyebrow at Harry's use of the suspect's name, which had just been released today. "There's been some speculation that a cop might have passed him the razor blade. Not a lot of tears being shed over his death"

"What if he's not the killer?"

"The cops seem to think he was. Apparently the guy confessed before he knocked himself off. They claim they're just tying up a few loose ends—that all evidence points to him." It struck Harry as just a little too neat.

197

"Well, I guess that's that then. Case closed." Preston grinned and Harry turned back to Anne-Marie, who was listening like someone who'd already heard the news.

"Let's go to the staff room," he suggested. "It should be pretty quiet at this time of day." Although it was a pokey little room, the staff room at least offered an assortment of comfortable, albeit tatty recliners and wingbacks. "So, how'd you get on today?" He was still shaken by the news about Holdman, but eager to hear her report.

"I've talked to a few people on the list. Mostly housewives, although there was one medical student who knew Robinson by reputation and wanted to be involved in his research. One guy refused to talk to me—Paul Simmons. And another one wasn't home. I've marked it on the sheet—which ones I went to, and whether I talked to them or not."

"Good. That will be useful."

"They all told me pretty much the same thing. They listened to sound recordings and viewed images, but their memories are pretty vague. No one had too many details. Although there was one strange detail that kept coming up—they all described cravings for very specific things during the time of testing. One was classical music, and the other three were food items. Muesli bars in one case, and meat in the other two. Which was quite odd, because one of the women was vegetarian, and the thought of eating meat really grossed her out."

"I had similar descriptions from the ones I interviewed. Strange cravings that could be completely out of character. Did you happen to interview a woman with dark hair? Or a man with a beard and a gold ring on his little finger? Or one with a limp and a strange mark on his right hand?" She gave him a strange look.

"I think Paul was wearing a ring, but that was on his wedding finger. And he was clean shaven. One of the women had dark hair. Why do you want to know?"

"One of the women I spoke to today described three people from a recurring dream she was having. Robinson was in it, too. It's possible the dream consists of images she saw in the sessions and then forgot. Maybe that's what happened to Pam Grinstone and Peter Holdman. The woman that you talked to, the one with dark hair—was it shoulder length?"

"No, short."

"Okay. I want to keep going through the lists until we can learn a bit more. In the meantime, keep an eye out for any of those three people. It's probably nothing, but you never know. The man with the beard wears it cropped pretty close, and is dark haired. I don't have much else on the other two." Anne-Marie nodded a little uncertainly.

"What exactly are you trying to find out?"

"I think Robinson has developed visual and audio stimuli that induce some kind of hypnotic trance. We already know he can stimulate desires in people that can be quite contrary to their normal personalities—like your meat-eating vegetarian. I had a fitness freak who couldn't stop drinking Coke. Advertisers have been throwing a lot of money at behavioral research, but there's always been strong support for the idea that desires can be stimulated at a subconscious level. Maybe Robinson's found a way to do it very efficiently, and even measure it. That's got to be worth a lot of money. Market Promise hasn't just spent ten million on interviews. Jo observed some pretty fancy equipment in use over there—to measure brain activity— so whatever he's doing might be quantifiable. But he seems to have had some casualties—people reporting very disturbing dreams. I want to see if there's any more."

"The research he's doing seems to raise some ethical issues, especially if he's getting vegetarians to eat meat, and fitness freaks to drink sugar."

"Yes, but the ethical implications go beyond forcing people's desires towards particular goods and services. Peter Holdman didn't have any criminal history before he participated. If he really was the killer, these murders might have been induced in some way." Her eyes widened in shock. "Or maybe it's just the images that are induced—maybe he just thought he was the killer."

"God, Harry, that's awful."

"Well, it's just a theory. I'm not saying it's true—just that I think we ought to check this place out a bit more."

"Are you going back out again?"

"I might stop at a couple of places on the way home. I have to talk to Burrows first." That wasn't a briefing he was particularly looking forward to.

~ * ~

While Harry was briefing Lou Burrows, Mario stood outside the door to Jo's apartment, knocking loudly. Although she looked better than she had yesterday morning, when he'd dropped her off, he was still struck by how pale and drawn she was. As he followed her into the sitting room, he noticed the dirty plates and cups piling up on her coffee table, which was normally kept as immaculately tidy as the rest of the apartment.

"Holdman committed suicide last night," he announced abruptly, unable to think of any other way to announce it.

"Too bad." She seemed almost uninterested.

"Yeah. Listen, Jo, I talked to Alton today. He's agreed you can come back to work next week, if you're feeling up to it. He wants you to come in first to talk to him. I can pick you up if you like— tomorrow morning, or Friday. Whatever suits. What do you think?" She didn't answer immediately.

"I don't know, Mario. I feel tired." Mario considered his words before speaking, treading carefully.

"Maybe you should talk to someone about that. Some of the detectives have been talking to Donaldson about this case, and I think she's okay. Couldn't hurt, right?" Jo didn't respond, so he blustered on, no longer careful. "I really think it would be good for you... to get back to work, get busy, you know." She gave him a weak smile.

"Perhaps you're right. Maybe I'll feel up to it by next week. I'll go in with you on Friday morning, if your offer still stands. Do you still think Holdman is the killer?" The sudden shift in the conversation disarmed Mario. He wasn't comfortable discussing the case with her, but didn't want it to show.

"There's still a few things we've got to sort out but yeah, seems like he is."

"Harry and I went to see Robinson's dentist yesterday. Robinson kept the mould they used to make his dentures. He could have used it to make himself a set of metal dentures." The information bothered him more than he wanted her to know, so he directed his concern at her instead.

"Jo, what are you doing going there with Harry? You know Alton doesn't want you working on this case any more." In fact, it was one of Alton's specifications when Mario pleaded Jo's case today.

"I know, but Harry was going anyway. I haven't followed up on it." She didn't mention her visit to Doctor Lui. While it bothered Mario that Robinson kept his denture mould, he didn't want to pursue it any further with Jo.

Thirty-nine

Harry hadn't had much luck with the rest of his interviews, and by the time he got home that night he was feeling pretty beat. He'd had a little more luck this afternoon with Burrows, who'd been surprisingly agreeable to him pursuing the Mountview story. With the proviso that he wrapped it up over the next few days. He tried to call Jo but she wasn't answering the phone. He tried the mobile, but that was switched off.

"Evening, Harry." He dropped the phone and spun round, stunned to see that last night's guests had returned.

"How'd you get in?" Alexander smiled at the question.

"We didn't think there was any need to bother with the door tonight. I hope we didn't startle you."

"Startle is understating it. I thought I might have dreamed you two last night, after you disappeared like that." Evelyn laughed, and the sound made Harry smile. They resumed the positions they'd had last night as if they'd never left.

"So, you guys are real?" Harry was still having a hard time adjusting to that.

"Yes, Harry, we're real."

"And you can appear and disappear at will?"

"Well, as we said last night, we have a different relationship to the space-time continuum than you. It only seems immediate to you."

"I was looking up this Storyteller on the Internet last night. Didn't come up with much. Just some cult called the Dark Force who referred to the devil as storyteller, and claimed he occupied another dimension. Is that what he is, this Storyteller—the devil? Did I go to hell on Monday?"

"Well, that's one way of seeing it, I suppose. And I guess there's an element of truth in that vision. After all, the Dark World has been driven by thousands of years of religion and occultism, as well as its more mundane sources. Excluding future beliefs and practices for the time being. So yes, there are various images of Hell driving the Dark World. Perhaps members of this cult, this Dark Force, have some awareness of that dimension, and that's how they've interpreted it— through their own religious traditions. Humans who've made contact with our worlds have used terms like heaven and hell to explain it."

"So there are people who know about these other worlds? People who have visited them?"

"Well, I wouldn't say it's a common occurrence, but for those who seek them out, the worlds can be accessed. Generally people only visit in dreams, or deep states of meditation. Some may obtain a brief glimpse, and because their own world is moving so fast they dismiss it as a fragment of their dream, barely remembered. But sometimes a glimpse is enough to create great works of art, if it is the Light World, or great destruction, if it is the Dark World. There are those throughout the Ages—artists, architects, storytellers—who have sought out the Light World, and in so doing been inspired to create works of beauty and splendor. They might see a fragment of such works in the Light World, and not realize it's there because they themselves have created it."

"I'm not sure I follow." Alexander explained with benevolent patience.

"The Light World is not really separate to the human world any more than the Dark World is. They're both the products of your own world. It's your world that creates the positive and negative energies that make up the Light and Dark Worlds. Humans create with the stories they tell. We don't create—we simply exist. But the Storyteller is breaking the rules—he's interfering in your world. He's using Robinson to tell his own stories."

"Why?"

"They feed his world. Every story of suffering and torment builds his world, makes it stronger."

"And weakens ours," Evelyn added sadly.

"So, there really is a battle between good and evil being waged on some higher dimension?" Harry found the possibility staggering, especially after all those years spent rebelling against his mother's careful attempts to mould him into the good Catholic boy.

"Well, it hasn't really been a battle until now," Alexander explained. "We balance each other out—the notion of a battle between good and evil is influenced by your own intellectual traditions. Light needs Darkness, to give itself meaning, just as Darkness needs Light. But the equilibrium is threatened by this interruption in your world—this attempt to make the forces of darkness greater than they are. We don't know what the end result will be, but we're starting to see repercussions in our world."

"But if the Dark World needs your world, why would this Storyteller try to destroy it? Wouldn't he just be destroying his own world?"

"We don't know what will happen, and we suspect he doesn't either. But even if he suspects, it's his nature to destroy."

"I don't understand why you've come here. Why you're telling me all this. What can I do?"

"We simply want you to continue doing what we've already watched you do. Investigate Robinson. Find out what he wants. And who else is involved."

"I'm just a reporter. Why me?" Alexander smiled.

"Who else, Harry? Investigating is what you do. The police aren't equipped to deal with this type of investigation."

"I hardly think I am either."

"Whether you think you are or not, you're connected to this story now. You have to seek out the others."

"The others? You mean like Pam Grinstone and Peter Holdman?" Another thought occurred to him. "Or the dark-haired lady, the man with the limp, and the man with the beard?"

"They're all involved, but you need to determine what everyone's role will be. The roles of Grinstone and Holdman have already been revealed— they are relatively minor players in this drama. But Robinson is involving others—your search is already revealing them to you."

"But I don't know who those people are."

"Then you have to find out."

"Why me?"

"As I've already said, you're connected. The others probably don't yet realize they're connected. It has to be revealed to them."

"So what do I do? Find these people, and tell them they're involved in some kind of battle between good and evil? Nobody's going to believe me. Why can't you just kill Robinson?"

"We can't kill anybody. We can't interfere in your world—we can only assist the players. Besides, if Robinson died, that would still leave the people he's infected with his thoughts. He's gotten into people's minds. And if he was gone, the Storyteller would simply use someone else. He certainly wouldn't be starved for choices—there's many people in your world who are willing to destroy." A note of sadness had entered Alexander's voice.

"Why does he need to use someone? Why can't he just do whatever he wants by himself."

"He'd die in your world. Those from our dimension can't remain here."

"But you're here now. You both seem okay."

"We can't stay here. Life is transient in your world. We don't know how long the Storyteller has lived already, but it could be thousands of years. Why relinquish that longevity just to live thirty or forty years in your world? Decades would be insignificant to him."

"Are you telling me that you and Evelyn are thousands of years old?" Harry couldn't keep the incredulity from his voice, and it was Evelyn who responded.

"Not thousands, but we've both seen a few centuries come and go. Although," she smiled, "Alexander has seen a few more than me."

"I'm having some difficulties with all of this." Alexander smiled at him.

"We understood that you would, Harry. But what you have to realize is that time works differently in your world. You could visit for what seemed to you like weeks, but which equated to a few hours in your time." Harry thought about that for a while.

"Is that what happened to Jo? When she was at Mountview?"

"Yes, although she didn't travel there physically. Someone from our world must take you to the other dimension. Although perhaps Robinson has found a way around that. Nevertheless, he took her there in her mind—she traveled with him. We don't know how long she was there for, but it can't have been long. It's too dangerous to stay long." Harry felt the pangs of concern.

"But she'll be okay?"

"She's a strong woman," Evelyn responded. "But she'll need help to get through her experiences. She's involved now, too. Whether Robinson planned to or not, he involved her when he took her to that world."

"I still don't understand what you're asking me to do. Even if I found these other people, how would I make them understand? I don't understand myself. I'm not even sure I believe what you're telling me. I admit you guys know things you shouldn't know, and are good at appearing and disappearing, but all this stuff about other worlds, it's—"

"Come with us," Alexander offered, standing and holding out his hand.

"What?" Harry watched as Evelyn also rose and extended her hand. He didn't understand what they meant, but he felt two hands touch his, and then the room began spinning crazily, and the contents of his stomach rose and fell as if he'd suddenly stepped onto a roller-coaster. A weirder ride than that time he'd experimented with acid. The room was fading from view, and he had to close his eyes to avoid the feeling of vertigo. When he opened them he was standing outside on a dirt path, with Alexander and Evelyn on either side of him, and in the far distance stood the most amazing castle he'd ever seen. As if it had been transported straight from the pages of some storybook fairytale, with its turrets reaching high into the deep blue sky, up into clouds so white it hurt his eyes to look at them. The castle seemed to shimmer against the blue background, drawing Harry closer, and he had to resist the urge to walk towards it.

~ * ~

"Where are we?" he asked, his voice brimming with awe.

"This is our home," Evelyn replied softly, "the only place where we could make you see."

"It doesn't seem real." Harry turned around slowly, his eyes gradually adjusting to the brightness of the colors. The fruit trees lining either side of the path seemed to shine, their emerald green leaves glittering in the sunlight. As he looked closer he identified one as an apple tree. He took a few tentative steps closer, unable to resist picking a huge, shining red apple from the orchard. As he went to take a cautious bite he looked back to where Evelyn and Alexander stood watching, checking that it was okay. They nodded, and the instant he bit into it his mouth exploded with the taste sensation. The very essence of apples was distilled into the sweet flesh, and as he rejoined them on the path he continued to take large bites of the fruit, enjoying the feel of its warm, sweet juice flowing down his chin. It was almost as if the apple replenished itself as he ate, continuing to provide him with fruit despite the repeated bites. He continued eating as he felt his eyes being dragged back to the castle. Even as he looked it seemed to change shape, talking on elements of a Renaissance Cathedral. With the apple finally finished, he let the core drop to the ground, and turned to Alexander.

"What is that place? Can we go there?"

"Not today, Harry; we have something to show you." Alexander took his hand as he spoke, and then they were taking long strides in the other direction, seeming to cover miles with each step, as if the normal laws of physics had been transcended. Evelyn was by their side as they swept over brilliant blue lakes and across grand canyons, over dozens of small villages where he could see frenzied activity taking place. The word 'village' occurred naturally to Harry, although normally he'd refer to such clusters of activity as towns. 'Village' seemed a better word for the cluster of buildings that appeared to be built from the surrounding rocks, and which looked like they'd been there for centuries. Finally they came to a swirling mass of gray wall and stopped. Harry gazed in wonder at the wall, which stretched high beyond his range of vision, and seemed to be made of thunderclouds. It looked as if they'd be able to walk right through it.

"What is it?"

"The borderland," Alexander responded. "It's moving in—there were villages here not long ago, but they've been pushed back, as the wall moved closer."

"Why is that happening?"

"It sometimes moves—back and forwards—over the centuries, but very gradually, and generally undulating back the same distance it moves forwards. We think this latest shift is the work of the Storyteller—expanding the Dark World, causing our own world to shrink." Harry's mind reeled at the enormity of what this meant—the idea that great chunks of this world could be eaten away. He stared at the wall, and a feeling of loss washed over him.

Forty

Harry woke the next morning feeling refreshed and driven, full of energy for the hunt ahead. He had only the vaguest memory of returning last night. He'd fallen straight into bed and slept the kind of sleep he couldn't remember having for years. Not since he was a boy. After a hurried coffee and shower, he was ready to talk to Geraldine Cross, the next person on his list.

Soon after his arrival at the Long Island residence, he realized he'd be talking to both Geraldine and Gary Cross, because Gary had taken a day off from the bank to 'catch up with a few things around the house.' At least, that was Geraldine's explanation. Gary didn't look like he cared much about catching up with anything. Geraldine answered the door in a fluffy pink dressing gown, clenching the material at the neck. The bones around her neck stuck out cruelly, and the outline of her bony shoulders protruded under the fluffy pink material. Her long nails matched the gown—a glaring, glossy pink. Too much color for the morning. Too much color for Geraldine.

Geraldine spoke into short, sudden yaps, and moved the same way: short, sudden bursts that took Harry by surprise. She reminded him of one of those little Chihuahuas, full of anxious energy. He'd put her age at late thirties, early forties. She had grayish eyes and a pinched, angular face and body. Unlike his wife, Gary expended very little energy at all. Slow-moving. It didn't take Harry long to work out that trying to engage Gary in conversation was a waste of time. He'd simply look over to Geraldine, who'd answer the question for him. He didn't even have to move his head much. Just his eyes. He was nondescript in every way. Average build, average height, average brown hair, thinning on top, faded brown eyes, average face. Harry could picture him down at the bank.

Harry quickly realized he didn't have to say much himself. All he had to do was ask the occasional question and let Geraldine talk. She was very emphatic. She'd been 'horrified' by her craving for fried food, 'devastated' by her inability to stop eating it. But although she had lots of opinions and commentary about Mountview, Geraldine really didn't have much to tell him. After an hour at her kitchen table, Harry was starting to feel like all his energy had been sucked out of him, and he understood Gary a little better.

The rest of the day passed in much the same way, with many descriptions of sometimes-unusual cravings, but not much about the trio from Tonia's dream. The initial enthusiasm with which he'd started the day had slowly ebbed away by the time he reached the house of Carol Burnett, whom he'd decided would be the last person he talked to today. Still in Queens, Harry pulled up at the two-story house with its large top-floor deck, and noted all the timber lying around in the yard. The woman who answered the door in her sweat pants and tee shirt had shoulder-length dark hair, and looked to be in her mid-thirties. She also looked hot and bothered.

"Carol Burnett?"

"Yes, are you the plumber?"

"No, sorry to disappoint you. My name's Harry. I'm doing follow-up interviews for Mountview Research Clinic. I see you're having some renovations done."

"Yes, my husband's doing the bathroom at the moment, and he's been waiting all day for the plumber to show up." She smiled, and the harassed look left her face.

"I don't want to take up too much of your time, but would it be all right to ask you a few questions?"

"Why not? But we might go upstairs to the deck, if that's okay? I've just made a pot of tea and left it out there. Would you like me to get you a cup?" She walked as she talked, and Harry rushed to catch up.

"I'm fine, Mrs. Burnett."

"Call me Carol. Right this way—look out for all that crap on the stairs. This place has been turned into a building site over the past few weeks. Luckily my son Bobby can sleep through anything." She talked over the sound of hammering as she led him up the stairs and along another corridor. "I've just put him down for an afternoon nap, although this late in the day I'm hoping he'll sleep right through. He normally goes down around two, but I've been helping Thomas with the bathroom. Not that I'm particularly handy or anything, but then, grouting's not brain surgery, is it?" The sound of hammering grew muted as they stepped out onto a small deck. She waved in the general direction of an outdoor pine table, with its matching pine and canvas chairs, and Harry took a seat.

"How old is your son?"

"Just turned two in July."

"Tough age."

"You're telling me. Nap time's the only time of day I get to enjoy a cuppa."

"Sorry to get you at such a bad time then."

"No, it's the best time really—when Bobby's asleep. I'm afraid I wouldn't be able to answer too many questions with him around."

"How'd you get on with him when you were doing the tests at Mountview?"

"Oh, it was difficult—that was about six months ago now, and Bobby had just started crawling. He was getting into everything. Well, he still is, which is a nightmare with all these renovations going on. But my mother lives just a few blocks away. She's a godsend. It's why we moved here, actually. To be closer to her, after I had the baby."

"So you haven't been here long?"

"Just over two years. We moved here while I was still pregnant. There's been so much to do, but it was all we could afford at the time. And during that first year, after Bobby was born, it was just impossible to get anything done. All those sleepless nights. For Thomas, too—it's not as if I do much of the DIY. Thomas has been doing most of the work on his weekends, and his days off. Like today. I suppose I'll have to do my share when it comes time to paint." She grinned. "But here I am rabbiting on about nothing. What did you want to ask me?"

"We're assessing memory. Can you tell me what you remember about the testing?"

"Well, it's funny really. I can't say I remember much. Doctor Robinson showed me a lot of pictures, and put on sound recordings, but everything is sort of blurred in my mind now. Nothing really stands out. I guess my mind's too full of diapers and renovations."

"Yeah, I guess it would be tough to think of much else at the moment."

"Tell me about it. These days I find it hard to believe I'll ever hold down a full-time job again. I was planning to return to work when Bobby turned one. Mum was going to help out with childcare. But so far it just hasn't happened. I'm exhausted just thinking about getting ready for work amidst all the morning bustle with Bobby. I can't imagine actually doing it. I feel a bit guilty about it, of course. We really do need the second income. We only took on this mortgage because we assumed I'd return to work. And there's so much more that needs doing around this place. I suppose we really should have bought something smaller. There's only the three of us, after all. We have talked about having another one, but I'm not sure now's the right time. Unless I want to commit to a couple more years at home. That's the reason I did the tests for Mountview—it was quite good money while it lasted. For a few afternoon's work. I don't suppose they're looking for people at the moment, are they?"

"Not at the moment, no, but I'll let Dorothy know you're interested, in case they need people later."

"Thanks, Harry. I don't suppose I've been much help to you, have I?"

"Hey, you've done fine. Most people don't remember much. Besides, whether you remember or not is not my concern—I just have to record what you tell me. It's all data. You haven't been having any unusual dreams or thoughts since you participated, have you?"

"Not that I can recall. What sort of thing do you mean?"

"Oh, nothing in particular. A few of the participants have recalled some of the images in their sleep, that's all."

"Not me I'm afraid. Once I fall into that bed at night I just crash. I never remember what I've dreamt about." Harry stood up.

"Well, thanks very much for your time today. I can see myself out if you'd like to finish your tea. Is it okay to use the stairs here?" The stairs off the deck led down into the front yard.

"Yes, be careful though. Thomas has been reinforcing some of them. He slipped on one the other day."

"Will do. Thanks, Carol." Harry had just started down the stairs when he jumped at the sound of a man yelling out behind him.

"Hey, be careful. A couple of those stairs are loose." Harry looked up to see Thomas Burnett standing beside his wife in khaki shorts and bare chest. He had a dark, closely shaved beard, and was wearing a bandage around his right ankle. These two details caused Harry to take his eyes of the stairs, and before he knew what was happening he felt his foot slipping through a step, and he was flying through the air. He hit the hard ground with a loud thump, and all the air was knocked from his body. As he gasped for breath he heard Thomas yelling above him.

"Stay where you are. Try not to move." And then Carol was kneeling beside him.

"Oh God, you poor man. Are you all right?" Harry's body ached all over, and it was an effort to reply.

"Yeah, I'm okay. My fault. I should have looked where I was going."

"Thomas startled you. Coming out like that and yelling. Can you stand up?" Without much dignity, Harry struggled into a sitting position, leaning against Carol to support himself. A sharp pain shot up his leg. "I think I might have sprained my ankle." Her voice was full of worried sympathy.

"Oh, you poor thing. Thomas did exactly the same thing. I shouldn't have let you use those stairs." She yelled in the direction of her husband. "Thomas, get the bandage. I'll bring him into the sitting room."

"Really, I'll be fine," Harry protested. "It's not broken or anything."

"You don't know that for sure. Anyway, even if it's just a sprain, you shouldn't be walking on it without a bandage. You'd better come inside with me. Now, can you put weight on it? Are you sure you haven't broken it?" Harry put his foot down gingerly, testing the weight. It was painful, but not unbearable.

"No, it's not broken." He allowed himself to be lead across the lawn, shuffling like an old man to keep the weight off his foot. Once inside, she deposited him on the sofa. Thomas turned up soon afterwards with a roll of bandage, some tape, and a sympathetic look on his face.

"Bad luck, pal. Did Carol tell you I did the same thing myself just a few days ago? Thomas Burnett by the way." Harry took his hand.

"Hi, Harry O'Brien. I was just talking to your wife about Mountview."

"Ah, right. Doing more research or something, are you?"

"No, just a follow-up visit."

"I see. Hope you weren't planning on visiting anyone else today."

"No. Guess I'll call it a day."

"Try and put your leg up on the sofa," Carol instructed. "I'm going to have to bandage over your jeans, unless you want me to cut the bottom off."

"Over the jeans is fine. Thanks, Carol." She wrapped it with a deft efficiency.

"You're not a nurse by any chance, are you?" She grinned.

"Nope. Financial manager."

"Well, you did a pretty good job there. Feels better already." Harry tried to stand up, and winced at the pain.

"Maybe you should rest awhile first." She was watching him with a worried expression. "I don't think you should walk on it right away."

"Really, I'm fine. I should get going."

"Are you sure you'll be able to drive?"

"Carol, don't fret," her husband intervened. "Let the man drive if he wants to." He grinned at Harry, prompting Harry to grin back. Looking at him, standing there beside his fretting wife, Harry found it hard to imagine him as the bearded man from Tonia's dream. He didn't seem the type to be tying up women. Maybe he was the man in the shadows—he had the limp. It struck Harry that, even though Tonia thought they might be two different men, they could be one and the same. Maybe he was only looking for one man—a man with a beard, gold ring, limp and a birthmark. He looked at Thomas's hands. There was a faded mark where his wedding ring would be. He mustn't wear it while he was working around the house. But there were no marks on his little fingers. And there were no birthmarks on either hand.

Forty-one

Every time he put his foot down on the accelerator a shooting pain ran up his leg. He hobbled up the two flights of stairs, pushed his key into the door, and flopped onto the couch, propping the injured ankle on a pillow. The phone was still sitting on the coffee table, so he tried Jo's home number. After letting it ring out, he tried the mobile. It wasn't on.

His thoughts shifted to Carol and Thomas Burnett. Was it possible Carol was the dark-haired woman? If so, what should he do about it? Of course, the dark-haired woman could be Tonia, or one of the many other women left on his list. Carol certainly seemed to be carrying a lot of guilt, but her husband hadn't struck him as the type to punish her for it. But then, maybe Harry had read him wrong. Perhaps he secretly resented the fact that she hadn't returned to work when she'd said she would, leaving him to support the family alone. She might have been the one who wanted a baby. Maybe the pressure of being the sole breadwinner, and the ongoing pressure of paying the mortgage and renovating the house alone, cause him to crack at some point in the near future. But Harry couldn't see it. Nevertheless, you never really knew what went on behind closed doors. Maybe the guy really would crack one day. And then maybe he'd change his mind.

Maybe he wasn't just the bearded man, but the man with the limp, hiding in the shadows, sorry about what he'd done and wanting to help. Wanting to rescue the woman he'd wronged.

But if he was the bearded man, why didn't he have a mark on his little finger? Maybe he only wore the ring occasionally. And if Tonia had misread the situation, and the bearded man was in fact the man with the limp, why didn't he have the birthmark? But maybe Tonia was wrong about that, too. She'd said he was lit up by the moon, so maybe the mark on his hand was a shadow. Or maybe something was yet to happen to his hand. It was only a dream after all—maybe the signs had been mixed up. Or maybe he shouldn't be taking it all so literally. But a metaphorical interpretation left him even further from discovering the players, as Alexander referred to them. And even if did find them, what was he supposed to say? Alexander and Evelyn had said they'd help, but where were they now? No one was going to believe Harry.

The weight of all these questions felt like a burden. Should he continue talking to people, or should he keep the Burnetts under surveillance while he tried to work out whether they were involved? But that would take time, and time was something Lou wouldn't give him. And neither, perhaps, would Robinson. Who knew what he was planning, now that another man had been charged for his crimes. The energy and drive that Harry had woken up with had been drained throughout the day, and now the remnants of it were being sucked away by the seemingly insurmountable nature of his assigned task.

Deciding to have an early night and sleep on it, Harry hobbled into the kitchen to fix himself an early dinner. He put the water on to boil as he collected tinned tomatoes, tuna and pasta from his poorly stocked cupboards, reflecting that he really had to get out and do some shopping over the next few days. But as the small kitchen started to fill with the smells of garlicky tomato, he stopped feeling so sorry for himself, and began to look forward to a quiet dinner in front of the television. Moving to the sink to drain the pasta, Harry reached out unthinkingly as the colander began to slide under the weight of water.

"Fuck, fuck, fuck," he screamed as the boiling water hit his hand. Rushing to the freezer, in the hope that the cold would ease the pain, Harry continued to curse under his breath. When he withdrew his hand from the freezer he was dismayed by its resemblance to a lobster claw. The skin was already blistering. "Fuck, just what I need. An infected hand to go with the sprained ankle." All he could find in the bathroom was a long bandage left over from a tennis injury a few months ago—no padding in sight. Wincing, he wrapped the overly long bandage around the blistered skin, before heading back to retrieve what was left of his pasta. His appetite now dissipated, he chewed discontentedly while watching the news coverage of Holdman's suicide.

Forty-two

While Harry slept—having retired early for the evening—Dan Williamson sat in front of the television. He'd been sitting alone for hours, the rest of his family having long gone to bed. Unable to sleep, he stared at the screen without really seeing it. When the police called on Tuesday to say they'd found Billy, and that he was alive, it had been the happiest day of his life. After trying to keep it together for so long, Dan had broken down and wept with relief. His wife had suddenly come back to life, and he'd thought everything was going to be okay.

But Billy had been traumatized by what that sick bastard had done to him, and when Dan first set eyes on him, and saw the dead look in his son's eyes, he thought he was going to weep again. At first they'd convinced themselves that his silence would pass. They listened to the police psychiatrist explain that many trauma survivors found it difficult to talk about what they'd been through.

"Just give him time," the psychiatrist had advised, and they'd been trying to do that. But it didn't seem to be working, and he wasn't eating either. They'd been back to the station today, and Doctor King had spent hours with Billy while they sat in the room, not knowing how to help. He just stared, breaking Dan's heart. And Shelly's.

Over the past few weeks Dan had watched his vivacious, outgoing wife descend into some dark place where he couldn't reach her, and just when he thought he'd gotten her back, he felt her slipping down again. She hadn't let Billy out of her sight since the police brought him back, and her constant fretting seemed to be eating away at her, stripping her of her flesh. She'd been losing weight since the day Billy was taken, but now she seemed to be wasting away, joining their son in his hunger strike. Since he got back, she'd been constantly trying to feed him, and it seemed that, if Billy wouldn't eat, than neither would she.

Billy's current state also meant that Shelly had to do everything else for him—bathe him, dress him. He didn't show any interest in doing any of these things for himself. She'd even moved a mattress into his room, sleeping on the floor beside his bed. Although Dan now had the extra security grills and locks installed, he knew her sense of safety had been profoundly violated. He understood it. He knew his wife was tortured by thoughts of what Billy must have endured. The same thoughts played through Dan's mind like a twenty-four hour a day movie. It was made worse by the fact that they didn't actually know—that Billy couldn't talk to them. The police had told them that he hadn't been sexually or physically abused, but Dan knew his child had suffered. He could see it in his eyes. He knew it was still early days—that it might be a while before Billy started to heal. He'd even accepted the fact that he might never be the same little boy again. But the last two days had seemed to last forever, stretching on for what seemed like weeks, and Dan didn't know how much more his family could take. He despaired at his son's state of mind.

When he saw tonight's news report about Holdman's suicide he'd been glad, hoping the man had suffered at least a fraction of what his son had suffered. But knowing the man was dead didn't make everything okay with Dan's family, and he wished there was something he could do. He'd been thinking about moving, helping his family forget by moving them out of the house where Billy was kidnapped. But he was also worried about money, and didn't know if the extra financial burden would put undue stress on them right now. He hadn't been to work in weeks, and while he had a lot of faith in the people who worked for him, he knew his prolonged absence wasn't good for business. One of the big contracts he'd been bidding for had already been lost, because he wasn't there to talk to the developers. But Dan had no idea how long it would be until he felt his family was safe without him. Right now, he couldn't bear the thought of leaving them, and he knew it might be some time before things returned to normal. Or as normal as they could be, anyway.

As he sat there with his glum thoughts, Dan heard a rustling outside the front door. He pressed the mute button on the remote, and listened again. Straining his ears, he heard what sounded like someone moving about in the bushes at the side of the house. The single-story house was shaped in an L-formation, with all the bedrooms at the back of the house, and Dan felt a rush of fear as he realized the sounds were moving towards the bedrooms. Jumping to his feet, he moved to the front door, undoing the new latches and peering out into the darkness. For a brief second he glimpsed what looked like a dark figure moving towards the back of the house. Rushing down the hallway to his bedroom, he took the recently acquired handgun from his bedside table, and raced back to his front door.

He was only gone a few minutes, but it was enough time for the darkly dressed stranger to enter his house. By the time Dan reached the front door, the stranger was already in the kitchen.

Forty-three

Moving as quickly and quietly as he could, Dan rounded the side of the house, catching another glimpse of what looked like a tall, dark figure. His heart pounding, he opened his mouth to yell, and was surprised by the rage in his voice.

"Who's there? Come out! I've got a gun!" Before anyone had a chance to respond, Dan heard a sound that almost stopped his heart. The sound of a child screaming in fear. Tearing back into his house, Dan ran down the corridor leading to the bedrooms. The door to the second room was wide open, and his wife was already there, holding the sobbing Gracie close to her chest. Shelly was staring at him with a horrified expression on her face, and it took him a few seconds to realize he was still holding the gun. He took Gracie's arm, and tried to make his voice calm.

"What is it, Gracie? What's wrong? Tell Daddy what's wrong." Gracie was trying to catch her breath in between sobs.

"A man was here. Watching me." Dan could hear his heart pounding in his ears.

"A man? Are you sure, Gracie? Where did he go?

"He was standing beside my bed, watching me. It was dark. His clothes were dark and I couldn't see his face. But I saw him and he scared me, Daddy." Dan stroked his daughter's head.

"It's okay, honey. Mommy and Daddy are here. The man's gone now. Can you tell Daddy where he went?" The beating of Dan's heart had started to slow as it dawned on him that his daughter had just had a bad dream. She was spooked, just like he'd been, by everything that had happened. It was understandable. But there was no way someone could have gotten into the house, and out again, without Dan seeing him.

"Daddy, I didn't see him go. Maybe he's in the closet."

"Okay, honey, Daddy will check the closet." Despite having convinced himself that he and his daughter were the victims of over-excited imaginations, Dan raised his gun as he approached the closet, using his free hand to turn the handle. A sense of relief rushed over him when he saw it was empty, but to convince his daughter his thrust his head inside and looked around carefully.

"No, sweetie, there's no one there." He closed the closet door and moved over to the bed, taking a seat beside his wife. "Maybe you had a bad dream, hey, Gracie? There's no bad man in your room." Gracie looked unconvinced.

"But I saw him, Daddy—he was tall. He was watching me." In the face of his daughter's conviction, Dan had a sudden chilling memory: he'd left the front door open.

"I'm just going to check the door," he told his wife, trying to keep the panic from his voice, but hearing it there just the same. He didn't get as far as the front door, stopping instead at the next room. The door was slightly ajar, but Shelly usually left it that way. "Billy," he whispered into the darkness, not wanting to wake his son if he'd managed to sleep through Gracie's scream. He crept over to the bed, relieved at the lump he saw there. Reaching out to touch his son, Dan felt the shock jolt through his arm when he realized the lump was a blanket. The bed was empty. Light flooded the room, and he turned to face the panic-stricken eyes of his wife. Staring at the bed, Shelly screamed like she was in child-birth all over again, but this time it was all going horribly wrong. Dan bolted away from the sound, out into their bedroom, the bathroom, then back to the sitting room, the kitchen, screaming his son's name like a man who'd lost his mind. Then he was at the still-open front door, running outside and screaming his son's name into the night air. Oh God, he thought, this can't be happening. I can't go through this again.

Forty-four

Harry woke with a plan. He was going to talk to Robinson, and confront him with what he already knew. Gauge his reaction. He wouldn't go to Mountview—it would be too easy to get turned away there. He had Robinson's address—he'd turn up at his house and threaten to publish what he already had unless Robinson agreed to talk to him. This afternoon would be best. After work. Hopefully Robinson wouldn't work too late at the Clinic. Maybe he'd get there early and try to talk to the housekeeper. Robinson's alibi had been bothering Harry, and he'd wondered if the housekeeper was covering for him.

In the meantime, he'd decided to focus on the men on his list. There were a lot less men than women, so they'd be quicker to eliminate. And if Thomas Burnett wasn't his bearded man, or his man in the shadows, then maybe he'd find the right man, or men. And if he didn't find him, or them, on the list, then maybe Burnett really was his guy. At least he'd get a better idea of how he should be concentrating his efforts. The guilty woman with dark hair was too difficult—it wasn't enough to go on. Besides, who the hell didn't feel guilty about something?

Feeling energized again, Harry sprang out of bed, and immediately had to sit back down again as the shooting pain reminded him of his sprained ankle. Limping into the bathroom, Harry sat on the toilet and started peeling the bandage off his ankle, peering down at the swelling. With the same care he began unwrapping the bandage on his hand, wincing as the skin stuck to the cloth. As the last of the bandage peeled away Harry stared at the wound in horror.

"You bastards," he raged at the empty room. "You fucking bastards."

"Is everything okay, Harry?" He jumped up as Alexander and Evelyn appeared before him, a look of concern on their faces. They seemed too big for the small bathroom—in their glamorous frock and suit—and as he stood there in his boxer shorts, Harry struggled to maintain the rage. He sat back down.

"You tricked me." The rage had dissipated into bewilderment, and his voice held the accusing tone of a small child. They smiled down at him like parents smiling fondly down on a child. A child who'd just thrown a tantrum, and had now decided to be reasonable.

"We didn't trick you," Evelyn responded in a condolatory tone. "But maybe we should talk about this outside; you look like you need some privacy. Perhaps we shouldn't have barged in here. Why don't you finish doing what you were doing, and meet us back outside." They left him alone, and Harry showered quickly and wrapped the towel around himself, averting his gaze as he limped past them with as much dignity as he could manage. When he'd changed and rejoined them on the sofa, he was gratified to see a steaming mug on the coffee table.

"The coffee is for you," Evelyn cajoled him. "White with no sugar, right?"

"Thanks," he replied begrudgingly. "Did you both know about this?" Harry held up the injured hand, unable to avert his own eyes from the crescent-shaped burn left by last night's accident. It was a mystery to him how the burn could be that shape. "Am I the man from Tonia's dream? The man with the limp and the mark on his hand?" Alexander held Harry's gaze as he replied.

"We don't know Tonia, but if you're asking whether you're the one who has to confront Robinson and the Storyteller, then yes, we suspected you were."

"What do you mean you suspected? You must have known."

"Harry, the future's not always crystal clear. Things become blurred when you look too closely. We came to you because we thought you were that person—you're the obvious person. But you had to confirm it."

"What do you mean 'obvious'? It's not obvious to me. I realize neither of you know me all that well, but let me clear something up for you both—I'm no hero. I'm just a reporter. I'm not particularly brave. Or good. Certainly not the type to fight the forces of evil." Alexander continued to smile throughout his diatribe.

"If you were too good, you wouldn't be able to enter the Dark House. The energy would be too contrary to your nature—it would destroy you. It's all right to have a dark side, Harry—you're human. We weren't looking for a saint. That's what the symbol on your hand represents. One point is darkness, one is light, and in the middle they maintain an equilibrium, balancing each other out. It means you're the chosen one." Harry wasn't concerned with the meaning of the crescent. He was concerned about what they were asking him to do.

"What is this dark house? And what do you mean it would destroy me if I was too good? How good do I have to be to get destroyed? Maybe I'm not as bad as you think."

"The Dark House is the house from Tonia's dream. It's the dark equivalent of the Palace of Light you saw last night, in our world." Harry thought it a little pretentious to refer to their house as a Palace, and the Storyteller's house as just a house. "The House of Darkness is an ugly place," Alexander explained with a smile. "That's why I wouldn't call it a Palace. But maybe they have another name for both buildings." Harry stared at Alexander in surprise.

"Were you reading my mind?" Alexander continued to smile enigmatically, saying nothing, until Harry was prompted to continue his questioning. "How did you know about Tonia's dream, if you don't know Tonia?"

"We don't know Tonia, but we know you, Harry. We've been watching you." Harry realized the idea wasn't as disturbing as it might sound.

"So why do I have to go to this Dark House? What's there?"

"It's the Center of the Dark World, just as our Palace is the center of our world. It's the focal point of all the negative energies emanating from your world, and the place where all dark forms are given life. It's the starting point for all dark possibilities. And when it's time for you to go there, you'll know why you have to go."

"Don't go getting all cryptic on me again, Alexander."

"I'm not trying to be cryptic. We just have to be careful not to interfere in your world."

"Why? Your pal the Storyteller doesn't seem to share your reservations about interfering."

"He's being careful, too. That's why he needs Robinson. Or at least, men like Robinson. If his role becomes too active, he risks changing his very nature."

"I don't understand."

"Like us, the Storyteller is the product of your world, albeit the product of hundreds or possibly thousands of years of your time. Once he exercises the dark energy that created him in the first place, he risks changing it, perhaps even dissipating it. He might even prompt the creation of a creature more powerful than himself. We don't really know what would happen, because interference is generally avoided. I doubt very much that he knows either." It took Harry a few minutes to digest what Alexander had told him.

"So, that's the reason you didn't tell me I was... what did you call it... 'the chosen one'? Who chose me? Are you saying that some kind of mystic force put that symbol on my hand?"

"Yes. That's the reason we didn't tell you. That and the fact that you would have rejected the knowledge. You needed to seek it out for yourself. The forces in the universe have marked you as the chosen one, but you need to find your own motivation to play that role."

"I'm not feeling all that motivated, to be completely honest with you."

"Then that may be still to come. It's not necessary for you to be completely convinced right now. When the time comes, you will be." Harry remained unconvinced.

"What about the others? The dark-haired woman, the bearded man? Who are they? Am I supposed to keep looking?"

"The truth will become clearer soon."

"So you keep suggesting. Any idea of a timeframe here?"

"Soon, Harry. And don't worry, we'll be right with you when the time comes. You won't be alone."

"That's not a huge consolation, Alexander—given your policy of non-interference and all." They both smiled gently and once more, as if by unspoken consensus, stood to take their leave. This time they used the front door.

Forty-five

Mario had been called out to the Williamson's house at around 2:15 that morning, after a neighbor rang 911 to report that Dan Williamson was standing in his front yard screaming at the top of his lungs. Shelly Williamson had been hysterical, and they'd resorted to getting Doctor King out of bed in the middle of the night to prescribe some sedatives. Mario told Dan that the killer was dead, and the kidnapper was probably someone who'd read about Billy's story in the paper. But he was starting to share Dan's doubts over whether they'd arrested the right guy.

"If it's someone else, his intent probably isn't to kill Billy," he'd tried to reassure the shocked father. But Dan Williamson knew his son was in mortal danger.

It had been a long night and Mario was regretting the fact that he'd coerced Jo into coming in with him that morning. It wasn't a great day for her to come in, particularly in light of Alton's stipulation that she wasn't to work this case any more. He was worried about her reaction to the news of Billy's kidnapping. Wearily, he parked the car in a no-parking zone, relieved her apartment was on the ground floor. He heard the shower going inside as he knocked on the door.

"I'm coming," Jo yelled, and as he stood on her doorstep he hoped he hadn't pushed her into this prematurely. Jo answered the door in her dressing gown, and while she was clearly making an effort, Mario detected that listless uncertainty he'd seen in her the other evening. It was as if she was trying to make an effort, but the dark cloud of apathy and uncertainty hovered just above her, threatening to descend at any minute.

"Sorry I'm not dressed; I won't be a minute. Help yourself to coffee—I just brewed a pot." Noting the mounting pile of crockery that had accumulated in the sitting room since his last visit, Mario headed for the kitchen, adding milk and about half a cup of sugar to the coffee. He sipped the sweet, hot brew appreciatively. It had been a long night, and Mario felt more like going home to bed then going into the precinct. Jo joined him a few minutes later, looking more casual than usual in dark corduroy jeans and a soft, button-down shirt.

"How you feeling, Jo?"

"Not too bad. Do I have time for coffee before we go? I only woke up twenty minutes ago."

"Sure, sit down, I'll get it." Mario felt the urge to look after her, to do something to help, and making the coffee was the best he could think of. As he poured the coffee he tried to think of a way to break the news gently, but he wasn't too good at that sort of thing.

"Jo, Billy Matheson was kidnapped again last night." She stared at him, a horrified expression clouding her green eyes.

"What? How?" He could hear the panic in her voice, and regretted having to tell her. But she'd hear it anyway, as soon as she got into work.

"We don't know. Best we can figure is the father went outside about 1:30 this morning. He was watching TV and thought he heard someone walking around the side of the house. He left the door open. Then he hears his little girl scream, and runs back inside, leaving the front door open. He finds his wife in with the daughter. Apparently the mother had been sleeping in Billy's room, but she woke up when she heard the scream. The daughter claimed there was a man in her room, watching her sleep. Dan reckons he and his wife were only in the daughter's room for five or six minutes, before he remembered leaving the door open. It must have been enough time for the kidnapper to get in and out. When Dan went to close the door, he stopped to check on Billy, and found him missing." Jo continued staring at him with that same horrified look on her face, making Mario wonder if she'd heard everything he said. When she finally spoke, her voice was flat.

"So he got in through the front door? He must have been waiting."

"Yeah, it seems the only way—Dan's got the place locked up like Fort Knox. New security windows in the bedrooms, extra locks on the front and back doors. The back door was still locked, so it's the only thing that makes sense. Best we can work out, the guy's watching outside, sees Dan watching TV, and creates a diversion to draw him outside. Then when Dan goes round the side of the house, he sneaks in the front door. Maybe he goes into the kitchen so Dan doesn't see him when he re-enters the house."

"So you don't think there was anyone in the daughter's room?"

"Doesn't make sense. Dan or his wife would have seen someone leaving the room. You remember their house, right? All the bedrooms at the back, in that L-shape. You have to go through the sitting room to get to the bedrooms. The master bedroom is at the back, then the daughter's, then Billy's. There's no way he could have gotten out of the daughter's room without being seen. Especially if he was heading for Billy's room. The mother just came from there."

"What about the noise Dan heard outside? What was that if the intruder was already in the house?"

"The guy's pretty jumpy. So's the daughter. I think both of them were imagining things. Dan could have heard the initial disturbance outside—maybe that was what our guy wanted him to hear. The diversion. Then he convinced himself he was following someone around the house. Our guy couldn't have been outside the house and inside the daughter's room at the same time. That'd mean there were two people, and it seems hard enough to believe one could have gotten in and out without being seen."

"Well, maybe the other guy never went in. Don't you think it's a pretty big coincidence that the kid wakes up and screams at exactly the same time that Dan is looking around outside? It's what got him back inside the house so fast he didn't bother closing the door. Got the mother out of Billy's room at the same time. I don't know, Mario—it all seems a bit too convenient to me." Mario had been having the same concerns, but he didn't want to raise them now. He shrugged.

"We haven't ruled out the fact that our guy might have had someone helping him. Although an extra person would increase the chances of being seen, and no one saw them. Dan didn't see a car or anything out the front, so he, or they, must have parked down the street. Maybe the other guy created the diversion, then went back to the car. It's possible. But it's also possible that Dan and his daughter were just spooked. The whole family is shook up at the moment—it wouldn't be surprising if they're hearing and seeing things."

"Could the daughter describe the man?"

"Nah. She said he was dressed in dark clothes, and his face was in the shadows." Although he knew he had to tell her about the kidnapping, her interest was making him nervous. Maybe she was better off with apathy. At the back of his mind Mario knew they were just circling around Robinson—neither of them were ready to mention his name yet.

"Who do you think did it?"

"We don't know. Maybe someone saw Billy on the TV, or read about him in the papers, and decided to copycat the crime."

"You still believe Holdman was the killer?"

"We don't have much else at the moment. There was a lot of evidence against him, Jo. I know you're not convinced it was him, but—well, maybe we should let this go for now. I wanted to fill you in on what was happening, but you're still off the case." He hadn't meant it to sound so blunt, but she didn't seem to take offence.

"Okay, guess we should get going then." He wasn't convinced she could let it go that easy, but he was happy to play along for the time being.

Forty-six

Harry's plans for the day had been shattered by the arrival of his visitors. After trying Jo's home number and mobile a few times, he decided to brave the stairs and the drive. He was getting worried. When no one answered the door, his worry turned to nervousness, so he rang Mario's mobile.

"Mario, it's Harry. I'm over at Jo's place and she's not in. Have you seen her?"

"Yeah, I picked her up this morning. We're at the precinct."

"Oh. She's returned to work then?" Harry felt the relief wash over him.

"Well, not officially. Officially she starts back on Monday. Listen, Harry, Jo mentioned you were following up on Robinson."

"Yeah. I've been talking to some of the people who participated in his tests, and I'm not convinced Holdman's your killer. But I'm not about to print anything without talking to you guys first, if that's what you're worried about."

"I'm worried about Jo. She needs to stay off this case. Captain's orders. And you're not helping matters. Besides, the case isn't closed—it could be dangerous."

"I got the impression from your Press Conference the other day that you guys considered it closed."

"Yeah, well, off the record, Billy Matheson was kidnapped again last night. It could be someone else." It took Harry a few moments to recover from the shock.

"Or, the killer might still be out there. Jesus, Mario, that poor kid. His poor parents."

"Just watch your back, Harry, that's all I'm saying. And try not to drag Jo into any of your investigations." Despite the reprimand, Harry knew Mario was just worried about Jo. And besides his concerns about Jo's state of mind, it can't have been easy to deal with parents who lost their son to a maniac not once but twice. Harry didn't know if he could cope with being a father—all that worry over everything that could go wrong. He tried to imagine what Dan must be going through, and knew he was nowhere close.

"How'd he do it? How'd he take Billy?"

"Same as the other times. Middle of the night. Although this time he got in and out through an open door rather than a window. Dan Williamson was outside investigating a noise. We don't want this to go to press, Harry."

"Yeah, okay. Listen, can you tell Jo I called? Ask her to ring me back when she's got a chance."

"I'll pass it on. Bye, Harry."

~ * ~

The meeting with Alton had been a humiliating experience. She had to sit quietly and listen to all the reasons she shouldn't have gone to Mountview on Monday. It seemed to take forever before he was done.

"You're a good detective, but I think this case got to you. That's why I've taken you off it. But I don't want things to go any further than that. If you think you're up to it, you can start back Monday."

"Thank you, sir." By the time she escaped his office Mario had gone to do interviews. He'd left a note on her desk saying he could give her a lift when he got back, but she knew he might be hours. She knew he must be interviewing the Williamson's neighbors, to see if anyone had seen anything. She didn't even feel like staying long enough to call a cab, deciding to ring from outside. Although Alton said he was keeping Monday's incident quiet, she knew word would have gotten around by now, and everyone would know she was off the case. As she stood on the pavement about to make the call, a blue Datsun pulled up.

"Hey, Jo." She smiled at the familiar face. "Do you need a lift?"

"Thanks, but I was just about to call a cab."

"Don't be silly—jump in." After a moment's hesitation, she took up the offer.

Forty-seven

Harry had decided to take the day off. He'd phoned Anne-Marie that morning and told her about the sprain, letting her know he wouldn't be back in till Monday. She hadn't been having much luck with her interviews, but he didn't tell her to stop. He'd spent most of the day sprawled out on the sofa, his foot on a pillow, trying to work out what his next move should be. In the end he'd decided to do nothing. Part of him was rebelling against the thought of dark houses and light palaces. He still wasn't sure he was up to the challenge of battling evil. The part of him rebelling against the idea just wanted to stay on the sofa. He'd tried Jo's number a few more times to see if she was home yet, but she still wasn't answering. At around five he ordered a pizza and tried the numbers again. Still no answer. He rang Mario.

"Hey, Mario, it's Harry. Did you give Jo my message?"

"What is it with you at the moment? You two getting back together or something?"

"Nothing like that. I'm just worried about her. She hasn't been herself since that encounter with Robinson."

"Yeah, all right. I gave her the message—I can't make her call."

"Are you still at work?"

"I'm just about to leave. Maria wants me to have dinner at home for a change. But Jo didn't hang around long today—she left before I got back. I'm not sure what time it was."

"Okay. Maybe I'll call over later."

"Maybe she just needs some space right now, Harry."

"Yeah, okay, I'll think about it first." But even before he'd finished the pizza Harry knew he was going over. He knew he was being a bit over the top at present, and might even be one of the people she was avoiding by turning off her phone. But he couldn't help himself. Standing outside her door, he hoped she wouldn't be unhappy to see him. When no one answered he knocked again, louder this time. Still no response.

"Jo," he yelled at the door, knocking again. Putting his ear against the wood, he listened for sounds within. There were none. "Damn," he muttered to himself, limping off in frustration. "Where is she?" Harry knew he was being a little irrational, expecting her to be home just because he wanted to see her. Nevertheless, as soon as he was back in the car, he rang Mario again.

"Hey, Mario. It's Harry again. Are you still at work?"

"Jesus, Harry, have you got me on speed dial or something? I'm leaving now."

"Do you think you can ask around—see what time Jo left today? I'm at her place and she's not here."

"Don't you think you're overreacting a bit? I mean, she's probably just at the shops or something. Or anywhere really. She's not working again till Monday."

"Just humor me, please." Mario sighed heavily into the phone.

"Yeah, all right. I'll call you back in five minutes." Harry waited impatiently, too anxious to feel foolish. He snatched at the phone on the first ring.

"Hey, Harry, Jones dropped her home around lunchtime. He said she was talking about getting away for a couple of days, so maybe she went through with it."

"Where would she go?"

"How would I know? She's a big girl—stop worrying. It would probably do her good to get away for the weekend."

"Yeah, okay. Maybe I am being a little over-anxious."

"You think?" Harry could hear the gentle sarcasm in his voice. "Talk to you later."

"Bye."

~ * ~

Harry couldn't let it drop. He continued to sit outside her apartment building, trying to think of where she might go for the weekend. She liked the beach, but he couldn't really see her heading for the coast in the midst of all this. She hadn't seemed in a holiday mood. Unless she went just to get away, like Mario said. Maybe she'd gone to stay with her Mum or sister. He still had Julie's number on his mobile. He realized it probably meant something that he hadn't deleted it after all this time. Hoping that Jo hadn't given her mother the full details of their breakup, Harry dialed the number.

"Hi, Julie, it's Harry O'Brien." She sounded genuinely pleased to hear from him.

"Harry! Hello, dear, what a surprise. What are you up to these days?"

"Still working for the Daily Courier. Actually, I was looking for Jo. She isn't answering her mobile, but she did say she might get away for the weekend. I wondered if she was with you."

"Sorry, Harry. I haven't seen her for almost two months. But I did speak to her last week—she never mentioned anything about coming here. Or going away. Are you two spending time together again?"

"We're just friends. Maybe she went to Sam's. Would you mind giving me Sam's number—it's kind of important."

"Oh?"

"Yeah, a work thing. I have some information for her, regarding a case she's been working on." He could hear Julie lose interest.

"Okay, dear. Do you have a pen?"

"Yes."

"The number is: 212-543-1256."

"Thanks, Julie. I really appreciate it. It's been nice talking to you again."

"You too, Harry. And if you manage to get hold of Josephine, tell her to call her mother."

"Will do. Bye."

He rang Sam's number immediately, but she hadn't heard from Jo either. Although Harry knew he was worrying for no clear reason, he'd felt uneasy about Jo since Monday, and he just couldn't shake that uneasiness. He knew she probably wouldn't appreciate him ringing Mario and her family to track her down, at the risk of making them worry too, but he just couldn't stop himself.

The nagging concern had been at the back of his mind since he'd talked to Tonia, but he hadn't allowed himself to bring it out and examine it until now. What if Jo was the dark-haired woman? Harry had looked for Anne-Marie's name on the list, but it hadn't been there. Jo's had. He knew he had to talk to her about what happened at Mountview. Since this morning's mind-altering glimpse of his hand, the nagging concern had fought harder for his attention. He hadn't even raised the possibility with Alexander and Evelyn, and he knew now that was because he didn't want them confirming it. He'd been content to leave it vague. But the truth will come out, according to Alexander. Harry was afraid that, when it did, he wouldn't like it.

Forty-eight

Mario had endured a long, exhausting day that had started at about 1:45 that morning, when he'd gotten the unwelcome call about Billy Matheson. He'd been dragging his feet at work for the last couple of hours, and had finally managed to get away from the place. He'd had to give a hand-over before he could leave for the weekend. His last weekend for the month, and then the roster changed, and he wouldn't get another weekend off for three or four months. He was looking forward to spending time with his family. After a long sleep in tomorrow morning.

Maria was cooking cannelloni for dinner, and for the first night this week Mario would be sitting down with his family to eat. His two girls were five and six, so they usually had dinner early, before he got home from work. He'd been looking forward to this dinner all afternoon. His wife was a great cook.

Mario's heart sank as he pulled into the driveway of his two-story brick home. He'd seen the silver Chevrolet Camaro as soon as he'd pulled in. Harry was walking over to the car before he'd even got his seatbelt off and his car door open.

"What are you doing here, Harry?"

"Waiting for you. This Detective Jones—he's got a beard and moustache, hasn't he?"

"Yeah. You would have met him at the Metro. Why?"

"Does he wear a gold ring on his little finger?"

"What the hell's this about?"

"Come on, Mario, it's important. Does he wear a ring?"

"Yeah, I think so. Yeah, he does. Are you going to tell me why you want to know?"

"This woman I talked to, the one who participated in Robinson's tests, had a dream that a bearded man with a gold ring on his little finger kidnapped a dark-haired woman. Mario, you've got to give me his address." Mario exploded.

"You've gotta be fucking kidding me with this shit. I've worked with Jones for over two years—he's a good Detective. A good guy. There's no way he'd kidnap another detective. What is it with you and all this dream shit, Harry?" Harry knew he couldn't tell Mario about his visitors or the dark world. Mario would think he was out of his mind.

"I know it sounds pretty bizarre, but—" Mario cut him off.

"Too fucking right it's bizarre." Harry pushed on.

"But I've been doing some research on Robinson's clinic. He's hypnotizing his subjects, putting all sorts of images and thoughts into their heads. I think the dreams are related to that. That's why Pam Grinstone and Peter Holdman, and Jo too, saw the things they did. He gets into people's minds and fucks with their heads. I've spoken to other people who participated in his tests. You've got to believe me, Mario. I'm not saying this Jones is a bad guy, but maybe Robinson got to him somehow. What about the day you guys brought Robinson in? Who interviewed him?"

"Petersen and Jones." Mario frowned. "Petersen left to drop Jo home, and Jones took over the interview. But that doesn't mean anything. It certainly doesn't prove he was in some kind of hypnotic trance. The whole interview is on tape—there wasn't any funny business going on. And Jones hasn't been acting weird or anything. I just talked to him today, about dropping Jo home. He seemed the same as usual."

"Mario, I know you don't believe me, but you've got to give me his address. Does he live alone?"

"Yeah, but I'm not giving you his address. What are you going to do—break into his apartment? He's a detective for Christ's sake—if he doesn't shoot you he'll arrest you. You can't just go around doing that kind of shit."

"Mario, please," Harry begged.

"What if Jones told the truth? That Jo decided to get away for the weekend. We've got no reason to believe she hasn't. Even if there was something to what this woman said—and I'm not saying there is—do you have any idea how many guys in this city have beards? Or how many women have dark-hair? Hell, my wife's a brunette. You should go home—put that foot up. What'd you do to it anyway?"

"Fell down some stairs. Listen, Mario, I know it sounds crazy, but you've got to trust me on this. Okay, so maybe I'm wrong. But what if I'm right? It's not just Jo we're talking about—it's Billy Matheson, too. If Robinson's involved, then Jo and Billy are connected."

"We don't know anything's happened to Jo."

"Okay, we don't know that for sure. But she's not at home, and the last time she was seen she was with a bearded guy who wears a gold ring on his little finger. Just like in the dream. I know lots of guys have beards, and lots of women have dark hair. But they also have to have some connection to Robinson. He was in the dream, too."

"Jones isn't the only bearded guy on the squad. Someone else could have talked to Robinson. Which is not to say I'm buying your story. I'm just saying, even if it were true, there's just not enough to pin this on Jones."

"But he was the last person to see Jo."

"Look, Harry, I'm sorry. I can't give you his address. If Jo doesn't turn up to work on Monday I'll look into it, okay?" As he met Mario's gaze Harry could see he wasn't going to back down over this. Frustrated, he returned to his car and drove off unhappily.

"Mario honey, is everything all right out here?" Mario turned at the sound of his wife's voice, and saw her framed in the doorway. He took a few steps forward, his voice heavy with regret.

"Hey, love. Everything's fine."

"I heard you pull up. I've been waiting for you to come inside. I heard voices—who was here?"

"Harry. Looking for Jo."

"Is everything all right?"

"Yeah. Listen, love, I've got to go back out for a little while."

"What's wrong? I thought we were having dinner together."

"So did I. I'm real sorry, Marie—I'll try to be quick. I just have to check on someone. You and the kids better start without me."

Forty-nine

Jo woke with a splitting headache, only to realize the recurring nightmare she'd been having had just come true. She was spread-eagled on the bed, naked, a gag around her mouth. She didn't know how long she'd been out. The last thing she remembered was the hand around her nose and mouth, the chemical smell on the handkerchief. She'd passed out immediately. Jo tried to scream, but all she could manage was a muffled, gagging sound. She struggled to sit up, but the obscene position she'd been left in prevented her from doing so. Her arms and legs were stretched wide and cuffed to the bedposts. As she regained full consciousness, she became aware of the throbbing pain in her shoulders and arms.

The room was empty. Jo tried another muffled scream, but no one came. Straining her ears, she listened for any sounds outside the room, but heard nothing. She couldn't understand why this was happening. Exposed and afraid, she yanked hard at the unrelenting handcuffs, tears of frustration forming in the corners of her eyes.

~ * ~

When Harry left Mario's he didn't go home, as Mario had advised. Instead he drove straight to JP's, knowing he was breaking one of his friend's cardinal rules: don't show up unannounced. Indeed, JP discouraged any visiting at all, unless you were making a payment. The tall, lanky African-American practically pulled him through the doorway, pushing him into the apartment.

"What are you doing here?" His voice was heavy with suspicion. Harry had long suspected that JP's paranoia was not solely related to his hacking activities, but had something to do with the copious amounts of dope Harry was sure he smoked. Because even now JP was wearing dark sunglasses, and Harry couldn't remember ever seeing his eyes.

"Sorry, JP, it's an emergency. I need an address for Simon Jones—a homicide detective." Harry felt JP watching him beneath the dark glasses.

"You got his tax file number or something I can use? Date of birth?"

"Sorry, that's all I've got. He's in his mid-thirties."

"Shit, man, you're not giving me much to work with here. Better have a seat if you're waiting."

"Thanks, JP. I really appreciate this."

"Don't waste your appreciation, man—hope you've brought your wallet." Harry nodded. It took JP about twenty minutes to get the information Harry needed. While he waited, Harry put in a call to Tonia, drawing a dark look from JP. He could see the eyebrows deepen into a frown above the glasses. Maybe he didn't approve of unsecured mobile calls. But he didn't say anything, and Harry prayed she hadn't gone out for the night. This time he was in luck.

"Tonia, it's Harry O'Brien—we talked on Wednesday."

"Yes, I remember. How are you?"

"Good. I'm calling about that dream you had. Can you remember anything about the location? Where the woman was tied up?"

"Not really. I just saw the bed. The bed and the woman." There was a brief pause on the other end of the line. "But I think she knew the place—she seemed to know where she was. I don't know how I know that—it just occurred to me now. That she knew. Why are you asking about this?"

"I'm just following up on a few things. I don't really have much at the moment, but if anything turns up I'll let you know."

"Do you think it's real? I mean, do you think this actually happens to someone?" There was anxiety in her voice, and Harry wished he could have done this some other way.

"I'm not sure. I don't want you to worry about it—it could be nothing. But if it is real, I'll let you know."

"Okay, well, I'll wait to hear from you then." There was another pause. "You really will tell me, if you find anything out, won't you, Harry?"

"I promise. Bye, Tonia."

"Bye." By the time he got off the phone, JP had the address for him. Harry gratefully handed over a hundred dollar bill as he took it.

Fifty

While Harry was sitting in JP's grungy den, Mario was busy cursing his name. Mario loved his food. He especially loved his wife's food. And he was particularly bitter about missing his wife's food that evening. Despite his deep-seated reservations about Harry's story, Mario knew he wouldn't be able to relax until he'd checked it out. And so, with considerable resentment, he'd driven to Simon's. He'd only been to his apartment once before, when he'd given Simon a lift home one night, but he remembered the address. As he stood on the doorstep, Mario wondered what the fuck he was going to say. Simon answered the door in sweat pants and a T-shirt, looking surprised to see him.

"Mario, what's up?"

"Do you mind if I come in for a minute?" Simon stepped aside.

"What's on your mind? Mario moved into the sitting room and took a seat, feeling Simon's inquisitive gaze following him.

"I'm worried about Jo. A friend of hers has been trying to contact her, and she's not answering the phone. Or her mobile."

"Maybe she went away for the weekend—like she said."

"Did she mention where she might go?"

"Sorry, Mario, it was a pretty casual conversation. Can I get you a beer or something?"

Yeah. Thanks. Mind if I use your toilet?"

"Go ahead. Second door on the left." Simon's one-bedroom apartment was small, and as he passed the bedroom on his way to the toilet, Mario peeped around the slightly open bedroom door, hoping Simon wouldn't come out of the kitchen at that moment and see him. Mario didn't even realize he'd been holding his breath until he released a sigh of relief at seeing the room empty. He moved quickly to the bathroom, cursing Harry under his breath. Back in the sitting room, he took a long sip from the beer.

"What's going on, Mario? Is something wrong with Jo?" Simon sounded genuinely concerned, and Mario wondered again what the hell he was doing here. "I know she was pretty freaked out on Monday, and Alton bumped her from the case. Do you think she's taking it bad or something?" Mario took another long sip, draining most of the bottle.

"Could be, I'm not real sure. This friend of hers was worried about her—I'm not sure why. This case has been a real bitch, hey? Maybe I'm getting a little jumpy myself—I've been worried about her this week. I thought she might have mentioned where she was going, that's all."

"Sorry, pal. But she seemed okay—I'm sure she'll be fine. She's a tough woman." As Mario drained the dregs of his beer, it occurred to him that Jo wasn't going to be too impressed about him and Harry trying to track her down all over the city. There was a reason she hadn't been answering her phone this week: she wanted to be left alone. Mario rose to leave.

"Thanks for the beer, Simon. And I'm sorry to drop in on you like this."

"Hey, don't sweat it. I keep an eye on my partner, too."

As Mario was coming down the stairs he saw the familiar Chevrolet pull up, and stomped angrily over to the car.

"How the fuck did you get this address?" Harry looked up in surprise, startled to see Mario hovering outside his window this time. He wound it down a little.

"I'm a journalist—can't reveal my sources."

"Don't jerk me around, O'Brien. I've had enough of your bullshit for one day." Mario looked seriously pissed off, and Harry tried a conciliatory tone.

"Did you go in?"

"I did. I even checked out the guy's bedroom. There's no one else there. Jones is enjoying a quiet night at home, which is what I should be doing right now. Have you had dinner tonight, Harry?"

"Ah, I got a pizza early on."

"Lucky you." Mario shot him a dark glare. "Well, I'm going home right now to have my dinner, which is probably cold. And I don't want to hear no more bullshit about dreams, or hypnotic trances, or bearded men. You got that?"

"Mario, I'm sorry about your dinner, but maybe Jones took her somewhere else?"

"Yeah, and where do you think that might be? He's a cop. He hasn't got extra homes all around the city, just lying vacant until he needs to stash women."

"What about Robinson's place? Tonia said the woman knew the place. Or the place where you found Billy? He—" Mario cut him off.

"This is bullshit, Harry. Jo doesn't know either of those places. She hasn't been there."

"Not physically. But she went to the place in the Bronx while she was under that hypnotic trance."

"I've had enough of this crap. It's still a crime scene, Harry, so don't go there. I'm going home. And I don't expect to be getting any more calls from you." Mario stomped off.

~ * ~

Jo didn't know how long she'd been tied up, but she'd watched the light slowly fade from the room as night fell. The throbbing pain in her arms and shoulders had gradually faded to a dull ache. She wondered why he hadn't come back for her, and struggled with her conflicting desire for something to happen—something that might give her a chance at escape—and the shame and fear of having him return. The shame of having him see her like this, totally exposed. The fear of what he might do to her in this position, completely vulnerable and open to him. Although she'd tried hard not to think about it, Jo had worked enough rape cases to know that her current position wasn't good.

Startled, she realized someone was at the front door.

Fifty-one

Harry didn't have any trouble finding the house. The address had been published by every journalist covering the story, including himself. He'd even been out with Eddie to get a few photos. The rambling, two-story house squatted on a half-acre of overgrown lawn in a run-down area of the Bronx. He could see its attraction as a place to stash bodies. There was a vacant lot on either side, and the nearest neighbors were housed in a run-down tenement block a few hundred feet away. Grabbing a heavy torch from the boot of his car, Harry made his way to the front door of the crumbling house. The police had left yellow tape around the door, but no one was watching. Deciding his foot wasn't up to kicking the door in, Harry crept around the house with his torch on, until he found a window low enough to crawl through. Shattering the glass with the torch, he wrapped his jacket around his hand and pushed the remaining glass through, before climbing into a dark room.

Shining the torch into the darkness, he found himself in a large, dusty room that might have been a dining room, if there were any dining furniture in it. The house smelled musty, and the air inside seemed heavier than it had outside, clinging to his skin like a wet glove. Shaking the glass from his jacket, he put it back on and took a cautious step forward, moving into the next room. Shining the torch ahead of him, he tried to make out where he was. The heavy drapes on the windows prevented him seeing anything outside the torch's beam, and it took a while to confirm that this room was also empty. Moving into the room on the right, Harry found himself in an old-fashioned kitchen that was surprisingly well-equipped, with a stove and a small fridge in one corner, and even a table and chairs. The smell of meat lingered in the poorly ventilated room, and Harry was quick to move out as soon as he'd confirmed it was empty. Moving back into the room he'd left, he started up the stairs on the far side of the room, hearing them creak under his feet.

Careful not to put too much weight on his ankle, Harry held tight to the banister with his left hand, and pulled himself upwards, wishing he'd brought a gun. Not that he owned a gun, but this was one of the few times in his life that he really wished he did. The weight of the torch in his right hand was comforting, but he'd rather be holding something that could kill. As he finally reached the top of the stairway he strained his ears, listening for any sounds of movement. Hearing nothing but an oppressive silence, he pushed open the first door, and shone his torch into the room. No furniture, no occupant. He moved on to the second bedroom, then the third, before reaching the bathroom. All the rooms were empty. Finally he reached the last door on the corridor, and flung the door open, shining his torch into its corners. Another empty room. Time to check out the basement, he told himself. It would have been the obvious place to start—the only place Jo would know—but the thought of it sent chills down Harry's spine.

Limping back down the stairs he returned to the large, empty room and moved through to a reception area, looking around for another door. Finding it, he entered a small, cramped room that made his skin crawl, and found the stairs leading downwards. Clutching his torch tightly, Harry moved cautiously. The air around him seemed to get thicker the further down he went, and he had to force himself to keep going. When he finally reached the bottom of the stairs, he found himself looking down a long, narrow corridor. A doorway led off to either side. Taking the left door first, Harry felt the sweat dripping from his hand as he turned the door handle. The smell of feces and urine, of human sweat and fear, assaulted his nostrils as soon as he stepped in. The smells of the past seemed not only trapped but intensified in this room, which seemed to keep out any fresh air, and Harry had to hold his breath to avoid gagging. Moving slowly now, he shone his torch into the darkness. But the darkness seemed to eat the torch's light, allowing only a feeble flicker to guide his way. He saw the thin mattress on the floor, and the buckets beside it. The realization that this was the place where Billy had been kept sent shivers up his spine. Harry backed away in the direction he'd come, afraid to turn his back on the room.

Back in the dark, narrow corridor, Harry had to take another deep breath to force himself into the next room. Gasping at the familiarity of the room—its direct resemblance to the room in Pam's dream—he took in the macabre-looking tank, the chains hanging from the ceiling. The stench was even worse in here, lingering beneath the smell of ammonia, and he had to fight the urge to flee. He forced himself to swing the torch around the room until he was satisfied it was empty. Wincing at the pain in his ankle he hurried back up the stairs, and limped quickly through the house, leaving the way he'd entered. Once outside he gulped greedily at the night air, trying to fill his lungs with the clean air, replacing the rancid air he'd already breathed in. Not until he felt himself breathing normally again did he realize just how much the house had affected him. It seemed to suck his breath away. Harry wasn't a particularly superstitious man, despite his Irish Catholic upbringing, but right now he believed he'd felt the presence of evil in that house, and he wanted to go home and wash it off his skin.

But he still hadn't found Jo, and he knew he couldn't go home until he had. Although he'd just wanted to get out of the house, from the moment he'd entered it, once he was actually out he had to face the disappointment of not finding Jo. Climbing back into the safety of his car, he closed his eyes and tried to think. Where would Jones have taken her? What other place would Jo know? The obviousness of it struck him with sudden clarity, and Harry wondered why it hadn't occurred to him earlier.

~ * ~

The biggest problem Harry faced was getting in. There were no windows he could climb through here. And even with two good feet he doubted he'd have the strength to kick the door in. Besides, the attempt would surely draw some attention, and the police might arrive before he'd managed to get in. He had no illusions about being able to count on Mario's help if he got busted for breaking and entering. He felt pretty confident Mario wouldn't lose too much sleep over the thought of Harry in a police cell. Harry's solution was to call a locksmith, who'd advised him there'd be an additional fee of three hundred dollars for the late night call out. Harry had readily agreed, and had stopped at an ATM on the way, driving as fast as he could to ensure he made it there before the locksmith.

The rush proved unnecessary—it was another forty minutes before the locksmith showed up.

"You O'Brien?" the large man queried.

"Yeah. Thanks for coming out. Left my keys inside, like an idiot."

"You'd be surprised how often it happens," the man grinned. Although Harry spent the entire time fretting that someone would walk by and say something, the locksmith worked on uninterrupted, and had the door open within fifteen minutes.

"Thanks, pal. How much do I owe you?"

"Four hundred. Plus one hundred and twenty for the new lock. That's five hundred twenty dollars total." Harry handed over the money, assuring the locksmith he'd be in on Monday to get a spare key cut.

Listening for any sounds within, Harry started at the muffled noises coming from the bedroom. Without his torch, he felt defenseless. Looking around for a weapon, he moved quickly into the kitchen, switching on a light and selecting the largest kitchen knife he could find. He moved quietly across the apartment, relying on the light from the kitchen to guide his way. With a beating heart, he reached for the door handle and turned it slowly. The room was enshrouded in darkness but the sounds coming from the bed had grown louder, more panicked. Reaching for the light switch, he caught a brief glimpse of Jo before he felt the hand across his face. As he started to lose consciousness, Harry felt a sharp prick in his right arm.

Fifty-two

For the past twenty minutes or so Jo had been straining to work out what was going on outside. She heard talking, and then the sound of buzzing. Uncertain about what was happening she tried screaming, but the screams were too muffled to carry far. When she heard someone enter the apartment she froze, thinking it must be Jones, returning to finish what he'd started. She struggled against the handcuffs, trying desperately to scream through the gag. The initial flash of light hurt her eyes, forcing her to blink, but in that brief second before blinking she'd thought she was hallucinating.

"Harry," she tried to yell, desperate to warn him, but all that came out was a muffled gagging sound. And then came the sound of metal falling to the floor, and Jo was forced to watch helplessly as Robinson dragged Harry's inert body to the chair in the corner of her bedroom. Lifting her head as far as she could Jo watched Robinson uncoil the thick rope from around his waist, where it had been hidden beneath his jacket. He held one of her carving knives in his hand, using it to cut the rope and tie each of Harry's legs to the legs of the chair. With the remaining rope he bound Harry's wrists together, then tied his arms to his side, threading the rope through the back of the chair. Only when he'd finished the job did he turn to Jo and smile, flashing those sinister metal teeth. Jo continued her attempts to scream, trying to will Harry to wake up, but the futility of her efforts just brought tears to her eyes. Robinson took a step closer to the bed.

"What's that you're saying, Josephine?" He smiled his sinister simile while yanking on the gag, pulling it down in one viciously quick motion. "Now remember," he smiled, "any screaming and that goes back on. And I may be forced to inflict some pain, on you and your friend over there."

"What have you done to Harry?" she demanded.

"Just a little something to knock him out for a while. A shot of Seconal and a little something extra. I don't imagine he'll be awake for a least an hour, but I have another shot with me in case he comes to. That should give us plenty of time to catch up, wouldn't you say?"

"Is that how you kidnapped those boys?" she demanded, her anger temporarily overriding her fear. "You drugged them? Just like you drugged me the other day? Did you give it to Jones too, so he could drug me?" Robinson smiled.

"Clever girl, Josephine. Although it was Pentothal on the handkerchiefs you and the kiddies inhaled. Doesn't last as long as what your friend's just taken."

"What you've given him is a hypnotic, isn't it? Is that what you use to hypnotize people?" He sat down on the bed, running his gloved finger along her cheek. She shuddered at the contact, the feel of him brushing against her naked body.

"Now, now, Josephine. I think it's better if I ask the questions. You're not really in a position to question me, are you? Quite a compromising position to find you in—I think I like it." His eyes moved over her body and she felt dirty. "Your colleague did quite a job."

"How did you make him do this to me?" The oily smile slid from his face, and he brought his roving eyes back to her face.

"Let me explain something to you, Josephine. I can't make anyone do anything they don't want to do. I simply drew upon the base instinct I saw in him, helped him awaken his own urges to ravish a beautiful young woman. Which you are, of course." He ran his finger in a slow line down her face, tracing a track down her stomach, towards her belly-button, and she recoiled with revulsion.

"Oh, don't be so precious, Josephine. I've got no use for your fishy old flesh. I prefer my flesh sweet, young and tender, remember? But that doesn't mean I wouldn't enjoy watching your detective friend ravish you. At the moment he's got no idea what he's done. He's completely forgotten about you." He leaned closer, the menacing teeth inches from her cheek. "But trust me on this, Josephine: at any moment I can help him remember what he's started. We can have him over in no time, to finish what he began."

"What have you done with Billy?"

"So, you're still intent on asking the questions, are you? You don't need to worry about him—I've put him in a safe place. We can visit him, if you like." He looked at her as if awaiting an answer, but pressed on when he received none. "But, we can talk about Billy later. He'll keep for now. I want to talk about you first."

"How did you get in here?" He shook his head at her, affecting a disappointed look.

"So many questions. If you must know, a friend of mine got the keys from your young detective."

"You have a friend?"

"Now, now, my dear, no one likes a bitch. Actually, he's a very good friend. Someone I'd like to introduce you to." Robinson rose and called out, "Storyteller", and suddenly, at the doorway, stood the ugliest man Jo had ever seen in her life. Dressed in a dark suit, the man looked like a mortician who was more than ready to join his clients. He appeared to be in his sixties, maybe even his seventies, with a face that had been ravaged by more than just time. As if AIDs or some other debilitating disease had befallen him in his old age, and was eating away at him from the inside. His face was traversed by deep crevices, and was an unnatural shade of yellow. As if jaundice had set in. A huge red boil sprouted from the crevices in his yellow forehead, and had drawn all the puckered skin surrounding it into a thick point that looked like it would erupt at the slightest touch. His eyes were small dark holes framed by a watery swamp of yellow.

"Josephine, I'd like you to meet my friend, the Storyteller. Storyteller, this is Josephine." He waved theatrically at each of them as he conducted his introduction, then slid over to the other side of the bed, politely vacating his position for the old man. The Storyteller took the proffered spot and smiled down at Jo with teeth that resembled rotting bits of yellowed bone embedded in a bleeding mess of raw flesh. Unable to avoid the smell of decay coming from his mouth, Jo shrank back in disgust, trying to draw herself up to avoid any physical contact.

"The Storyteller has been entertaining himself in your bathroom. You see, we arrived quite some time ago, but he had a feeling that your friend over there was on his way, so when we heard him outside with the locksmith we waited in the bathroom. The Storyteller likes to make a dramatic entrance, so we delayed his appearance for dramatic effect. Quite effective, don't you think?" Jo was struggling to overcome the horror and disgust she felt at having them on either side of her, with the old man breathing his toxic fumes on her naked body. She fought to find her voice.

"Do you two usually work together?" It came out weaker, more vulnerable than she would have liked.

"Quite frankly, my dear, he's got skills you wouldn't believe. He's proven quite invaluable to me, in terms of searching out young children in accessible rooms. He can sniff them out." As if to demonstrate, the old man sniffed the air deeply, his big, purple nose twitching. Jo found her eyes drawn to the gaping black pores on that purple organ in horrified fascination. "Not to mention prisons," Robinson added.

"So it was your friend who gave Holdman the razor," she asked, catching his point and wondering if he also had something to do with Pam Grinstone's suicide. Robinson smiled at that before dismissing the question.

"Of course, the relationship is not all one-way. The Storyteller also benefits from my service to him."

"Does he eat small children, too?"

"No, Josephine, his thing is watching." In fact, the Storyteller was watching now. He was leaning back watching the exchange between Josephine and Robinson like an interested moviegoer, his watery gaze shifting from one to the other. "In fact, he was quite looking forward to watching you and your young detective, but that's one story we might have to play out later." The old man licked his thin, cracked lips and gave her a lascivious grin, epitomizing the image of the dirty old man. He reached out with a gnarled, claw-like hand and rested it on Jo's stomach, making her skin crawl.

"I don't know, Terry," the old man spoke at last. "Maybe there's time for more than one story." Until he spoke, Jo had assumed Robinson was in charge, but the menacing authority in the old man's dusty voice hinted at something else. When Robinson replied, it was with an almost deferential tone.

"Of course, Storyteller, whatever you want. But first we have to get her to the house."

"What house? Where are you taking me?" Ignoring her panicked questions, Robinson reached across the bed and lifted the old man's claw from Jo's stomach. Holding hands, the two of them leaned over her, smiling their ugly smiles. The metal and the yellow stumps swam in front of her eyes, clouding her vision, until Jo thought she was going to pass out from the smell of the old man's fetid breath. Then Robinson was staring into her eyes, and she couldn't break the gaze. Staring into the darkness of his eyes, she felt everything around her slip away, until only the darkness remained.

Fifty-three

Harry felt someone slapping his cheek and calling his name.

"Harry, can you hear me? You have to wake up." The slapping made his head swim, which in turn made him aware that his head felt like it was being crushed in a vice. He came to indignantly.

"Stop slapping me," he exploded, opening his eyes to see images of Alexander and Evelyn swimming before him. Evelyn had her hand raised as if she was going to hit him again, and he reached out to stop her.

"I just tapped you, Harry. Does your head hurt?" Her voice and eyes were full of motherly concern.

"Arrgh, like you wouldn't believe." He tried to sit up. With the realization that he was tied up came the memory of what had happed.

"Is Jo okay?" He strained his neck to see around Evelyn and Alexander, and Alexander took a step back so that he could see the bed behind him. Still handcuffed in the same spread-eagled position, she looked like she'd fallen asleep. Or lost consciousness.

"Untie me! We have to get her free before he comes back." Alexander bent to pick up the carving knife Harry had dropped earlier, the one Robinson had used to cut his ropes. He sawed at the ropes until they were severed, and Harry leapt free from the chair before he'd had time to remember the pain in his head and ankle.

"Whoa," he managed, as the room swum before his eyes.

"Are you okay, Harry?" Evelyn was still wearing the look of concern.

"Yeah, I'm fine. We're going to need bolt cutters or something to get those handcuffs off." He moved closer to the bed, looking around him in what he knew was a futile search for something to cut the cuffs.

"Jo! Jo, can you hear me? Wake up, Jo!" He turned back to Alexander and Evelyn, startled to see that Alexander had disappeared. Staring at Evelyn he implored her to help. "He must have given her something. I remember a shot in my arm just before I went down. Must have been some kind of tranquillizer. He must have given her the same. We have to get her up."

"She's not asleep, Harry." Evelyn's voice was gentle. "Robinson has taken her to the Dark World."

"What? But she's here." As suddenly as he'd disappeared, Alexander was back, a pair of bolt cutters in his hand. Struck dumb by the sudden reappearance, Harry watched as he deftly clipped the chains restraining her arms, before moving down to her ankles. Harry tried to avert his eyes from her naked body.

"We need to cover her up," he said, and Evelyn nodded at the suggestion. Ignoring the pile of clothes on the far side of the bed, she walked over to Jo's wardrobe and withdrew some loose pants and a tee shirt.

"These should be easier to get on than jeans," she explained. Alexander lifted the dead weight of her body while Evelyn and Harry struggled to pull the clothes on. The cut handcuffs still dangled from her arms and ankles, and while Alexander tried to get the nose of the cutters under the cuffs, Harry turned back to Evelyn.

"What did you mean, about him taking her to the Dark World? How can she still be here?"

"He hasn't taken her physical body, just her consciousness."

"Why would he do that?"

"It means she can't die in the other world."

"Well, at least that's a good thing, right?" Alexander finally had the cuffs off, and he looked up now and met Evelyn's gaze. As they exchanged looks something passed between them that Harry didn't quite understand. But they must have reached some kind of silent consensus, because Evelyn explained gently.

"Well, perhaps it is. But it also means he can keep her there for a long time. If her body doesn't die..." She didn't finish the sentence, and Harry felt the ripple of horror in his colon as he realized what she meant.

"You mean he wants to keep her alive so he can play with her? Even if she dies there she's still alive here? So that he could kill her more than once? Kill her and revive her? For an eternity?" The enormity of it made his mind reel.

"Well, a month of your time would seem like an eternity in that world. Of course she couldn't stay alive in this world for an eternity—she'd have to be fed and cared for just to last a month." Evelyn spoke cautiously, careful of Harry's feelings.

"But why leave her body here to be found? Surely he's putting himself at risk."

"Robinson didn't put her here. It won't be his fingerprints that are found on the body."

"God! Jones!" It came out as a gasp.

"There's something else, Harry. If Jo loses her mind, like the children did, she won't be able to implicate anyone. Even if she were institutionalized, Robinson could use her as his plaything in the other realm. But apart from that, Robinson is getting more careless. Despite having Jones bring her here, he seems less concerned about getting caught than he was before. Perhaps he used Jones for convenience, rather than to hide his tracks. He seems less concerned with hiding his identity in your world, and more interested in what's happening in the other world. Why else reveal himself to Jo, and to you? He's deranged. He believes himself immune in your world. He revealed far too much to Jo the other day. He knew she was a detective, and didn't care. The Storyteller was here with him tonight—things are drawing to a conclusion." Harry stared at her, at Alexander, the anger building within him.

"You mean you were here? You saw them? Why did you let them tie me up? I thought you were supposed to be helping me." He couldn't stop the angry tirade of questions. "Why did you let him take Jo? And what about Billy?" As he thought of Jo and Billy, Harry felt the anger mounting. How could they just let it happen? How could they watch and do nothing? It was Evelyn who responded, her voice gentle.

"Harry, we couldn't risk letting the Storyteller see us. He can't know we're helping you. It's best if they underestimate you. He sensed you were coming here tonight, and warned Robinson. But so far, he just sees you as her friend. He might sense there's something about you, but he doesn't know we're helping you. He doesn't know you've been to our world, that you've eaten the apple from our orchard."

"What's the apple got to do with anything?" Just the mention of it aroused a craving in him, despite the turmoil he was in.

"It nourished you, Harry. It's given you strength, even if you don't realize it yet. You'll need all the strength you have to withstand the horrors of the Dark House. You have to go there, Harry, to rescue them. The Storyteller is drawing power from this story. He has made Robinson more than he could have ever been by himself. We will have to go soon. We don't know what Robinson intends for you. Maybe he'll come back for you, and we can't be here when he does. But you need us to get there. We couldn't risk being seen. He'd guess you were coming."

"You said I've been there before—the other day at work."

"Yes, like Jo you went there mentally, not physically. We have to take you, just as the Storyteller took Robinson. The first time at least—perhaps Robinson can go alone. But you can't, and it's time." Despite his desperate need to go after Jo, Harry felt unprepared.

"I really need a cigarette first, okay?" He fumbled in his jacket for the packet. Under the circumstances he figured Jo would forgive him for smoking in her bedroom. As Alexander and Evelyn watched on silently, he drew the smoke deep into his lungs, feeling a little calmer. When he was done he extinguished the butt on the outside of the packet, before slipping it back into the pack.

"Right, let's go then." He went for a nonchalant grin, but felt it falter on his face as they reached out for his hands. Suddenly he was back on the roller-coaster, sucking in his breath as his body zoomed upwards, the room swirling into a distant memory. And then they were going down, and all the breath was leaving his body, and finally his feet were on firm surface again, and he was clutching their hands tightly. Blinking, he tried to clear his vision. He blinked again, but everything remained the same. It was as if they'd landed in the middle of a giant thundercloud. Whichever way he looked, all he could see were gray swirls of nothingness.

"Where are we?" It was Alexander who replied, his voice coming from the swirls of gray that had obscured his face and body.

"We're at the border."

"The border?"

"Yes, where we came the other day. This is the border between our world and the Storyteller's. It safe here—we can't be seen."

"How do we get into the Storyteller's world? I can't see anything." Harry experimented by stretching out his arm, but it was swallowed up by the gray, his fingers no longer visible. Alexander cleared his throat.

"We'll point you in the right direction. But, Harry, I'm afraid you've misunderstood us. We aren't going—you are. We can't go with you. You have to go alone." The panic hit him.

"You're kidding me, right? I don't even have a weapon."

"A weapon wouldn't be much good to you in there anyway. Things change. You'll have to use whatever comes to hand. The forces in there would destroy us. We have to survive to take you back to your world, or you'll be trapped here."

"You could have told me that before we left."

"Why? Do you think it would have made a difference? Do you think you wouldn't have come? Do you still believe you had a choice?" Harry thought about Jo and Billy, and realized Alexander was right.

"So, what's the plan? I just go into that world, find the house, and then what?"

"You won't have to look for the house, Harry. But you will have to look for Jo and Billy. You must find them and rescue them—bring them out of that place so that we can take them back to your world. Hopefully it's not too late for them, although we have grave concerns for the boy."

"That's not much of a plan."

"You are stronger than you realize, Harry. We're not trying to mislead you—you won't find it easy. It's very easy to lose your way in the Dark House. You could wander around for an eternity and not find them. But have faith in your own strength; be guided by your own instincts. Feel your way."

"That's not very comforting."

"We'll still be there to help you, if you need us."

"I thought you were staying here. How can you help me from here?"

"We can watch from here. We'll know if you need us. Our thoughts will be with you." Harry desperately needed another cigarette, but he knew he'd just be postponing the inevitable.

"Well, I guess I'm as ready as I'm ever going to be. Which way do I go?"

Fifty-four

Jo had passed out for a few minutes, and when she came to she felt like she'd woken up in hell. She was back in the dentist's chair from Robinson's office, only this time she was naked. Her wrists and ankles were bound in the same way as before. And there, right in front of her, was Billy Matheson, hanging from the ceiling, just like the last time she'd seen him. His arms were handcuffed to the chains, his thin legs hanging free as he dangled in the air. It was the nightmare she'd been having for days. It was all coming true. And this, the image she'd been unable to erase from her mind, the point in her dream that always woke her up in a heavy sweat, was being re-enacted. She'd woken up in time to see what happened next.

Jo swung the chair as hard as she could with her restricted body, and saw the giant tank, and beside it, the demon from her dream. In this new nightmare he was joined by an even uglier demon, and they both stood watching her with expectant looks on their evil faces. As she turned her chair to face them, Robinson slid noiselessly across the room, while the old man shuffled a few steps closer. Both were illuminated by the light reflecting off the back wall, which made their faces glimmer. Standing by her side now, Robinson spoke.

"Ah, Josephine, you've come to. I'm afraid the journey proved a little difficult for you."

"How did I get here?"

"No need to concern yourself with the details, my dear. Suffice to say, you're here now. Safe and sound." His serpent-like pronunciation of the 's' sounds made him sound more sinister than ever, and he narrowed his eyes into reptilian slits before turning to his friend.

"Allow me to get you a chair, Storyteller." Slithering across the room noiselessly, he dragged forward a chair Jo recognized from the other day, and placed it carefully beside Jo. He waved at it magnanimously, as if he'd just conjured it up from thin air, a magician's trick demanding applause. The old man shuffled over, and Robinson addressed him in a grandiose tone.

"You may as well make yourself comfortable, old friend. I have a show to perform." He leaned into Jo's chair, and she shrunk back from him. "A performance you might recall, my dear, from the other day. But, of course, that was merely a dress rehearsal. Today is the real thing. And it's going to be a tough performance to top, I assure you. The pressure will be on. We will have to think of something really creative for your reporter friend." Jo froze at the reference to Harry. The Storyteller seemed to be enjoying himself, nodding along slowly and grinning like a deranged lunatic. A thin stream of spittle had formed at the corner of his crusty old lips, and was dripping down the cracks of his grisly chin.

"Although I must be honest with you, Josephine," Robinson continued theatrically. "Torture is not really my thing. Now, you see Billy over there," he waved dramatically in Billy's direction. "I see him simply as sweet, ripe flesh in which to sink my teeth. Of course, I know it will cause him considerable pain, but that is really beside the point. The point being, of course," he flashed his metal teeth at her, "my own pleasure. Nevertheless, I am a professional. If torture is required of me, I'm sure I can accommodate my audience." He leaned in closer, whispering in her ear like a man taking someone into his confidence. "You see, Josephine, the Storyteller has given me so much. And sometimes one has to give something back, don't you agree?" He ended his monologue with a theatrical sigh.

"Enough of your jabbering, Robinson," the old man barked, spraying spittle at both of them. "Get on with it." Robinson stood up stiffly, as if he'd been slighted by the old man's tone. When he responded, the stance was matched by his stiff tone.

"Of course, Storyteller. As you wish."

Fifty-five

Harry stumbled through the fog in the direction Alexander had indicated, and within a few minutes he'd noticed the air become thicker and heavier, while at the same time more translucent. Another minute, and he was on a winding path lit by the moonlight, leading up to what was the ugliest building Harry had seen in his entire life. About a hundred feet in the distance, it was just like Tonia had described: an enormous public toilet block. Yet even as Harry stared it seemed to change shape, morphing into what Harry considered to be the worst example of public housing ever built—a filthy, decaying tenement block for the poor and dispossessed. He took a few, hesitant steps along the path, limping forward reluctantly. His sprained ankle ached at the motion, and his legs felt heavier than usual. Walking seemed a much bigger effort than normal, as if the building itself was repelling him, trying to force him back the way he'd come. He could feel the thick forest encroaching on either side of the path. The gnarled, leafless trees were the same dark color as everything else in this landscape, barely touched by the moonlight. The moon focused its pale light on the path, leaving the trees to fall back into the shadows.

Harry willed himself forward, trying to ignore the scrambling sounds coming from the forest. He tried not to think of what creatures might live amongst those lifeless trees. Tried to ignore the feeling that whatever they were, they were watching him. He could hear the beat of his heart in his ears, thumping loudly, and felt the sweat forming on his forehead. He forced himself to march forward in tune to the beating of his heart. The building still seemed about a hundred feet away, as if he hadn't yet covered any distance at all. As he stared at it, trying to imagine what wretches might inhabit such a place, it began to change shape again, taking on the characteristics of a prison. Forcing himself to keep the building in sight, to try to close the gap, Harry pushed on, ignoring the growing ache in his legs. It was like walking through water; his legs were tired already.

Pushing himself forward, Harry stumbled over a rock and nearly fell, and as he cast his eyes downward he recoiled in horror. It wasn't a rock at all, but some ugly gray bug, like an oversized, discolored cockroach. The path was littered with them. What he'd mistaken for stones were actually alive, and the crunching underneath his sneakers had been the crunching of living things. Harry forced his eyes back up and ahead, fighting the urge to turn back, to flee to the borderland. And to the magical world beyond, which offered comfort and safety, a haven from this world of dark horror. Which would embrace him like a mother embraces a frightened child, and erase the images of this world from his mind. Harry took comfort in the thought of that world, and in the thought of his friends watching him from the borderland, and found the courage to push on. They believed in him.

One foot in front of the other, Harry walked and walked, until his legs were numb. It seemed like hours must have passed, but finally the hundred feet had become eighty feet, then seventy, until he'd reached the final ten feet, and they went quickly. As if they really were only ten feet. And then Harry found himself at the doorway of that dark monstrosity, his hand outstretched to turn the knob. As his fingers touched the greasy brass, Harry felt a jolt of pain pass through his body—as if he'd been hit with a bolt of electricity—and he was thrown backwards, landing face-up on the ground. Shocked and dazed, it took him a few minutes to realize he was lying in a sea of bugs, and the realization forced him to his feet. He swatted frantically at his body in a desperate attempt to kill the things that were now crawling all over him. He swatted at his jeans and jacket, and scraped the back of his neck with his hand, feeling the thick growth hanging there. He pulled his hand away to reveal a thick gray leech, fat with his blood. He raked his hands through his hair, and patted down his face and neck until he was sure nothing remained attached to him. And then he turned back to face the door, wondering what to do next. The thought that he had walked all this way, only to be turned away at the door, filled him with a despair that threatened to bring him down again. And then a voice spoke to him, whispering gently in his ear.

"Try it again, Harry." He spun around, looking for the source of the voice. There was no one there. Maybe it was a trick. Some malevolent presence that wanted to see him electrocuted.

"Go on," she urged again, and Harry's suspicions began to subside. It wasn't Evelyn, but there was something about the voice that reminded him of her. It was gentle, almost maternal, and he found it difficult to associate that voice with malevolence. With a renewed strength he approached the door for a second time, reaching out more carefully this time. So that this time, when the bolt hit him, he was more prepared. He raised his other hand and rested it against the door, bracing his body to absorb the shock. Refusing to let go of the doorknob for a second time, Harry gritted his teeth against the pain and turned. The door swung open.

Fifty-six

Harry entered the house cautiously. His original impression of the building was confirmed when he realized he was standing in some nightmarish public toilet block. The smell of piss and shit was overwhelming, and Harry had to pinch in his nostrils in an attempt to filter out some of the stench. His stomach rebelled against the odor, and he had to fight the urge to regurgitate the contents of his stomach. Stalls stretched along the far wall as far as he could see, and there was no other exit within sight. Still fighting the urge to vomit, he took a few tentative steps towards the first stall, and heard the sounds of splashing beneath his feet. Looking down, Harry wondered if a pipe had burst, because the floor was covered in dirty water. At least, he told himself it was water, hoping he was right.

Harry pushed open the first stall, cringing as he touched the filthy door, wishing he had a glove or something to protect himself. The toilet bowl was overflowing, dripping its contents onto the concrete floor, and Harry saw the feces rising to the top of the porcelain bowl. The smell was horrifying. He stepped back, trying to turn away from the smell, but his reflexes had been completely disarmed this time. The contents of his stomach joined the filthy water, swirling around in the rest of the waste. As soon as he'd finished, Harry felt his stomach rising once more to his throat, and he had to bend over again, vomiting until there was nothing left. As he watched the small bits of pizza join the dirty flow beneath him Harry was stunned by the memory of eating earlier that night. It seemed like months ago now. Then the dry retching began, and by the time he was finished Harry's whole body felt weak. He'd never felt so filthy in his entire life—he wanted to climb into a clean, hot shower and scrub every inch of his body. But he couldn't.

Wiping his face on the sleeve of his jacket, Harry steadied himself to push open the door to the second stall, then the third, then the forth, looking for some kind of exit out of this place. Not all the stalls had doors—he only had to peer into those that didn't—but all of them were filthy. Brown-smeared toilet paper littered the floor of some, swirling in the dirty water, and others featured used and discarded sanitary napkins. Others had feces or blood smeared on the walls. Most of the stalls were flooded. Harry stumbled along numbly, something in his brain telling him that the exit could be anywhere, and that he had to keep looking. The stalls stretched out before him in a never-ending row, and the only way he could face them was by emptying his mind.

About a third of the way along Harry pushed open a stall and was shocked out of his numbness when he realized it was occupied. As he pushed on the door he could feel the weight on the other side, and could hear the grunt from inside. The toilet seemed to open up to accommodate its occupants, defying the laws of physics. A junkie, looking moments from death, sat on the filthy toilet bowl, trying to maneuver a syringe into an arm covered in pustulous boils. His acquaintance, a filthy-looking youth with wasted eyes and a face ravaged by imminent death, squeezed out from behind the door, where Harry had unwittingly pinned him.

"Do you know where the exit is?" he implored the man with the needle. The man just stared back blankly before shrugging his shoulders, flinging his head back as the needle found its mark.

Harry left them to it and continued along the stalls. In one stall he interrupted a woman with her pants around her knees as she sat on the toilet, the overflowing water seeping up beneath her wide bottom.

"Do you know where the exit is?" he pleaded, and she frowned at him. Pulling the door closed after him he continued along.

Almost to the end now, he pushed open a door to reveal a huge, hairy bear of a man standing naked in the stall, sodomizing a young boy. The boy's pants hung down around his ankles, soaking up the filthy water. This stall seemed larger then the others, and Harry watched in horror as the man's hairy back moved up and down, glistening with sweat as he pushed against the boy like a piston. Seeing the blood dripping from between the boy's legs, he grabbed the man around the neck and tried to pull him off. The man roared as if he'd been mortally wounded, and the boy turned to face Harry, his black eyes dead and unseeing. The man scrambled back to the boy, who turned back to face the dirty wall.

Harry left them to it, bending over to dry retch outside the stall. Stealing himself to continue he pushed on, the end finally in sight, but with no exit in view. The thought that he might have to go back the way he'd come, traveling that distance again, this time knowing it was all in vain—for the only exit led outside—almost threatened to cripple him with despair. But Harry forced himself to continue, telling himself that there had to be another way out. Four stalls down, and Harry had reached the second-last stall. He yanked the door open, no longer concerned with germs, and saw an empty cubicle. This one had a doorway where the back wall should be.

Fifty-seven

"Wait!" Jo practically screamed the word, as Robinson slid towards the boy. He looked back at her with a serpentine smile, waiting for her to continue. "I can tell from your friend's name that he enjoys a good story, am I right?" Jo forced herself to speak calmly, to keep the revulsion from her voice.

"What did you have in mind, Josephine?"

"I want to know about the other children. You could tell us both. The police checked your background—we couldn't find anything on you. But you must have a history, right? A man like you—you must have indulged your desires before now. How did you manage to conceal it? How did you stay hidden from the police?"

"Well now, that is an interesting story." Robinson took a few steps towards her, away from Billy. "Although I'm not sure my friend will find it equally fascinating. You see, he's heard it all before. Been there, done that, so to speak. Haven't you, Storyteller?" The old man nodded, a demented giggle escaping his cracked old lips.

"He always was a bad boy," the old man cackled. "Especially after he got rid of his family." Jo jumped on the information.

"How did you do that? I thought you were in boarding school when your family had the accident."

"Sure I was, Josephine," he smiled wickedly. "But I was also in dear old Dad's head. He never stood a chance. It was his own fault, of course—he was already far too prohibitive. Coming up to the school puffed up with threats after I bit a few of the boys—all quite harmless fun. I'd never let myself be detected so easily—there was never anything serious. It was easy when I traveled. Especially within the poorer countries. You really can buy as many young children as you want in the Third World. Did you know that, Josephine?" She shrugged in response, unable to speak, still struggling to mask her disgust. "There's always the problem of disposing of the bodies, of course, but if one is careful, there's not too much that can go wrong. The death of a few homeless children tends to go unnoticed, as long as no glaringly obvious patterns emerge. I had to cut them up in those days—I didn't have these." He flashed his teeth at her. "But then, that helped in a way, too. Corpses with a few bits of flesh sliced off aren't as uncommon as the corpses I've been leaving behind lately. Still, one has to weigh the disadvantages against the pleasures, and this has all been very pleasurable for me. I believe I've been relatively prudent."

"Not completely," Jo intervened. "I talked to your dentist. He told me about the mould you took away. I presume that was to make those things you're wearing now." His eyes flashed with displeasure, and the Storyteller cackled in the background. Robinson's voice took on a threatening edge.

"You're a nosy little bitch, aren't you, Josephine? Guess it's lucky you won't be able to talk to anyone after today." He switched tones suddenly, moving back into the persona of the friendly storyteller. "Of course, once I decided to give up traveling and concentrate on my research, I was free to start exploring my desires in greater depth. With only myself and Margaret left at home, it really was quite simple."

"Margaret? Is she your housekeeper?"

"My housekeeper, and for many years my nanny. She adores me, you know. A few Valium in the tea at night and the poor dear doesn't have a clue what's going on."

"So that's why she gave you those alibis? She was unconscious at the time. She didn't even realize you weren't home all those nights."

"You do realize, don't you, dear, that you'll never get the opportunity to use this information? There's nothing connecting me to any of those crimes."

"Two of the people involved in your research killed themselves, after seeing the crimes you committed."

"Two suicides out of hundreds of participants. I hardly think that's going to strike anyone as unusual. I doubt that percentage is much higher then the national average, my dear. It's certainly not something anyone could build a case on."

"Maybe not, but it will reflect badly on your research." He threw back his head and laughed.

"My research. Oh you are a precious fool, Josephine. I don't give a damn about what the advertisers want. Do you really think I care what people do with their money? What they buy? I needed the advertisers' funds; I was never interested in the same desires that they were. I'm interested in darker desires. In using those desires to encourage people to enact stories the advertisers could never dream of. Think of me as the director, and my friend over there as the producer. The technologies we've developed will be used to bring more people under our control. It's going to be an exciting time, Josephine—such a pity you'll miss it. Although we are planning to bring some of the excitement back to you, so don't feel too left out." Jo's mind rebelled against what he was telling her, momentarily closing down in shock, so that it took her a while to respond.

"So, have you always had this special ability to hypnotize people? To get into their minds?"

"It's not as difficult as you might imagine. The visual and audio productions I've developed for the advertisers prove that anybody can do it, if they know how." Jo shuddered at the thought of a world viewed through Robinson's eyes.

Fifty-eight

Harry entered the cubicle and walked straight through into another room. It was even darker than the toilet block, the only light seeming to emanate from the walls themselves. A pale, unnatural glow that was insufficient to give him an idea of the room's size and dimensions. Much of the room was hidden in shadows, and he had to press his left hand against the wall to guide himself through the darkness. He could hear faint moans and groans coming from somewhere in the distance, but tried to block them out as he groped his way forward.

The room appeared to defy the normal laws of physics, seeming to stretch on forever. It was more than thirty minutes later, by his estimation, that Harry finally reached a corner. As he looked down at his hand to guide himself around the corner, he felt the icy hand of terror clutching at his bowels. The walls were moving. There were people trapped in them. The faint glow of the walls illuminated images of slaves being driven forward by cruel overseers, their legs chained together so that they stumbled as they moved. The fat, cruel faces of their white masters leered as they brought the whips down on the slaves' lacerated backs, the black skins glistening with sweat and blood. Snatching his hand away in horror, Harry tried to stumble forward without the wall to guide him, and tripped. On his knees he was unable to avoid the images closer to the ground, of women and children being beaten. As their images became clearer, their screams of pain and suffering became louder, and soon the screams and sobs for mercy were almost too much for him to bear. He clamped his hands across his ears in an attempt to block the sounds, and scrambled back to his feet. As he struggled to catch his breath Harry felt the walls closing in on him, the darkness threatening to swallow him up. The panic welled, and he gulped at the musty air, desperate for breath.

"Don't look at the images, Harry. Nothing can hurt you unless you allow it into your mind. You have to keep going. Try to forget the images, and just keep moving." It was the voice from outside, whispering in his ear.

"Who are you?" he pleaded. "I can't see you." A middle-aged woman suddenly appeared before him, her smile lit up by a light that seemed to emanate from within, rather than the unnatural glow of the walls. There was something about her sweet, smiling face that struck Harry as familiar, but it took him a few minutes to place it. Alice from the Brady Bunch. Although less submissive. She seemed completely out of place in this house, and Harry wondered if he was hallucinating.

"I'm Alice," she told him. You've go to be kidding me, Harry thought. But he didn't say it. "I'm a friend of Alex and Evelyn. They sent me to watch over you."

"I thought it was too dangerous for..." Harry wondered how to finish the sentence, and finally decided on "people like you." She chuckled—a rich, throaty sound that comforted him.

"Oh, I've been around for a long time, Harry. Alex and Evelyn are mere babes compared to me. I come from a time when, let's just say, goodness had to be a little cruel to survive. I've got a bit of the dark force in me. I've needed it over the centuries." Harry found it difficult to believe that this sweet, motherly woman could possibly have a dark side, but he didn't interrupt. "Which is not to say that I find this atmosphere healthy. I can't remain in this form for long—I might be seen. But I'll be here. Try to ignore the images and just keep moving—you're going the right way."

"But how will I know if I stop going the right way? What if I take a wrong turn?"

"You'll know the right way to go. You just have to follow the darkness into the black heart of the house. That's where you'll find what you're looking for. And here," she offered, reaching into the folds of her matronly dress. "Take these with you. You might need them along the way. Maybe the boy will need them." In the center of her outstretched palm sat four bright red balls, about half the size of ping pong balls.

"What are they?"

"Cherries." The banality of her answer struck Harry.

"I don't understand."

"They're from the Light World. Like the apple. They can give strength and nourishment to whoever eats them. They may come in handy." He stuffed the cherries into his jacket, noticing that she was already fading away, her light growing less bright.

"Wait! Alice! What if I get lost?"

"I'm here," she whispered in his ear. "Keep going." Strengthened once more, this time by her appearance, Harry returned his left hand to the wall with determined resolution, blocking the images as he guided himself forward. He moved faster now, and it wasn't long before he'd reached another doorway.

Fifty-nine

The doorway opened onto a long, narrow corridor. Doorways led off in either direction along the corridor, stretching out in a long row like the cubicles in the toilet block, so that Harry despaired of ever finding the right door. Alexander's words about being lost for an eternity rang in his mind as looked glumly in each direction, wondering how the hell he was going to choose a door. He opened the one directly in front of him and peered inside, seeing the same unnatural glow coming from these walls that he had observed in the last room. As Alexander's words floated through his head, he remembered his advice to 'feel' his way, and be guided by his instincts. Deciding to start with the doors to his left, he walked along the corridor, brushing his hand against the doorknobs as he moved. About five doors down Harry experienced the same jolt of energy he'd felt at the main entrance, and knew this was the right one.

Opening the door, he was immediately assaulted by the sounds of babies crying, young children screaming, and had to fight the urge to slam it closed again. Leaving the door open, he tentatively placed his left hand against the nearest wall, averting his eyes from the horrific images he'd glimpsed only briefly, but which had instantly been singed into his brain. A pile of dead and dying babies, piled up in some macabre pyramid. A child being set alight by a man with a cruel smile. Moving along cautiously, one foot in front of the other in a careful shuffle, his hand hit something hard, something jutting from the wall. Groping in the dark, his fingers grabbed onto the steel banister. As he tentatively stretched out his foot, he felt the ground disappear beneath it. He'd come to a staircase. The stairs led down, into the bowels of the house. Or its heart.

Clutching the banister Harry made his descent slowly. Unable to see the stairs, he moved carefully, keeping his eyes straight ahead. At one point the screams seemed to grow louder, startling him into glancing up. His eyes could not avoid the images on the wall, and for a moment he stood transfixed, staring at images of fetuses trapped in jars, suspended in some kind of fluid. Like you might expect to see in some kind of medical laboratory. And as he stared, one of the fetuses grew bigger and bigger, until it was a fully developed baby, its sad eyes staring at him, its mouth opening in a scream. The staring eyes startled him and he stumbled, almost falling down the stairs. Picking himself up mid-tumble, his heart racing, he spoke to himself, trying to comfort himself just as Alice had done.

"Be careful, Harry. Just look ahead. You have to keep going." The steps seemed to be endless, stretching forever downwards. But he knew he must be getting closer to the bottom, because he could feel the dark energy coming up to meet him, trying to force him back. Whatever was down there didn't want him coming closer. He forced himself to keep moving, descending further and further downwards, into air that was becoming heavier and heavier. It was increasingly difficult to breathe.

When he finally reached the bottom of the stairway he gasped for breath, and experienced a weird sense of déjà vu. The bottom of the staircase opened onto another narrow corridor, this time with only two doors: one leading to the left, the other to the right. He went to the left first, following a pattern that was already established. Harry gasped as he realized he'd been in this room only hours before. He recognized the mattress, the buckets, and above all, the stench. The room was empty.

Closing the door behind him, he stared at the door to his right, remembering the tank, the chains from the ceiling. His heart was pounding as he reached for the doorknob, the sweat now dripping down his face. In one swift movement he pushed it open, and ran screaming into the room. All the fear Harry had felt in the house, all the horror and disgust and revulsion, came bubbling out of him in the madman's scream—a mad warrior cry that sounded alien even to his own ears. He moved with a madman's speed and precision, knowing the layout of the room without having to look, seeing the chains in his mind's eye. And there he was, beneath the chained body of the young boy. He tackled the surprised doctor with everything he had, knocking him to the floor before he'd realized what was happening. In that moment, Robinson was the only thing he saw. He didn't look at Billy dangling from the chains, or at Jo watching him with a look of amazed disbelief. Or at the old man who'd stood up to watch, and seemed to be unfolding his tired old limbs in a way that defied the laws of physics, growing taller and taller with each passing second. The old man seemed to draw on the darkness in the room to give himself a height and substance that he hadn't had moments before.

Sixty

Harry straddled Robinson, his legs on either side of the man's torso, pinning him down, while his hands stretched out to take the man's neck. And then Harry was squeezing with a strength he didn't realize he had, squeezing the breath out of the man, feeling the windpipe beneath his thumbs and wanting to hear it crush open. A murderous rage had built within him, making his blood boil, and he was gratified to see Robinson's face turning purple. Then the whispering started in his ear, and this time he didn't want to listen.

"Robinson is only a man, Harry; you can't take his life. Vengeful murder only feeds the energy here."

"I can't let him live," Harry protested. "Prison won't stop him. He's too dangerous. There's no other way." But his grip loosened slightly, and Robinson gasped greedily at the air, trying to fill his windpipe with it.

"He gets into people's minds through their eyes," the voice whispered. "You can destroy his eyes without destroying him." Harry looked over to Jo, who was watching him talk to himself, a bewildered expression on her face. He saw the old man watching gleefully from the sidelines, the spittle forming a thin stream down his chin. Seeing him, Harry understood that the old man wanted him

283

to kill Robinson. Whether he was an ally or not, the old man was too caught up in the sport of it to help Robinson. But even as Harry watched, for that brief moment in time, he saw the old man's attention shift. He watched him sniff the air and bellow.

"Where are you, you dried up old cunt? I can smell the decaying perfume of your unused pussy. You don't belong here! Show yourself!"

The powerful rage in his voice took them all by momentary surprise. He was no longer the old man, but a powerful force, and Robinson took advantage of the brief lapse in Harry's attention, the slight relaxation of his grip, to fling his head upwards, out of Harry's grasp. His mouth found Harry's shoulder and he clamped down. Harry screamed in pain as the razor-sharp metal cut through the jacket and thin cotton T-shirt to find the flesh beneath, clamping down like a vice. An agonizing spasm of pain shot up his arm, momentarily debilitating him. Wildly, he reached out with his hands, blindly searching for Robinson's head. Finding it, he tried to push it from his shoulder, but Robinson's mouth remained tightly fixed to his flesh. Seeking out the eyes, Harry pressed his thumbs deep into the gelatinous tissue, digging deeper as he heard Robinson's roar of pain. The doctor's grip on his shoulder loosened as Harry continued to push down on the eyes. He felt the tissue give way under his thumbs as Robinson's head rolled back onto the concrete floor with a loud crack. And still he refused to let go, pushing deeper until he felt the tissue tear away from the sockets, allowing him to dig his thumbs under the tissue and use the extra leverage to push upwards, until he felt the eye sockets give way. Not until he saw the bloody tissue and eyeballs come loose did he release the pressure. The sound of Robinson's enraged roars echoed loudly through the room, like the sound of a bull being castrated, so that even the old man stopped sniffing and grabbing at the air to watch.

"Where's the keys to the handcuffs," Harry yelled into Robinson's bloodied face, but the tormented doctor just spat in response. The thick globule of spit hit Harry in the face, and he grabbed the doctor's head in both hands and slammed it against the concrete. The loud crack would have signaled a terminal injury for a weaker man, but Robinson seemed to have superhuman strength in this place, and managed to moan his protest. Nevertheless, his head went slack in Harry's hands as he teetered on the edge of consciousness, and Harry used the opportunity to start rummaging through Robinson's pockets. He continued to straddle the doctor, letting his hands roam behind himself, and when Robinson regained full consciousness and tried to resist the search, Harry moved his hands down to Robinson's balls. Grabbing the vulnerable flesh in his fist he yanked viciously, and the doctor's moans turned to tortured screams. Robinson tried to curl his legs up in a defensive posture, but Harry kept him pinned down, checking his jacket. He felt the surge of triumph when his fingers touched the metal, and as he jumped off the doctor's hands moved immediately to his balls. Harry gave him a few more kicks with his good foot to keep him down, but he needn't have bothered—the doctor was in no position to get up yet. So while Robinson continued to moan and hold his balls, Harry reached up and unlocked Billy's wrists, tucking the handcuffs into the top of his jeans when he finished.

As he turned towards Jo, the feeling of metal pressing into his stomach, the old man stepped forward and spat at Harry.

"You don't think I'd let you go as easy as that, do you?" Harry took a swing at him, surprised at how easily he sidestepped the punch. The graceful agility belied his apparent years.

"What are you going to do, old man?" Harry challenged, pulling Billy past him as he moved towards Jo. The room suddenly filled with the sounds of thousands of agonized screams, the sounds of children and babies crying, sounds which almost brought Harry to a standstill. They were far louder than anything he'd heard coming from the walls, and he had to clamp his hands across his ears to stop his eardrums from bursting. The walls of the room started to glow, and Harry had to look away from the images he saw there. They were worse than anything he'd seen yet. He dragged Billy over to Jo's chair and began tugging at the leather straps binding her wrists and ankles. When he finally managed to free her, he tried to drag her to her feet, but she was like a dead weight, staring straight ahead. Her freed hands went to her ears as she tried to block the horrible sounds. For a terrifying moment Harry was paralyzed by despair, looking at Jo and Billy as they stood speechless and motionless, unable to help themselves. He despaired at finding the strength to help them all. But he forced himself to take action, to move through the despair. He stripped off his jacket and T-shirt, wincing at the pain in his shoulder, and pulled the T-shirt over Jo's head. As he wrapped the jacket around her waist, he screamed in her ear, praying she'd hear him.

"Jo, you have to block them out. They're not real; just ignore them."

"He's holding the knife to her neck." Jo's terrified reply was barely a whisper, and Harry had to bend over her to catch it. He swung around, but saw only the old man. Robinson was still lying on the floor, clutching his tortured manhood. Billy stood beside them, the same transfixed stare on his face that Jo had on hers. Unfortunately, there was no way for Billy to tell them what he was seeing.

"Who is it, Jo? What do you see?"

"He's got Sam."

"Sam? Your sister? No, Jo, Sam's not here. This house is playing with your mind. It's the old man's trick to keep you here. You've got to fight it. We've got to get out of here." Tears began rolling down her cheek.

"I can't. I can't leave Sam here. There's others too—Mandy, and Tony, and James." Harry slapped her face, hard, his hand stinging with the impact. "No, Jo, they're not. Samantha's at home—safe. I talked to her earlier tonight."

"You did?" Her eyes met his, and for a brief moment he saw a flicker of her former self reflected there.

"Yes. And the others are dead. But Billy's not. He's here, and he's alive. We have to get him out of this place. He needs us. You have to be strong, so that we can save him." The flicker in her eyes grew stronger.

"Billy?"

"Yes, look, Jo, he's here. We have to get out now or you know what will happen to him." He grabbed Billy's hand and pushed him forward, urging Jo to take his hand. "Come on, I know the way out." From behind them came the blood-curdling roar of the old man's rage, and Harry turned to see him filling himself out with the sound until he towered above them all. Still looking backwards, he pushed Jo and Billy ahead of him, not wanting them to see.

"You can't leave. I'm not finished with you yet." From behind the old man Alice suddenly materialized, looking pale and somehow less substantial than Harry remembered her.

"I believe you were calling me, Storyteller." He spun around, and she called out to Harry, "Get them out of here! Now!" He pushed them towards the stairs, urging Jo to move quickly.

"To the left, Jo, up the stairs. Don't look at the walls." She had Billy's hand now, and was dragging the boy with her. Harry followed behind, and as they left the room he took one final look back. Alice and the Storyteller were flinging themselves across the room in a manner which defied the laws of gravity. Despite her claim that she was old enough to survive in this place, Harry could see she was faltering already. He didn't know how long she'd be able to hold back the Storyteller.

Reaching the stairway he urged them on, encouraging them up the stairs so that they reached the top far more quickly then he'd been able to descend it. The terrible sounds of battle pursued them, drowning out all other sounds, and Harry tried not to imagine what Alice was enduring.

"Turn right, Jo! There's a door to your right about eight feet along. Just keep going." He was right behind her when she found the door, and as she pushed it open he took her hand. "Keep hold of Billy's hand. The doorway is across the room." The moans and groans were more audible here, although the sounds of battle still shook the walls.

"Harry, what's that noise?"

"Just ignore it—it's in the wall. It can't get out. It can't hurt you. Just trust me, Jo, everything will be okay. I came through this way."

"Jesus, Harry, what is this place?" Deciding that an explanation could wait, he didn't reply. Groping their way across the darkness without the walls for guidance, they finally reached the edge of the room, and Harry moved to the front, fumbling along the wall until he found the doorway. From the bowels of the house he heard heavy footsteps thundering up the stairway. Someone was following them. Jo heard it, too.

"Someone is coming, Harry."

"Maybe it's just the sounds coming from the walls." He pushed the door open and dragged her through the cubicle stall. Pulling Billy along beside her, it took her a few seconds to realize where they were, and when she did her face fell in horror.

"Don't think about it, Jo. We're almost out now. There's a doorway at the end of the room. It's the only way out, so hold your breath." They were running through the filthy water when Harry heard their pursuer reach the top of the stairs. His voice rang out as though he was right there with them, in that room, although Harry knew he wasn't.

"Did you think I'd let you get away? I don't need eyes to see you in this house! I can smell you, you bastards!" Robinson had made it to his feet and sounded mighty pissed. "When I get you, you'll all suffer like you've never imagined suffering in your life. Do you hear me?" Harry could see the terror in Jo's eyes.

"Jo, we're still ahead of him. He sounds closer than he is. Just keep running." Dragging Billy with her she reached the exit, with Harry right behind them, and then they were outside.

"Follow the path," he gasped between breaths. "I'm right behind you. Don't look back." Robinson's enraged roars continued to follow them outside the house.

"You can't get away from here, you fools." He sounded close, but Harry tried to convince himself it was just a trick, refusing to look back. An idea struck him, and he caught up with Jo.

"Jo, listen to me for a moment. You're not physically here. That means you're not bound by the same laws of physics. You can run as fast as your mind allows you to run. So I want you to fly down that path, until you reach the gray shadows. There's people inside who will help you—go inside the shadows." Jo looked at him as if he'd lost his mind.

"What do you mean I'm not physically here? Of course I'm here."

"I saw you tonight. You're still in your bedroom. Jones tied you up, remember? You're just dreaming this. Listen, I don't have time to explain—you just have to believe me." Harry was running out of breath, trying to talk and run at the some time. "Get Billy to safety!" For a few moments he thought it hadn't worked. She hadn't believed him, or he'd been wrong about it, but suddenly she picked up speed. She looked back at him and hesitated, slowing down as she saw the distance between them.

"Harry, take my hand," she yelled.

"No, you go ahead. You have to get Billy away from here. I'll be okay. Trust me, I know what I'm doing." Harry sounded more confident than he felt. He hoped he knew what he was doing. He continued running behind them until he saw them enter the gray shadows of the border land, and then he slowed down, jogging at a pace that he thought Robinson could meet. He could feel him approaching from behind, could hear his murderous demands for blood. He didn't allow himself to turn and look yet, although he desperately wanted to know just how close he was. Picking up speed slightly, he moved forward, fighting the urge to put as much distance as possible between Robinson and himself. Finally, only a few feet from the borderland, Harry stopped and turned to face his opponent. Despite his awkward stumbling, his flailing arm movements, the blind man was moving fast, and heading straight for Harry.

Sixty-one

"What do you want, Robinson?" Harry's voice was steady and calm, belying the utter terror he felt. Robinson roared and charged at him, ramming him with all the power of a bulldozer, so that Harry was knocked to the ground. Robinson fell on top of him and the two men were rolling in a sea of bugs and leeches to which Robinson seemed impervious. Harry had to pretend they weren't real, but the distraction lost him any advantage his eyes might have given him, and soon Robinson was on top of him. The blood streamed from his eyes as he reached for Harry's throat. Harry pushed both hands forward at once, and as he felt one of them find Robinson's face, he crunched his fingers and pressed them into the bloody eye socket, gratified to hear Robinson's roar of pain. Harry pushed the bellowing doctor off him, rolling over so that he could get back on top. Straddling the blind man, he screamed at the top of his voice.

"Where are you now, Storyteller? I've got your man here—don't you want him back?" He pulled one of the handcuffs from the top of his jeans, clicking them over Robinson's wrists before rolling off him and dragging him to his feet. Suddenly the old man was standing before them, larger than ever, grinning like a madman.

"Your friend put up a brave fight, boy," the old man leered, "but she was a tired old cunt in the end. She suffered incredibly, in case you're curious." Harry dragged Robinson a couple more feet, looking over his shoulder at the Storyteller and forcing himself not to think about Alice.

"Well, I have a story you might enjoy, old man. I'm going to join Jo and Billy so they can watch me tear the good doctor apart. I'm going to rip his balls off and shove them down his throat." The old man grinned widely, the stream of saliva flowing freely now. "Should be quite a show," Harry grinned back. He pulled Robinson another foot, so that they were at the edge of the borderland. The old man took a few steps, and Harry poked Robinson in the eye again to make him scream. As they stumbled into the borderland, Harry could see the Storyteller right behind them.

Harry felt the air shimmer and shake around him, and heard the sounds of the old man screaming. He continued to drag Robinson along, until the air started to clear, and then he sunk to the ground exhausted, pulling Robinson down with him. Robinson started to moan and Harry looked up to see the gray shadows darken, then flash brightly as if lit by lightening. Alexander and Evelyn pulled the Storyteller into their world, and his screams of pain filled the air around them, darkening the skies. As the Storyteller fell to his knees Harry reached into his jacket for the cherries Alice had given him, and thrust the fruit down the old man's throat, holding his hand over his mouth so that he couldn't spit them out. He choked and sputtered as Harry thrust his fingers down his throat, feeling the rotting teeth biting down on his fingers as he forced the fruit in. The old man started choking, and his mouth began splitting open as red blisters formed at the corners of his lips. They looked like they'd been washed in acid. Robinson's moans were drowned out by the sound of the old man's screams.

Alexander and Evelyn stood watching, before reaching down together and placing a hand under each of Harry's arms. They brought him to his feet in time to watch the old man shudder for the last time, then explode into a ball of black dust. He left nothing behind. Harry began to pass out, and felt the strong arms holding him up.

Sixty-two

When Harry opened his eyes the first thing he saw was Jo lying beside him, looking serene in a bed of soft, white linen, dressed in some kind of long, white tunic. A deep feeling of contentment washed over him as he lay there, easing the horror of the past hours. She opened her eyes a few seconds after him, and he was profoundly happy to see that the flicker of light he'd observed earlier had not faded from her eyes. It was actually stronger. The sounds of gentle murmuring brought them both to a sitting position at the same time, and they saw Alexander seated in the corner. He spoke quietly to Billy while feeding him slices of apple.

Harry looked around him, drinking in the details of the massive room: the soft, sumptuous furnishings; the enormous four-poster bed, complete with soft, white drapes. Everything else in the room was decorated in warm shades of white that made him feel clean again. Indeed, someone must have washed his body, for he actually was clean again, and dressed in fresh jeans and a crisp, white T-shirt. Even his jacket, which was slung over a chair, looked like it had been cleaned. Billy had been washed too, and changed into clean shorts and T-shirt. He was watching Alexander with something Harry hadn't seen in his eyes since he'd met him: signs of life. For the first time that night Billy spoke.

"I remember your voice," he told Alexander. "You were with me at that other house. With the ladies."

"Yes, Billy, we were there." Alexander smiled kindly, and as Jo and Harry watched Billy smiled back, tentatively at first, but then wider. Alexander looked up at Harry.

"We were with Billy the whole time, but Robinson's hold over him proved too strong. We thought he was lost, until you brought him back. Alice would have been pleased." Remembering what had happened, Harry experienced a flood of loss disproportionate to the length of their acquaintance.

"Alexander, I'm sorry about Alice." Alexander smiled sadly, and the grief crept into his voice.

"She knew how it would end. For herself, anyway. We didn't know if we'd be able to destroy the Storyteller; we have you to thank for that. For knowing what to do. We couldn't tell you what to do, so we didn't know how it would all turn out. We were waiting to see. But Alice would have been proud of her role in things." Alexander cleared his throat, and when he spoke again it was with a quiet authority. "We should be getting back to your world now. Billy's parents will be anxious to see him. Are you both feeling rested enough to make the journey?" Jo stared at Alexander with bewilderment, speechless for the time being. Harry still had a lot of questions.

"What about Evelyn? And Robinson?"

"They're both fine. Evelyn is in the next room with him. We'll have to take him back with you; he can't stay here. I'm afraid he's not enjoying his visit very much." There was a knock at the door, and an attractive young woman in a glittering green tunic entered, bowing slightly before Alexander.

"Your Majesty, your wife wishes to know if our guests are ready to travel."

"Thank you, Cassandra. Please tell Evelyn we're ready." The young woman departed with another bow, and Harry stared at his friend with a newfound awe.

"Are you two royalty or something?" Alexander stood to his feet, taking Billy's hand in his.

"Something like that," he replied modestly, brushing away the question. "Are you ready to depart?" Harry nodded, and he and Jo got to their feet as Evelyn entered, leading a subdued doctor by his still-handcuffed hands. Someone had taped white gauze over his empty eye sockets, and he allowed himself to be led forward like a docile patient. Harry reached for his jacket and moved to the front of the bed, standing next to Jo. He took her hand in his, and reached out to Billy with his other hand. Jo continued to stare in wonder as Evelyn reached for her free hand, and when the whole group was joined the room began to shimmer. Harry felt the familiar rush in his stomach and gripped Jo's and Billy's hands tighter, trying to reassure them. Then they were all descending. Harry blinked and the image of Jo's bedroom cleared, and he realized he was only holding Billy's hand.

Jo was back in bed, the tunic replaced with the pants and tee shirt that Harry and Evelyn had dressed her in earlier. She was sitting up as if she'd just woken from a dream, only to find that all the characters from her dream were now surrounding her bed. The room was still shrouded in darkness, in contrast to the brightness they'd just left. As he glanced at Jo's digital alarm clock, Harry was amazed to see it was only 9:30.

"Is it still Friday?" he asked Alexander, the sense of wonder finding its way into his voice. Alexander nodded, and addressed Harry solemnly.

"Do you still have the other handcuff, and the keys?" Evelyn and Alexander still held Robinson by each hand. Harry was surprised to find the other handcuff still shoved down the front of his jeans, and he pulled it out, along with the key from his jacket. Alexander pushed Robinson back into the chair that Harry was tied to only an hour before, and deftly undid the cuffs. He clicked it to one arm of the chair before attaching the other handcuff. Taking the rope they'd previously cut off Harry, Alexander bound Robinson's arms and ankles, securing him in the chair. Satisfied with the job he'd done, Alexander straightened up and addressed Harry.

"Are you going to be all right with him? And with getting Billy back to his parents?" Harry nodded, and Alexander bent down and whispered something into Billy's ear. Billy nodded solemnly in response to whatever Alexander told him. As Alexander straightened up Evelyn came forward and gave the boy a hug, and Alexander turned his attention to Harry.

"Thanks for everything you've done. We'll be watching over you, just in case you ever need our help." Harry took his hand, suddenly overcome by that sense of loss he'd felt earlier, when he remembered Alice. As if sensing his feelings, Evelyn came forward and hugged him, kissing him on the cheek, before leaning over and kissing the bewildered-looking Jo. And then they were gone, and for a brief moment Harry felt like weeping. He glanced over at Billy, who looked like he was feeling the same way, and moved forward to put his arm around the boy.

"Your mum and dad are going to be pleased to see you again, Billy." Billy brightened instantly, and Harry turned to Jo. "I think we should ring Mario—someone has to take him in." He jerked his head in Robinson's direction, and Jo was immediately galvanized into action, waking properly from what she'd thought might be a dream, even though it didn't seem like it.

Sixty-three

Mario was standing in Jo's kitchen twenty minutes later, a dumbfounded expression on his face as he watched them drink hot chocolate with Billy.

"Where's Robinson?"

"In the bedroom," Jo answered matter-of-factly. "He's tied up." Mario rushed off to check the story, and came back with the same dumbfounded look on his face.

"What went on here tonight, Jo? And what the fuck happened to the guy's eyes?"

"We'll explain everything later. First, we have to take Billy home to his parents. Is someone coming to help you with Robinson?"

"Patterson and Evans are on their way. How'd he get in here? Robinson, I mean?" Jo spoke calmly and evenly, as if she was telling the truth. They'd already decided they couldn't tell anyone the real story.

"He had my keys. From when he knocked me out earlier today, after Jones dropped me home. He tied me to the bed. Harry got a locksmith and came in, and untied me." Mario looked from Jo to Harry, as if he couldn't believe what they were telling him.

"And he brought Billy with him?" They could hear the disbelief in his voice. It was Billy who answered this time.

"Yes, sir. And this man and lady rescued me. The man in there is the bad man who took me last time." Mario's jaw dropped at the sound of Billy's voice, and Harry looked down into his hot chocolate, a little ashamed at having Billy lie like that. Not that it was a complete lie—they had rescued him.

When Harry and Jo initially discussed what to tell the police, they'd almost forgotten he was in the room with them. Only when Harry looked over at Billy and saw him watching them did he realize that this might be even more difficult for a young boy to explain than it was going to be for them. He had no idea how Billy was coping with everything he'd been through. He'd knelt beside Billy and tried to explain.

"Billy, I know this might be hard for you to understand, but Jo and I are worried that other people—well, that other people might not understand about the dark house, where the bad man lived, or the Light Palace, where Alexander and Evelyn lived."

"And Alice," Billy had added.

"And Alice," Harry agreed. "If people haven't been there—and most people haven't, Billy—they wouldn't understand. They might think that we're making up stories. Do you understand what I'm telling you?" Billy had nodded gravely.

"Yes. Alexander already explained it to me. We're special. And we can only talk about it with each other." Harry smiled, a sense of relief washing over him.

"That's right, Billy. And if ever you want to talk about what happened, you can ring Jo or me. Isn't that right, Jo?" She nodded, smiling down at Billy. "We're going to leave our numbers with your parents, in case you ever want to talk to us. About anything." Billy had nodded solemnly, his serious brown eyes meeting Harry's in a spirit of understanding.

~ * ~

As they made their way up the driveway that Harry had walked just over a week ago, his heart rose at the change in circumstances. Although it was almost eleven o'clock at night, he knew their visit would be welcomed. He squeezed Billy's hand as they approached the front door, glancing across at Jo. She held Billy's other hand in hers, and smiled at Harry across Billy's head.

Harry heard the doorbell ringing inside, and then Dan Williamson was standing shirtless before them, looking like he'd aged ten years since Harry had last seen him. His eyes widened in disbelief at the sight of his son, and for a few seconds he stood frozen, as if he couldn't trust what he was seeing.

"Billy," he finally whispered, the disbelief heavy in his voice.

"Daddy," Billy replied, and the big man fell to his knees, tears streaming down his cheeks as he took his son in his broad arms.

"Dan," came a woman's voice behind him. When Shelly Williamson saw her son in her husband's arms she started weeping too, kneeling on the doorway beside them.

"Mummy, everything is okay now," he consoled his tearful mother, and she looked from her son, to Harry and Jo, in amazement. Her arms remained wrapped around her husband and son as she wept even louder.

"I know, Billy. I'm crying because I'm so happy you're home."

Although the Williamsons invited them in, eager to show their overflowing gratitude with cups of coffee and anything else they might want, Jo and Harry insisted they had to get down to the precinct to give a report. Assuring the ecstatic, grateful parents that the right man was really in custody this time, they said their goodnights, letting them know that, for tonight at least, the police would be leaving them in peace. Harry hugged Billy before he left, reminding him to call if he ever wanted to talk.

~ * ~

Down at the precinct Mario kept shaking his head in disbelief at the idea of Robinson breaking into Jo's apartment with Billy, ready to give her a grisly performance before killing her, too. He apologized to Harry for not believing something was wrong with Jo, but Harry merely shrugged.

"Yeah, well, I guess the story seemed a little far-fetched. I don't think I would have believed me either. Besides, I didn't have all the details straight anyway."

At around one a.m. on Saturday morning Harry finally drove Jo home, feeling utterly drained.

"Why don't you spend the night here," she invited. You're clearly exhausted, and I could really use the company right now. I'm not sure I'm ready to stay in my apartment alone. Besides, I've still got a lot of questions for you, although they might have to wait for morning." Harry nodded.

Once inside they were too tired even for coffee, and Jo conceded that the questions really would have to wait until morning.

"Do you want me to sleep on the couch?"

"I think I've slept beside you often enough to trust you to keep your hands to yourself." Harry grinned, and tried to work up the courage to say what he'd wanted to say all night. Even before he spoke, he knew he should probably leave it until tomorrow, when they were less tired, but he didn't think he could hold off any longer.

"Jo," he began hesitantly, "there's something I really need to say to you. Something I've been wanting to say to you all week. My feelings for you haven't changed... they're just as strong as they ever were. I'm really sorry about what happened... in the past. But if it's any consolation, I've been faithful to you since we split up." He hadn't looked at her while he spoke, knowing he'd lose his courage the minute he met her gaze. But as he looked up now, and saw her troubled expression, he knew he'd made a mistake.

"Harry, I don't know what to say. I didn't mean to give you the wrong impression by asking you to stay. I'm grateful for everything you've done for me, but I asked you to stay as a friend, not a lover." Harry felt like he'd just been kicked in the guts. The bite Robinson had given him was nothing compared with this.

"Yeah, of course. No big deal. I promise I'll keep my hands to myself."

Sixty-four

Harry had crept out before Jo was awake, going back to his own apartment to write up the story of Robinson's capture. When he'd finished he'd emailed it in to Lou. Then he'd rung Anne-Marie and filled her in on the details of Robinson's research. She was horrified to learn he was the killer, but excited about doing the story. After the initial excitement wore off, she became shyer, asking Harry if she could talk to him about something. He'd agreed reluctantly, and she began telling him about the date she had with Paul that night. She had some reservations, and wanted to know if Harry thought it was a bad idea to date someone from work. Harry wondered why she was talking to him about this. He also wondered whether he should warn her off, but after careful consideration decided against it. Somehow, he figured she wouldn't take too much crap from Preston. Maybe they wouldn't be such a bad match after all. Sure she was only twenty-three, but then, Preston had the emotional capacity of a man in his early twenties. And he suspected Anne-Marie was a lot tougher than he'd originally given her credit for.

"Thanks, Harry," she'd gushed. "It's just that I didn't have anyone else to talk to about this—no one who knew us both, and could offer an informed opinion. And you've been so good to me since I've been working at the Courier—I knew you'd be the right person to ask."

300

And now he was on the highway, leaving the city for some as yet undetermined destination. Probably coastal. In his email to Lou he'd told his editor not to expect him in until later in the week. He'd done enough overtime lately to cover a few days off.

"How was Alton about you taking more days off?"

"He was fine. He's just happy to have Robinson locked up. Told me to take as long as I needed, as long as I didn't need more than a few days." Her laughter filled the car, and Harry felt happier than he could remember feeling in his life, excited at the journey ahead. He was glad he hadn't kept his promise to keep his hands to himself last night. And that, in the end, she'd decided that saving her life, and possibly her soul, probably made up for his past indiscretion—"as long as it never happens again." He'd promised solemnly, happy to commit his life to this woman.

"I thought that when we get back from wherever it is we're going I might give Sam a call. We should invite her and her new boyfriend over for dinner. What do you think?"

"Hey, as long as we get to spend a few days alone together first, I don't mind what plans you make. I've been suffering quite a dry spell you know." She rolled her eyes and turned on the radio, and Harry fought the urge to sing along to the sappy love song that was playing.

Meet

Kathy Anderson

Kathy Anderson lives in North Queensland, Australia. Dark Forces is her second novel. Her first, Imposter (2007), was published by the e-publisher, Speculative Fiction Review.